THE
SHADOWHAND
COVENANT

THE
SHADOWHAND
COVENANT

BRIAN ★ FARREY

illustrated by
BRETT HELQUIST

HARPER

An Imprint of HarperCollins*Publishers*

For Benji, an honorary Grimjinx

ISBN 978-0-06-204931-5

Typography by Megan Stitt

13 14 15 16 17 CG/RRDH 10 9 8 7 6 5 4 3 2 1

❖

First Edition

Also by Brian Farrey

The Vengekeep Prophecies

· CONTENTS ·

PART ONE:
★ THE SHADOWHANDS ★

CHAPTER 1: *Good–Bye to Nanni* 3

CHAPTER 2: *The Summons* 12

CHAPTER 3: *The Shadowhands* 25

CHAPTER 4: *Ambush*. 40

CHAPTER 5: *Underground*. 59

CHAPTER 6: *Attack of the Vessapedes*. 75

CHAPTER 7: *Tinderjack* 85

CHAPTER 8: *The Sarosan Plight*. 97

CHAPTER 9: *A Sinister Message* 107

CHAPTER 10: *Escape* 126

CHAPTER 11: *The Smell of Blood* 139

· C O N T E N T S ·

PART TWO:
★ THE COVENANT ★

CHAPTER 12: *Return to Redvalor* 161

CHAPTER 13: *The Robberies* 173

CHAPTER 14: *Finding the Traitor* 186

CHAPTER 15: *The Dagger.* 199

CHAPTER 16: *The Horror in the Walls* 210

CHAPTER 17: *A Deadly Oasis.* 223

CHAPTER 18: *The Nursery* 231

CHAPTER 19: *The Last Shadowhand.* 239

CHAPTER 20: *Shimmerhex* 250

CHAPTER 21: *The Final Trap.* 261

· C O N T E N T S ·

PART THREE:
⋆ THE SOURCEFIRE ⋆

CHAPTER 22: *Underground. Again.* 273

CHAPTER 23: *The Traitor's Story* 288

CHAPTER 24: *The Palatinate Palace* 295

CHAPTER 25: *An Impossible Menagerie.* 306

CHAPTER 26: *Unexpected Rescue* 322

CHAPTER 27: *The Labyrinth of Glass.* 332

CHAPTER 28: *Another Tribunal.* 342

CHAPTER 29: *A Last Request* 356

CHAPTER 30: *Exile* 364

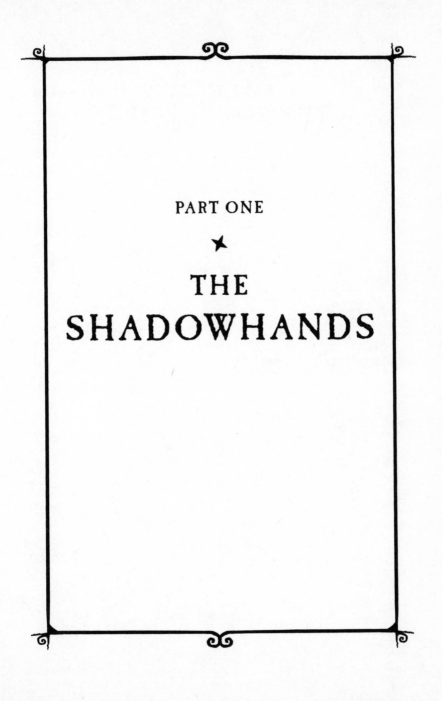

PART ONE

★

THE
SHADOWHANDS

1

Good-Bye to Nanni

"Whenever things seem to be exactly as they should,
lay down money that they're not."

—*Ancient par-Goblin proverb*

It was exactly the funeral Nanni always wanted.

The morning sun glistened off the fresh sheen of snow across the hillside. The nip in the winter air, crisp and clean, chilled without being too cold. Huddled together for warmth, the crowd of mourners stood around the freshly dug grave in the cemetery just outside Vengekeep as a hemmon chirped in the nearby trees.

I brushed snow from the lenses of my silver-framed glasses and gave my sister Aubrin's gloved hand a squeeze.

She looked up, eyes swollen with tears, and returned a fragile smile. To my right stood Da, wearing the traditional burgundy shawl of mourning, staring down at his feet as though looking at the grave would be too much. Ma's arm reached around his shoulders from the other side, comforting the bereaved son.

While we were never what you might call religious, we still thought it proper to hire a vicarman to say a few words about my grandmother, whom we called Nanni. He stood near the casket, talking about all the lives she'd touched and how much she meant to us, the Grimjinx family. When he spoke of how much Nanni loved making singemeat stew, Da released a loud, heaving sob. I put my free hand on his forearm as Ma whispered loudly, "Be brave, love."

Talian Strom, Vengekeep's town-state mage, uttered a single word. His spellsphere sparkled, and the heavy casket descended into the frozen earth. Nearby, the widow Bellatin tugged on the strings of an oxina and played a plaintive song. Da stepped forward, scooped up a handful of dirt, and said in staggered breaths, "Ma . . . Nanni . . . you'll be missed. Always." He tossed the soil into the grave, then returned to Ma's waiting arms, where he broke down crying.

The mourners—dozens and dozens of our neighbors in Vengekeep—waited in line to pay their respects. We hardly knew them. Many were among the wealthiest people in the town-state, no doubt hoping to impress Da—the town Protectorate—by simply showing up.

We stood at the edge of the cemetery, receiving the well-wishers one by one. Aubrin was the bravest of all. She looked everyone in the eye and thanked them sincerely for coming. Ma spoke for Da, who eventually had to withdraw when his sobbing overtook him. He murmured excuses, then walked back toward the town-state gates and home.

I shook hands and accepted condolences with a stoic face. As the line of mourners thinned, I found my best friend, Callie Strom, in a modest crimson dress. Teary-eyed, she pulled me into a tight hug.

"She was a lovely woman, Jaxter," she said, her voice broken. "I can't believe she's gone. I keep thinking we'll see her again."

I coughed and gave Callie a look. She lifted a handkerchief to her eyes and moved on to Ma. Once the receiving line was finished, Aubrin tugged at my sleeve.

"Can we go home yet? Everyone here looks so grave."

I groaned. She hadn't spoken a word for the first ten years of her life, and now that she was talking, she couldn't stop making bad jokes. "Why don't you head back to the house and help Da? Ma can finish up here."

Aubrin raised an eyebrow. "What about you?"

I looked up toward the rim of the valley that surrounded Vengekeep. "I have a quick stop to make and then I'll be along."

I hugged Aubrin, then trudged up the valley slope through the snow. I glanced back at Vengekeep. I hadn't seen my hometown for nearly six months. I couldn't have guessed the reason that had finally brought me back.

At the top of the hill, a large, gray, copper-trimmed carriage drawn by four silver-maned mang waited near the edge of the forest. On my approach, the footman, who'd been hugging himself to stay warm, leaped off his perch.

"Oya, Tren," I said to him with a wink. Tren winked back. I stood beside the carriage and took a deep breath. More than a little nervous, I nodded at Tren, who opened the carriage door. I climbed inside.

Red velvet lined the carriage's interior. I sank down in the rounded bench at the fore, my back to the mang out front.

Sitting across from me, the Dowager Annestra Soranna, wrapped in a thick fur serape, inspected an unruly stack of parchments on her lap. She leafed through the pages, frowning at what she saw and clicking her tongue with disapproval.

I studied her quietly. Silence between us had been the norm recently. Right now, I couldn't tell if she was still upset with me or just busy. In training me to be a thief, my parents had taught me how to read people's thoughts and emotions based solely on their body language. But when the Dowager worked on official state business, she was inscrutable.

"How did it go?" she asked absently, absorbed in her reading.

"A beautiful service from start to finish," I reported. "Callie sang a lovely dirge. Something about ladygills blossoming in the spring. Or was it autumn? Not sure. Wasn't really paying attention. Anyway, there was quite a turnout. I wish Nanni could have seen it. She'd have loved it."

The Dowager nodded, but I wasn't sure she'd heard me. Shortly before we'd left Redvalor Castle three days ago, she'd received an urgent message. A herald from her brother, the High Laird who ruled all the Five Provinces, had arrived and delivered the parcel of parchment now before her. The entire trip, the Dowager had pored over the papers and grown increasingly distressed with what she read.

I said, "Don't tell me. The High Laird has decided to give up his post for a life as a novelist."

The Dowager snorted. When she looked up, I finally saw the warmhearted woman to whom I'd been apprenticed these last six months. She had a slight, odd smile on her lips, eyes that flittered about, and a gentle sway to her head. Even with the tension between us, it felt good to make her laugh.

"Not exactly," she said. "Although maybe I'll recommend it to him. Honestly, Jaxter, I moved into Redvalor Castle so I wouldn't have to deal with things like this. Missing artifacts, suspicious thefts . . . And he's got no one to blame but himself. If he'd listened to my advice . . ."

Her voice trailed off as she turned another page of the High Laird's report. Since moving to Redvalor Castle to do research with the Dowager, I'd learned that frenzied missives from her brother seeking advice were commonplace. She, not he, had been groomed by their father to be High Laird. Sometimes it showed in her brother's hasty decisions. He spent a lot of time consulting her, often *after* he'd made terrible mistakes.

The Dowager set her papers aside. "You do understand why I couldn't join you at the service, don't you, Jaxter?" she asked delicately.

"Of course," I said. "It's for the best that you stayed away. Everyone understands. Besides, it's all over now."

The Dowager gazed out the window at Vengekeep. Last night's snow had painted the walls surrounding the town-state, making them hard to see against the blanket of white that covered the valley. "That must have been very difficult for you."

I shook my head and grinned. "Nah. Not really. I'm starved. You ready to eat?"

★

When the Dowager and I arrived at Ma and Da's house, we found Da dancing jubilantly around the kitchen, making a show of dropping chopped vegetables into a boiling kettle and singing a silly jingle about par-Goblins. Ma knelt near the fireplace to check on the two plump gekbeaks roasting on the spit. Aubrin sat curled up in a large, plush chair in the corner, scribbling furiously into her black leather journal.

My sister had turned eleven last month and had taken a

sudden interest in writing. Now, whenever I saw her, she was holding a small leather-bound book, scribbling away. As I walked past, I snatched playfully at her journal. She pulled it to her chest with a smile and wagged a finger at me.

"It's not time," she said. That's what she always said when someone tried to read her journal. No one knew why.

Ma swept across the room to take the Dowager's fur. "Dowager Soranna," Ma cooed, bowing respectfully, "we are honored to have you in our home."

"Please," the Dowager said, her head lilting side to side, "call me Annestra. I think it's a perfectly lovely name. The problem with having a lovely name and being a member of the royal family is that no one ever uses your lovely name."

"Annestra it is," Ma said as Da stepped forward to shake the Dowager's hand and show her to the dinner table.

I answered a knock at the door and nearly fell over as Callie burst into the house, threw her arms around me, and wailed, "Oh, Jaxter! The pain! The loss! However will you get by?"

"Be respectful," I warned, pushing her gently away. "This is a house of mourning."

Callie giggled. She'd changed from her funeral dress

back into the gray robes she was required to wear as Talian's apprentice mage. She gave me a mock curtsy. "I thought my performance was brilliant."

"This morning, yes," I said. "But you were a bit over the top just now."

Ma pulled the gekbeaks from the fire just as Aubrin brought bowls full of boiled vegetables to the table. Once we all took our seats, Da poured ashwine for the adults, while Aubrin, Callie, and I helped ourselves to glasses of mangmilk. Ma struck her glass with a fork and stood, raising her arm in a toast.

"To Nanni!" she said. "May she rest in peace!"

We all raised our glasses and repeated, "To Nanni!"

Just then, we heard a creak as the back door in the kitchen opened. Turning, we watched a hooded figure carrying a large cloth sack waddle in. The sack dropped with a metallic crash as the figure pulled back the hood to reveal Nanni, grinning widely.

"You didn't start without me, did you?"

2

The Summons

"The difference between a good lie and a great lie is
six years in gaol."

—*Graydin Grimjinx, sole perpetrator of the Second Aviard Nestvault Pillage*

O nce everyone had a full plate, Da explained.

"It's an old thieving tradition," he boasted to the
Dowager, who was eyeing Nanni's loot bag with a great deal
of discomfort. "When you decide to retire, you fake your
death, have your accomplices throw a big funeral, and then
rob the houses of the mourners as they cry over your grave."

The Dowager nodded nervously. I'd explained all this
to her when I first got the letter from Da three weeks ago,
announcing Nanni's imminent funeral. The Dowager's

mischievous side had agreed to accompany me back to Vengekeep so I could take part, but the side of her that remained very aware she was the High Laird's sister kept her from enjoying the festivities fully. No telling what people might do if they believed she was in on the deception.

"Of course, it's a very old custom. Not many practice it these days," Ma said sweetly, as if trying to comfort the Dowager.

Da raised his cup to Nanni again. "But how could we say no to giving Nanni such a fine send-off?"

The Dowager managed a weak smile. "So," she said, after steeling herself with a swallow of ashwine, "you're retiring. How lovely. Where will you go?"

Nanni, who'd been rooting around in the bag of stuff she'd just nicked, almost missed the question. "Hrm? Oh, yes. Time to rest these weary bones. I've found a lovely cottage in Angel Cove. Nice little seaside town just south of Vesta." She pulled an elegant copper candelabrum from her bag and all us Grimjinxes oohed with envy. "This should just about cover the down payment."

The Dowager choked on her ashwine. She knew our family code meant that we never stole from the poor. But theft was still theft. Officially, the Dowager disapproved of my family's shady history. Unofficially, she was fascinated by the guile that went into planning and executing criminal activities.

Granted, those activities had decreased sharply in the past months. After Ma had accidentally woven a tapestry from fateskein that nearly destroyed Vengekeep, our family decided to go easy on the heists and try a new adventure: being normal.

None of us was very good at it, but at least we gave it a shot.

Nowadays, Ma and Da tried to earn an honest living, with Da serving as Vengekeep's Protectorate and Ma making dolls in the phydollotry shop. Still, the par-Goblins always said, "An unused tool is a rusty tool." With Da in a position to make sure that any sort of substantial charges would go away, my family indulged in just enough thieving to stay at the top of their game.

But the Dowager was clearly torn between showing her admiration and being offended at the very idea of dining with thieves. So, she chose a halfway point: total denial.

"I'm sure you'll enjoy retirement," the Dowager said, poking at her food with her fork.

"Retirement beats living like a fugitive," Nanni said, raising her glass in the air.

"Yes," Ma said softly, "I imagine that's how the Sarosans are feeling these days."

I looked up sharply at Ma, but her eyes were already down on her plate. She'd promised she wouldn't talk politics while the Dowager was here. But Ma being Ma, she couldn't resist a gentle challenge.

To be fair, news about the Sarosan plight dominated conversations everywhere you went in the Provinces. And like many people, Ma had been following the story with great interest. A month earlier, the High Laird had ordered that everyone belonging to the nomadic tribe submit themselves for interrogation. No explanations, just a demand for compliance.

The Sarosans were peace-loving people. Some of their leaders sought an audience with the High Laird to discuss the problem. They were promptly arrested and a royal decree named all Sarosans as enemies of the state, to be arrested on sight. The remaining nomads had scattered and now lived in hiding. Some law-advocates had pressed the High Laird's court for an explanation. But the High Laird refused to

justify his orders, and as a result, there was unrest throughout the Provinces. Everyone feared they would be the next
ones asked to surrender for interrogation.

"Ma . . . ," I said quietly.

But Ma just smiled and passed a plate of steamed vaxis
root around. "I'm only saying that it's very strange, given that
no formal charges have been brought against the Sarosans.
The worst they've ever done is bore people by roaming
around, preaching against the use of magic. And if being
boring is a crime, they should have locked Castellan Jorn up
years ago."

Privately, the Dowager had no problems criticizing her
brother and his often erratic policies. When the High Laird
ordered the arrest of the Sarosans, she ranted to me for hours
over how foolish it all was. But here, she put on her best
"head of state" face. She squared her shoulders and said, "I'm
sure all our thoughts are with the Sarosans and the High
Laird as well."

"So, Callie," I said, quickly changing the subject, "you're
looking very smart in your apprentice robes. I imagine
Talian's got you casting all sorts of spells by now."

Callie harrumphed. "Hardly. I can't get a spellsphere

until I'm sixteen, and I hear it takes a year just to learn how to speak the magical tongue properly." Then she beamed. "But Talian says our lessons are going well. He might let me try casting a simple glamour next week."

Everyone raised their glasses to Callie.

I nudged her with my elbow. "Maybe before the Dowager and I go back to Redvalor, you can give us a tour of Talian's place."

Callie stiffened. "Actually . . . I have to leave right after dinner. Talian and I are being evacuated by the Palatinate tonight."

Everyone's face went from pride in Callie to looks of severe discomfort. Leave it to me to try to steer the conversation away from politics, only to land right back in the thick of the mess again.

The Palatinate, the body that governed the use of magic in the Five Provinces, had announced earlier this week that they believed the anti-magic Sarosans were a threat because they refused to turn themselves in. For their own protection, all mages had been ordered to report to the Palatinate palace in Tarana Province until the "Sarosan menace" had been dealt with.

"Yes, a lot of people are upset about these evacuations," Ma said, doing a terrible job of sounding innocent. "I'm no law-advocate—"

"And bless you for that," Nanni muttered.

"—but I believe the High Laird's Law states that all citizens are entitled to the benefits of magic. That's why every town-state is assigned a mage. To assist, to protect . . . Some might interpret the Palatinate's order as defying the High Laird's Law."

Well, at least she wasn't attacking the High Laird.

"Except I'm pretty sure the High Laird approved their plan," she continued.

So much for not attacking the High Laird.

"It's true, Allia, that none of us here are law-advocates," the Dowager said slowly.

"Bless us all!" Nanni cried out. I think she may have had one too many glasses of ashwine.

"And maybe as such," the Dowager continued, "it's best if we left legal interpretation to them and found more pleasant topics of conversation."

"Dessert!" Da said quickly and loudly. "Anyone for dessert? I made burnwillow crumble. Nanni's favorite."

It wasn't time for dessert. In fact, we'd all barely touched the food on our plates. I offered a silent prayer to any deity willing to listen that someone would change the subject.

"So what are you and the Dowager working on at Redvalor Castle?"

I should have been more specific in my prayer about which subjects were off-limits.

Aubrin, sensing how tense I'd become, was doing her best to get us off politics. But asking about life at Redvalor Castle only made my neck muscles tense up more.

I'd written letters to my family, bragging about all the research the Dowager and I were doing, all the discoveries we'd made. For all they knew, I was doing exactly what I'd always wanted.

The fact was that the past six months at Redvalor Castle hadn't been nearly as wonderful as I'd led my family to believe.

They'd hardly been any kind of wonderful, actually.

At the start, I'd approached my studies with enthusiasm. We spent weeks in the Dowager's greenhouse, cataloging the rare, magic-resistant plants she'd rescued from extinction. But then, we'd moved on to topics I was less excited about.

Like the migratory patterns and eating habits of vessapedes. Who needs to know that?

Apparently, the Dowager.

We spent three months crawling around underground, tromping through vessapede warrens and studying their lives. For the record, vessapede lives consist mainly of burrowing tunnels and eating.

Their food of choice? Faces. Yes, faces. No one knows why, exactly. That was what the Dowager wanted to find out. And since the maggot-like giants were basically mindless animals, you couldn't just go up and ask them why they ate faces. Try that and you soon wouldn't have anything to ask with!

It was toward the end of our time among the vessapedes that the Dowager and I began arguing. We bickered about everything. It got so bad at one point that we communicated only by passing notes back and forth, using her majordomo, Oxric, as a courier.

It may seem disrespectful, but I had been raised by my parents to question everything and everyone. I'm sure the Dowager wasn't used to being questioned. As her apprentice, I should have been more obedient. But I wanted to study plants. Or the stars. Or anything that didn't end with run-ning and screaming.

By the time we got the letter about Nanni's "funeral," we'd both been suspecting that maybe this apprenticeship wasn't working. We'd agreed to take the trip to Vengekeep, cool down, and then see if we really wanted to continue working together. Now, facing the family who thought I was having the time of my life, that was all very hard to admit.

The Dowager and I exchanged the briefest of looks, nei-ther of us ready to admit what was wrong. Then, just as she had defended her brother, she tried to put the best face on the situation.

Her stiffness vanished and her childlike eyes lit up. "We haven't *stopped* working since Jaxter arrived. We successfully cross-pollinated a wraithweed plant with a duskgnat bush, we spent some time underground studying vessapedes—"

Three months. *Three. Months.*

"—and soon, we hope to start translating *The Kolohendriseenax Formulary* into par-Goblin." Nearly out of breath with excitement, the Dowager finished.

Now *that* interested me. Knowing the Dowager had a soft spot for learning new languages, I'd suggested translating the *Formulary*, the rare, definitive text on magic-resistant plants, into ancient par-Goblin as a way of teaching her the language. The Dowager liked the challenge of the project. I liked that it didn't involve face eating.

My family stared back, smiling and blinking and doing their best to pretend they understood everything the Dowager had said.

"Well," Da said with great enthusiasm.

"Isn't that . . . ," Nanni said. She spent a couple of moments searching for the right word, then quickly looked away, pretending she hadn't spoken in the first place.

"Fascinating!" Ma finally said.

The Dowager smiled. My parents stood and raised their glasses.

"Another toast!" Da proclaimed.

"To Jaxter and Dowager Soranna," Ma said. "May their work continue to bring them happiness."

Happiness. Right. If we didn't kill each other first.

We'd all just put our mouths to our glasses when a loud *thud* sounded from the front door. We looked at one another; no one else was expected. Nanni dove under the table. She was, after all, dead. Da set his glass down, moved across the living room, and opened the door.

A cold winter breeze spilled into the room, rustling a sheet of parchment that had been attached to the outside of our door. With a dagger. Da examined the parchment, his face growing ashen.

"Nanni," he said in a voice I recognized as Da trying to be very calm when, in fact, he wasn't, "I don't believe we've given the Dowager the grand tour of the house. Would you and Aubrin mind showing her the upstairs?"

Nanni and Aubrin instantly knew something was up. Nanni stood and offered her arm to the Dowager. "Wait'll you see my room, dearie. Tiniest thing ever. You'll understand why I'm so eager to move."

"Callie too," Da said, his eyes never leaving the parchment stuck to the door.

Callie had seen the upstairs of our house several times. She opened her mouth to say as much, but I caught her eye and shook my head ever so slightly. Aubrin took Callie by the hand, and they followed Nanni and the Dowager upstairs. I was about to join them when Da said, "Jaxter, stick around."

Da yanked the dagger, took the parchment, and shut the door. He joined us at the table and laid the paper out.

A message in coarse handwriting took up the top half of the parchment. It said simply:

Allia GrimJinx
Ona GrimJinx
Jaxter GrimJinx
The Clocktower Inn
20 Minutes

There was no signature. Just a large black handprint on the bottom of the parchment.

"By the Seven!" Ma whispered, her brow crinkling.

Da stroked his chin. I finally understood why it was so important that the others leave the room. I'd never seen anything like this before, but I knew it by reputation.

"The Shadowhands," I said breathlessly.

Da gave a curt nod. "We've been summoned."

And while my knowledge was limited to hearsay, I knew that one thing you didn't do—if you valued your life—was ignore a summons from the Shadowhands.

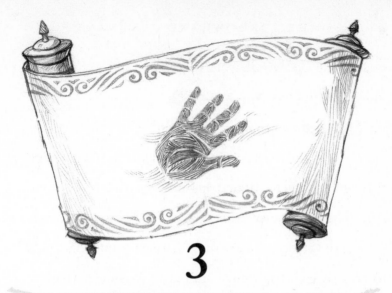

3

The Shadowhands

"Necessity forges alliances.
Reality sets them asunder."

—*Quorris Grimjinx, thief-bard of Rewtayne Falls*

The three of us stood gaping at the parchment, like we were afraid it might leap up and bite us. Ma fingered her braid of ebony hair while Da folded his hands behind his head, sure signs they were both deep in thought.

"What could they want with us?" Da asked. "I mean, I understand summoning you and me. But why our son?"

"It's all very odd," Ma said, shaking her head. "It's broad daylight out. Shadowhands only ever send a summons at night. And they would have had to evade the Dowager's guards outside. Needlessly dangerous. This is either terribly urgent or . . ."

Da raised an eyebrow. "You think it's a fake?"

I stood up. "One way to find out." I started digging through the twelve drawstring pouches that hung from my belt. They contained what *The Kolohendriseenax Formulary* called "the essentials of nature." Twelve plants that could be used to detect and, if mixed just right, counteract magic.

I scooped up handfuls of amberberry pollen, tallis root, and roxpepper dust, ground them together in a mortar from the kitchen, then sprinkled the powder over the handprint at the bottom of the parchment.

We waited, eyeing one another nervously. Then I took a deep breath. "Here goes."

I blew the concoction off the parchment. The outer edge of the handprint glowed with a thin line of blue light that faded a moment later. No doubt about it. Only Shadowhands knew the secret to making imprimatur ink.

"Right, then," Ma said, pulling our coats off the hooks on the wall. "Best not be late for a summons."

Da tucked the parchment into his pocket and called upstairs to Nanni, telling her we'd be back soon. Then the three of us bundled up and headed out into the snowy streets. We kept quiet as people passed, bowing their heads and expressing their condolences to Da. He looked confused, then remembered he was in "mourning."

"Maybe this is a good thing," I said. "Maybe you're being invited to join!"

Some thieves scraped by day to day, hoping not to get caught. Others worked hard to improve their skills, trying to attain the title of master thief. But beyond all that, the highest honor any thief could be given was an invitation to join the Shadowhands.

The Shadowhands were the most elite thieves-for-hire in all the Five Provinces. They'd worked in complete secrecy for centuries, pulling off some of the most daring and elaborate heists anyone could imagine. My aunt Menia once told me that my ancestor Andion Grimjinx had been one of the Shadowhands' founding members. Da, of course, denied this later. Because, as the par-Goblins say, "The ignorance of denial shelters the foolish."

That's how the Shadowhands operated: behind a veil of total anonymity. They were so secretive that anyone you knew could be a Shadowhand, posing as a common citizen to hide their true nature. The baker down the street, the nanny for the neighbor's children . . . *Anyone*. You had to be the absolute best of the best to even be considered to join their ranks. And if they sent you an invitation, you'd better think long and hard about it. Because joining meant signing the Shadowhand Covenant. And that was serious business.

Granted, I had no idea what the Shadowhand Covenant *was*, but I knew it was serious.

Ma and Da smirked. "I doubt it," Da said jovially. "They wouldn't send a summons to the three of us if they were only inviting your ma and me."

We arrived at the Clocktower Inn, situated on the ground floor of Vengekeep's only clock tower, and walked inside. Despite it being a bright day out, the inside of the inn was dark as pitch. Shutters blocked all the windows, leaving only the dwindling light from a fireplace near the bar to illuminate a path for us. Faint candles flickered on the dining tables. A handful of patrons sat nursing their quaichs filled with blaze-ale.

Ma scanned the room, looking for a sign of our contact. She pointed to the far corner, the darkest part of the inn. Unlike the rest of the candles, which flickered with a soft yellow light, the candle in the corner appeared red and muted, as if it were behind a piece of glass.

"That's the Shadowhand signal," Ma said softly.

I asked, "How do you know—?"

Ma silenced me with a finger to her lips. We moved across the room and approached the corner table. A figure sat, back to the wall, submerged in shadow. Da cast an eye around to make sure no one was listening. We stayed at a respectful distance and waited to be addressed.

"Thank you for coming."

It was relatively warm in the inn, but ice shot down my back as I recognized the voice. The figure leaned forward into the candlelight, revealing the hardened face of Maloch Oxter.

Maloch and I had grown up together, the closest of friends. I showed him how to pick locks and do sleight of hand; he protected me from the other children whose stuff I'd nicked. Then, about two years ago, that all changed for no reason. One minute we were friends, the next he was treating me like a demented gekbeak. Tripping me, shoving me. It got worse when he was made apprentice to Aronas, captain of Vengekeep's stateguard.

He became obsessed with catching my family stealing, relentlessly following us around town. Seven months ago, when Callie and I tried to sneak out of Vengekeep to get the ingredients we needed to destroy the fateskein tapestry, Maloch had nearly beaten me to a pulp in the catacombs beneath the city. When you're a Grimjinx, you expect to have enemies. But I'd never dreamed my worst would be someone I once trusted.

Maloch ran his hand over his impossibly short hair and waited for us to respond.

"Maloch Oxter," Ma scolded, her eyes ablaze, "you have no idea what you're playing at. It's very, very dangerous to impersonate a Shadowhand." She lowered her voice. "They have spies everywhere, and if they were to catch you . . . Not even your father with his wealth and power could protect—"

"Save your breath, Ma," I said, glaring down at my former friend. "He's not playing a game. It's a setup. Any minute now, Captain Aronas and his men are going to storm the place and arrest us for conspiracy."

Aronas had never liked our family. We knew it hadn't been easy for him when Da became his boss six months ago. I wouldn't put it past him to entrap us.

Maloch turned to Ma. "This is no game, Mrs. Grimjinx. The summons I sent was authentic. You must have verified that. I sent it on behalf of my father. *He's* a Shadowhand."

The three of us gaped, unbelieving. Maloch's father, Yab Oxter, owned and ran Vengekeep's most prestigious bank. He was a well-respected member of the community, whom many guessed would be named the next castellan if Jorn ever retired. He gave generously to charities and had absolutely no tolerance for crime, often making impassioned speeches to the town-state council in favor of harsher penalties for criminals. He was everything a Shadowhand wasn't.

Which, of course, was the perfect disguise for a Shadowhand.

But I didn't trust Maloch. I couldn't. "I don't believe him. This is a trick. We should just walk away—"

"Shut up, Jaxter," Maloch said. "We can't talk here. We have to—"

"Just hold on, everyone," Da said. He peered at Maloch as if trying to see into his little black heart. Then he turned to Ma and said, "Allia?"

Ma straightened her back, looked Maloch in the eye, and said, "*Ker aminus sortinnel rev hil narjak?*"

Ma's ancient par-Goblin was perfectly accented, each word enunciated to avoid confusion. Not that there should be any confusion. I was convinced Maloch didn't know anything but the handful of par-Goblin words I'd taught him years ago.

Maloch stuck out his chin. *"Shera tuo mer."*

I fumed. His accent, perfect. His enunciation, clear as a bell. But his answer made no sense whatsoever, and I assumed he'd blown it.

But Ma nodded at Da, and he nodded back.

"Where should we go?" Da asked quietly.

"Maloch's house," Ma said. "Jaxter and I will go first. Maloch, you follow at a distance. No one will think it odd if you're watching us from afar. Ona, you pick another route. We'll all meet behind the house."

Maloch slid from his seat. Before I could protest, Ma clamped her arm around my shoulders and guided me out into the cold streets. We'd gotten only a few steps down the road when we heard the door to the inn close behind us. Maloch was now pretending to follow us.

"Okay," I said to Ma, "I get it. You trust him because he

knew the answer to your question. What was all that about? You asked him, 'Where does the solitary heart rest?' He said, 'In the eclipse.' That doesn't even make any sense."

Ma smiled and waved to people walking past and whispered through her smile, "It's not supposed to make sense. It's how Shadowhands recognize one another. Get the answer wrong and you're liable to end up with a dagger in your gizzard."

Codes between thieves were common. I knew a few basic ones that simply identified me as a thief, meant to solicit help from other thieves when in a tight spot. So, naturally, the Shadowhands had developed their own special system. Sure, things like the lone red candle were general knowledge among thieves because it was to the Shadowhands' advantage. But a code like this eclipse thing had to be the most secret of secrets in order to work and keep anyone—

"Hang on," I said, maybe a bit too loudly. I lowered my voice and said, "How do *you* know the Shadowhand passcode?"

Ma breathed loudly through her nose and peeked over her shoulder to make sure Maloch was still following at a discreet distance. "Because, Jaxter," she said plainly, "I was a Shadowhand."

I stopped in my tracks, but Ma gripped my arm tightly and kept me moving forward.

"Keep going," she whispered, a smile never leaving her lips. "If a Shadowhand is sending his son to collect us, there must be unimaginable danger involved. Someone might be watching. We can't do anything suspicious. Just pretend we're out for a stroll and act normally."

I plastered a fake smile on my face and pretended to point out a flock of birds flying overhead. "'Act normally?'" I said through clenched teeth. "Someone I hate claims to be the son of a Shadowhand and suddenly you tell me that *I'm one too*. There's nothing normal about this."

"Oh, stop making a fuss," she chided. "It's really not that big a deal."

My mother didn't do humble very well.

"Out with it then," I said. "What's the story?"

She sighed. "Not much to tell. Honest. It was a long time ago. Just after your da and I got married. Word about my forgery skills had gotten around, I was summoned, and I accepted the invite. Tripled our income for a while, I can tell you. Oh, the heists we pulled . . ."

"So what happened? You said you *were* a Shadowhand." Then a thought occurred to me. "Or . . . or are you . . . ?"

"No, son, I'm not still a Shadowhand. And, yes, I know that's what I'd say if I were still a Shadowhand, but I give you my word that I'm not. I gave it up just after you were born. We settled down here in Vengekeep, and glamorous as the Shadowhand life was, it was far too dangerous for a new mother. So I walked away."

"And they let you?" I didn't imagine that was easy. She knew the identities of her fellow Shadowhands and all their secrets. It didn't seem like something you just walked away from.

"They asked me to reconsider, but when I told them no . . . well, yes, I walked away. They knew I would keep quiet. I'd signed the Shadowhand Covenant, and breaking it would have meant placing my family in more danger than anything all the High Laird's troops could've mustered. I'm bound to the Covenant. For the rest of my life."

I didn't like the sound of that last bit.

"Did you know that Mr. Oxter is a Shadowhand?" I asked.

She shook her head. "Hadn't a clue. He must have joined after I left. But chances are he knew I was. He'd have seen my name on the Covenant."

I was about to ask Ma what being bound to the Covenant meant exactly, but we'd arrived at the Oxter house. Three stories high with copper trim around the windows, it put most other houses in town to shame. We slipped down the alley between the Oxter house and the pie shop next door. Ma and I waited near the back door until Maloch showed up, followed shortly by Da.

Once inside, Maloch led us through to the dining room. A long table with ten chairs sat below a massive crystal chandelier. A light coat of dust covered everything. It looked like it had been some time since the room had been used.

Maloch reached behind a large hutch containing colored glass plates and pulled a hidden lever. The whirring of gears filled the air as the hutch slid to the side, revealing a small room beyond. Maloch led us in, allowing the hutch to close behind us.

Da lit an oil lamp atop an old, ornate desk at the center

of the room. Piles of parchment camouflaged the desk's surface. Ma looked around.

"Maloch, I thought you were bringing us to see your father," she said.

Maloch didn't say anything. He produced a key from his pocket, unlocked the middle drawer of the desk, and pulled out a green leather-bound book, which he handed to Ma. She squinted at the pages, then fluttered her eyes.

"Oof!" Ma said with a bemused chuckle. " 'S been a while since I've had to read shadowscript. Give me a mo."

I looked over her shoulder at the writing in the book. I didn't recognize the language—it looked like a bunch of meaningless symbols—and guessed it was a special code used only by Shadowhands. On closer inspection, I saw that the writing was moving. I would focus on one character, and a moment later, it would squirm on the page and shift into a new symbol. In a blink, it would shift again to something entirely different. Each character transformed among three different shapes. I found it harder and harder to focus on the page, as every symbol wriggled and contorted. I finally had to look away.

Ma ran her finger across the yellowed parchment. "You

just have to know which symbols mean something and which are rubbish." She sifted through the book slowly, her face growing more concerned with each page turn. She stopped on what looked like a list, where each line was crossed out. Ma looked up at Maloch with a mix of fear and astonishment in her eyes.

"Maloch . . . ," she said, her voice cracking. "Do you realize—?"

"I can't read it, but Da told me what it says," Maloch said. "Now you know why he wanted *you* to see it."

I kept an eye on the sliding hutch, still expecting an ambush from Aronas and his men at any moment. "So why are you doing your father's dirty work for him?" I asked. "Why didn't he come to Ma himself?"

"My father is missing!" Maloch whirled on me, clenching his fists. He was a head taller than me, with arms like fence posts. He was ready to tear me apart. But I could hear the concern and fear in his voice. "He's been gone for two weeks now. And he told me that if he was ever gone for that long without checking in, I was to get your ma and bring her here."

"Why her?"

"She's a *Shadowhand*. Are you really that thick, Jaxter?" Maloch said as he turned and punched the wall.

Da raised his hands. "All right, everyone. Calm down. What's it say, Allia?" He pointed to the book.

I stepped forward. "Yeah. You're retired. Why not ask the other Shadowhands for help?"

"Because," Ma said, looking up from the book with sad eyes, "the Shadowhands are vanishing."

4

Ambush

"However long the vessapede, the tail will come."

—Sirilias Grimjinx, liaison to the par-Goblin Rogue Triumvirate

"What do you mean . . . vanishing?" I asked.

Ma snapped the book shut and stood. "This house isn't safe anymore. Maloch, go upstairs and pack a bag. You're staying with us until we can get things situated."

"And then we're looking for my da?" Maloch asked.

Ma ignored his question as she pillaged the desk drawers. "We won't bother splitting up on the way home. Too risky. We need to stay close. Go, Maloch." Scowling, Maloch obeyed.

Da found a burlap sack and began filling it with whatever Ma pulled from the desk. "What is all this, Allia?"

A lifetime of thieving had taught my parents to be cool in all situations. And in those moments when things got really rough and Da started to worry, Ma always stayed collected and unfazed. So, watching her scramble to get us out of the house, her eyes dark and distant, I couldn't help but panic a little. I just had no idea what I was panicking about.

Ma thumbed through the green book. "Yab Oxter first noticed that other Shadowhands were disappearing about a month ago. One by one, he lost contact, and he grew suspicious. He started to document what he knew about the disappearances."

She held out the book, showing the squirming shadowscript. "He left here two weeks ago to look for the last three Shadowhands: Alvar Oro, Bennis Carra, and Dylis Jareen."

"How many are missing?" I asked.

Ma tucked the book into the sack. "There are only ever twelve active Shadowhands at a time. Makes it easier for everyone to trust each other. It sounds like Yab is gone now too. Who knows if the three listed here are still around?"

She and Da both took the small dirks they kept strapped near their ankles and hid them up their sleeves for easier access. I'd seen them do this only a handful of times before. Always when the danger was very, very real.

"Ma, I've never seen you this scared," I said.

Ma put her hands on my shoulders. "Jaxter, these are the Shadowhands. No one in the Five Provinces is better at moving in secret and staying hidden. If someone has been eliminating them . . . that's someone you should be scared of."

★

Once Maloch returned with his things, we left for home. Ma made me walk ahead with Maloch while she and Da kept an eye on us from behind.

"So," I said, looking down at my feet as we walked, "you're a thief."

Maloch could hardly keep from smiling. "Since the day I was born."

He sounded smug, and it made my chest burn.

"And when we were kids, and I showed you how to pick a lock—"

"I already knew how," he said, grinning even wider. I hated that grin.

"And all the times your da pushed to have our family arrested . . ."

At this, Maloch laughed. "Best way to make sure no one suspected he was a Shadowhand."

And then I did the bravest thing I think I've ever done. Braver than facing down magma men. Braver than dodging hordes of killer balanx skeletons. I turned and slugged Maloch as hard as I could in the arm.

It was like punching a fleshy wall. I probably did more damage to my knuckles than to him. I'm not even sure he felt it. Still, he looked at me, annoyed. "What was that for?"

"That," I said, trying to sound intimidating, "was for treating me like a total garfluk these past few years. I can't believe that all this time you've really been a thief in training."

His eyes lit up. "You gotta admit, Jaxter, I had everyone fooled. 'The greatest role you'll ever play is the role that others believe in.'"

I hated that he was a better thief than me. I hated that he and his father had hoodwinked my family all these years. But more than anything, I hated that he was quoting par-Goblin proverbs to me. I wanted to hit him again . . . but the feeling hadn't returned to my hand after the last blow. "You beat me up in the catacombs!"

The memory, over six months old, was still fresh in my mind. Callie and I had been searching for a secret way out of the town-state when Maloch attacked, pretending to arrest me.

He rolled his eyes. "Jaxter, if I'd wanted to hurt you in the catacombs, you'd never have left there on your own two feet. I was holding back."

"You could have said something," I complained.

"Whatever," Maloch said. "Doesn't really matter for you, does it? You're not a thief anymore."

I wanted to retort but couldn't. Instead, I just punched him in that meaty arm of his again. I heard something in my hand pop.

"If you'd like," he said softly, "I could teach you how to throw a punch."

I suspected that the offer was less about teaching me self-defense and more about demonstrating a real punch by using my face as his target, so I kept to myself the rest of the walk home.

★

When we arrived at my parents' house, the sun was setting and we found the Dowager's carriage pulled up to the front door. The Dowager was waiting outside.

"There you are!" she said in her singsong voice. "I was getting worried. And who's your friend?"

I coughed at the idea that Maloch was my friend. "This," I said, looking her in the eyes, "is Maloch Oxter."

The Dowager's nose wrinkled. "*The* Maloch Oxter?"

Maloch frowned. "What's that supposed to mean?"

The Dowager tilted her head, studying Maloch's face. "He doesn't *look* evil, Jaxter. I thought you said—"

Before Maloch could reply, Da clamped his hand around Maloch's mouth and ushered him toward the house. As Da fought to get Maloch through the door, Ma curtsied politely.

"Lovely to see you again, Annestra. Forgive us, but we have an urgent matter to attend to. You know. Phydollotry shop business." She then turned and helped Da pull Maloch into the house, closing the door behind them.

The Dowager smiled sweetly after them. "For rogues,

your parents are such nice people. We should visit them again. For now, it's time we were getting back."

I started. "Really? So soon?"

"I'm afraid so. My brother is expecting a response from me regarding those missing artifacts. I'm sorry we have to leave earlier than we'd planned."

My heart thumped in my chest. Going back meant working on the translation of *The Kolohendriseenax Formulary*. But it might also mean crawling around underground after vessapedes again. Or maybe tromping around the fireglades of Yonick Province, seeing if we could outrun a sanguibeast.

I had a hunch we couldn't.

The one thing I knew for sure: my fear of dying overrode my love of learning. I wasn't sure I could take much more. But I thought about what Maloch said: *You're not a thief anymore.* And it made my brow burn to admit he was right. Studying science was the only thing that came naturally to me. If I didn't go back with the Dowager, what would I do?

"Right," I said absently. "I, uh . . . I'll just go get my things."

The Dowager climbed into the carriage as I entered the

house. Ma and Da bent over the kitchen table, studying a map of the Five Provinces. Nanni and Aubrin sat nearby, Aubrin writing so quickly in one of her journals that I thought her hand might fall off. Maloch paced back and forth, yelling at them all.

"I came to you to help find my father—," he was saying.

"We have no idea where he is, Maloch," Da said patiently. "Right now, our best bet is to try to warn the remaining Shadowhands that someone is after them. Your da left us with enough information to go on. This is what he wanted. That's why he kept records. Once the remaining Shadowhands have been warned, I'm sure they'll launch an effort to find your da and everyone else who's gone missing."

Ma pointed to the map. "We can be in Aldria in two days."

Da looked to Nanni. "Mind putting off your retirement just a mite? Watch Aubrin and Maloch until we get back?"

Maloch stomped his foot. "I will not let her watch me."

"No problem, kid, I didn't want to watch you anyway," Nanni said, turning her nose up in the air.

Ma went to the closet and pulled out two large back-packs. One of the perils of being a Grimjinx is that you have to be ready at a moment's notice to flee, in case you're ever chased by an angry mob. It's happened more times than I can count. As a result, Ma and Da kept a stash of emergency supplies, already separated into packs. We could live off those packs for days.

"If you're going to find the Shadowhands, then I'm coming with you," Maloch said firmly.

"Maloch, we have no idea what we're up against," Ma said. "Ona and I are old hats at this. The search will go much faster if it's just the two of us."

Maloch stood there, silently fuming. I didn't know what to think. What Ma and Da said made sense, but if I were in Maloch's shoes, I wouldn't wait around, hoping someone would look for Da at some point. Instead of arguing, he turned and tromped upstairs.

As Ma and Da checked their packs, I realized I couldn't leave with the Dowager. I needed more time to decide if I wanted to continue my apprenticeship. I reached into the closet and helped myself to another pack. "If you wait just a few minutes, I can—"

Da took the pack from my hands. "Hold hard, young man. Where are you going?"

Ma shook her head. "You have an apprenticeship, mister. Responsibilities. Your place is in Redvalor Castle now. Your da and I will take care of this, and we'll send you a letter when it's all through. Don't keep the Dowager waiting."

I opened my mouth to speak. Everything I wanted to say—how miserable I was, how the apprenticeship wasn't what I thought it would be, how the Dowager and I had argued endlessly for the last two months—just sat there at the back of my throat. Ma and Da had been so supportive of me. If any other young thief had told his parents he wanted to leave the family business and study plants, he'd have been locked in his bedroom until he could pick the lock and get out himself. But Ma and Da wanted me to be happy and do whatever I wanted. How could I admit that maybe what I wanted wasn't what I'd thought I wanted?

My shoulders slumped. Ma and Da gave Nanni, Aubrin, and me quick hugs, then slipped out the back door.

"Come on, Aubrin," Nanni said, taking my sister's hand. "We've got another mouth to feed." She glanced up the stairs to where Maloch had gone. "And it looks like a big one. Time to go shopping."

"But you're dead, remember?" Aubrin asked. "If you think

you'll go unnoticed, you don't have a ghost of a chance."

Nanni shook her head at the joke. "I think I liked it better when you didn't speak." She threw a cowl over her head
to disguise her face. "If anyone notices, you can tell them I'm
your nanni's evil twin sister. That should scare the nosy ones
away."

And with that, they left. I glanced out the window at the
Dowager's carriage. An idea formed. Before I lost my nerve,
I ran outside.

"Oh, good," the Dowager said as I crawled into the seat
across from her, "we can leave. You know how much I hate
traveling at night. The rogues who prey on night travelers
aren't nearly as nice as your parents."

"Listen," I said slowly, avoiding her eyes, "Maloch's
father. He's missing. My parents are going to look for him
and I . . . I think I should go with them."

I figured that if I headed out now, I could catch up and
talk them into letting me join them. Tell them I wanted
one last adventure before returning to Redvalor. They'd buy
that. I hoped.

The Dowager's eyes grew sad. "Is this . . . about our
problems?"

I stammered, "N-no, no . . . I just want to help my parents. Then I'll come back to Redvalor so we can start translating the *Formulary.* Just give me a week. Maybe two."

The Dowager studied me. I felt sick lying. I didn't know for sure that I *would* return to Redvalor.

"If you must, you must," she said, smiling as the singsong returned to her voice. "Oh, I will miss you, Jaxter. Arguments aside, we've had some good times these past few months."

If you don't count vessapedes trying to eat our faces, I thought. But I said, "I've learned so much from you. Thank you." The Dowager looked confused, and I realized it sounded like I was saying good-bye permanently. So I added, "We can talk more when I get back."

"Take as long as you need to help your parents. But I'll expect you to go right to work on the translation when you return."

I held both hands over my heart. "Thief's honor."

I bounded from the carriage and waved as it pulled away. Once it was out of sight, I ran into the house and took an emergency pack from the closet. Ma and Da could only have just left the town-state gates. Catching up would be easy. Convincing them to let me join the search . . . Well, I couldn't let the fact that I'd failed once stop me. As my great-great-aunt Gola Grimjinx always said, "The thief who tries twice can only die once."

Come to think of it, that wasn't a very good saying.

I took the back door into the alley. I'd only made it half-way down the passage when something large and heavy fell on me from above.

I hit the ground, the air rushing from my lungs. Head spinning from the impact, I looked around to find Maloch sprawled out next to me, shaking his head.

"What are you doing in the alley?" he asked.

I looked up and noticed that my second-floor bedroom window was open.

"What are you doing jumping out of windows?" I said back to him.

Maloch crawled around on his hands and knees, retrieving the contents from his backpack, which had spilled all over the alley.

"Should have known better than to trust a Grimjinx," he growled, shoving a length of rope, a grappling hook, and a sextant into his pack. "If no one else will help me, I'll find my da myself." He tugged at his sleeve to conceal the small silver dagger in a sheath on his forearm.

I leaped to my feet to block him from leaving the alley. Not that there was anything I could do if he chose to push past me. But I like to think it looked valiant.

"Steady on, Maloch. It's like Ma and Da said, we have no clue where he might be—"

"I don't give a zoc what your parents said!" Maloch said loudly. "They've got their way of searching, I've got mine."

He shoved me with his shoulder and stormed out into the streets as night fell on Vengekeep. The way I saw it, I had three choices. Choice One: continue with my original plan, track down my parents, and join them on their quest to warn the Shadowhands. Choice Two: find Nanni and hope that she could help me convince Maloch to stay and leave things to my parents. Either of these would have been safe, sane things to do.

So why did I go with Choice Three: follow Maloch and try to stop him myself?

I broke into a sprint to catch up with him. "This is completely naff-nut, Maloch. You have no idea where to start looking."

Maloch only walked faster to keep ahead. "Da was on his way to the village of Skona. I'll start there."

"Yeah," I said, practically running to keep up with him, "but you don't even know if he made it to Skona. Look, Ma and Da are looking for the remaining Shadowhands. They've got more practice tracking people down than anyone. They'll find your da."

"The only person I can rely on to find my da is me."

We turned to find a lamplighter touching her flaming pole to one of the oil lamps that dotted every street corner. When she looked our way, Maloch darted between two buildings. I leaped after him, crouched in total darkness. Once the lamplighter had moved on, Maloch slipped back onto the street and I followed.

"Go home, Jaxter," Maloch said. "You're not coming with me."

I laughed. "I'm not planning on going anywhere with you, you garfluk. I wouldn't if you asked me."

"Well, I'm not asking."

"Well, I'm not going. I'm trying to get you to be sensible and come back with me."

He chuckled. "Not a chance."

Suddenly, he stopped. Not watching where I was going, I ran into him and fell to the ground. "Not nice," I said, picking myself up.

He looked side to side, then took off walking again, faster than ever.

I raced to catch up. "If you don't slow down and listen, I can't tell you all the great reasons to stay—"

"We're being followed," he said, pulling me closer. I quickened my pace and searched for our pursuers. "Don't look around, you idiot!"

He was right. Looking around was conspicuous. Amateur mistake . . . and he didn't make it. I did.

Have I mentioned that I hated the idea he was a better thief than me?

He bobbed his head to the left. "Two of 'em. In the shadows behind us."

I shot the quickest of glances, and sure enough, I spotted two hunched figures jumping from shadow to shadow, staying close.

"This way," Maloch said as he pulled us down another alley. The farther we went, the darker it got. We'd only made it about halfway down the alley when a tall, broad-shouldered man stepped out ahead to block our exit. Whirling around, I saw that our two pursuers were now guarding the entrance.

The shadows in the alley started to stir. Four . . . then five . . . soon, eight men had emerged from the darkness and formed a circle around us. It was a trap. They'd intentionally let Maloch know they were following and steered us down this alley on purpose.

The idea that maybe Maloch wasn't such a brilliant thief after all gave me little comfort as the eight men advanced slowly.

I stepped away from the alley's entrance until my back met Maloch's. From the corner of my eye, I saw him raise his arms, so I threw up my own hands in surrender. I looked again to see that Maloch had his fists up. He wasn't giving up. He wanted to fight.

"Oh, zoc," I swore, bringing my hands down to chest level and making the most pathetic fists ever. "You know, there's no shame in screaming like babies for help."

"No way," Maloch said, shifting his weight from foot to foot.

Our attackers appeared weaponless. They were tall and lean, dressed in tattered clothes, long hair pulled back into tails. "Who are they?"

"If someone's after Shadowhands," Maloch said, "they might be going after the families too."

Oh. So they were here for Maloch. My Grimjinx survival instinct kicked in. But before I could even step aside and say, "He's all yours," the men charged at us.

My right hand dove into a pouch on my hip. I pulled out a handful of powdered roxpepper seeds and threw it in the face of the man closest to me. His head pitched back as he howled in pain. I couldn't blame him. His eyes would sting for a week. You don't mess with roxpepper.

Before I could grab more from my pouch, two sets of hands squeezed my arms and yanked me forward. I struggled, thrashing around and trying to stomp on their bare feet. But I weighed next to nothing, and keeping me subdued wasn't a problem.

Maloch, however, was another story. As an apprentice to the stateguard, he'd been trained in kioro, the ancient Satyran fighting art, and it showed. Maloch whirled and spun, throwing fists and kicks in every direction, most of them landing with more force than I imagine these guys thought a twelve-year-old could muster. It was actually kind of impressive. Not that I'd tell him that.

Maloch managed to hold his own until five of them attacked him all at once. They wrestled him to the ground, and Maloch went down fighting. I opened my mouth to try plan B—the screaming-like-a-baby idea—but someone clamped a wet rag over my face. The earthy smell of camma bark infused in seris oil overwhelmed me, and I gasped in panic. According to the *Formulary*, the combination made a powerful sleeping draught. Gasping was a mistake. The heady aroma sent my head spinning. I was out cold a moment later.

5

Underground

"The friendlier the smile, the deeper the cut."

—*Ancient par-Goblin proverb*

When I awoke, I drew a deep breath in through my nose and found my nostrils filled with dirt. My head throbbed. I pushed my glasses, which were dangling from the tip of my nose, as far up as they could go. It took a moment for my vision to clear. My mouth was completely dry. I knew to expect this after waking from a camma bark and seris oil infusion. Even so, I chose to blame Maloch for how awful I felt. It seemed right.

Sitting up, I dug what dirt I could out of my nose and

looked around. The round room was made entirely of earth. *Underground,* I thought. The black ceiling, walls, and floor glimmered with an eerie purple glow as pinpricks of light burned like tiny stars all around.

Not a good sign.

When I stood, a rush of dizziness nearly sent me to my knees. I reached out and touched the wall, which felt soft and moist. Pulling back my hand, I sniffed my fingertips. They smelled vaguely of warm mangmilk.

Definitely not a good sign. The sooner I got out of here— wherever here was—the better.

I took two steps and tripped. For once, it wasn't my fault. In the dim light, I'd failed to notice Maloch in a lump next to me.

Thick rope bound his wrists to his ankles. A dirty rag had been shoved into his mouth. He didn't look comfortable. I guessed that from the way he was wincing.

"Sorry, did I kick you when I tripped?" I asked, pushing myself up to all fours. "Well, might not be so bad if I did. I owe you a kick or two for everything you've done to me over the years. Maybe three." I surveyed the scene. Just a few steps away, an opening led from the chamber to a tunnel where more purple light, embedded in the walls, sparkled. This appeared to be the only way out. "How long have you been awake?"

Maloch began squirming. He was muttering, which I guessed was really cursing. I listened for evidence we were being guarded. I heard nothing.

"No guard. No door to block our escape. Too easy, wouldn't you say, Maloch?" I took a cautious step toward the entrance, scooped up a handful of purple sparkling dirt, and tossed it over the threshold. Nothing happened. "Still could be booby-trapped, I suppose. What do you think?"

Maloch had stopped thrashing around and was now screaming full volume into his gag.

"You know, Maloch, I like you this way: quiet. Well, not exactly quiet. But 'nonverbal' is definitely an improvement." If he could have, he'd have murdered me with his eyes. His grunting became a steady, low, dangerous roar. I sighed. "Still, as much as I hate to say this, we're sort of stuck together here, and we won't get very far if we can't talk."

I yanked the rag from his mouth. He sucked in a massive breath, then spent a few moments heaving and coughing.

"I'm going . . . to pound you . . . you little zochead . . . ," he sputtered, his voice hoarse from all the restrained screaming.

I shook my head and tsked. "Not a persuasive argument for me to untie you."

"Why did they tie me up and not you?" he asked.

I held up my hands and ticked off the reasons. "You're disagreeable, you kicked several of them in the head, you're ornery, you called some of their mothers terrible names, you smell funny—that might not be a reason for tying you up, but I thought it worth mentioning—and, if your theory is right, you're the son of a Shadowhand and very valuable to them."

"Then untie me before they check in on us."

I examined the ropes. "Every time you move, you make the knots tighter. I need something to cut through them." I kicked around in the dirt, hoping to find a sharp-edged stone.

Maloch smacked his lips. "Do you see any water? I'm thirsty."

"That'll be the aftereffects of the sleeping draught. I'm thirsty too. And hungry." I reached for my copy of *The Kolohendriseenax Formulary*, which I kept on my belt with my pouches, only to discover that all three—belt, book, and pouches—were missing. I squeezed my eyes shut and tried to recall what the book said about camma bark/seris oil infusion. "It's a pretty potent sleeping draught. My guess is we could have been out for as long as a day. Maybe a little longer."

"Yeah, that's fascinating. *Now untie me!*"

I'll admit: I was taking my time. Maloch had spent two years tormenting me. I didn't mind seeing *him* helpless for a change. But truthfully, the purple, twinkling glow all around us worried me far more than I'd let on. We needed to leave quickly.

I knelt over him and wormed my fingers into the knots. "Listen, we have to be careful. The thing about these caves is—"

From behind, in the direction of our only exit, I heard voices. Our captors were coming. I tugged as hard as I could at the ropes, but the knots wouldn't budge.

"Move away from him or I'll cut out your liver!"

I turned slowly, hands in the air. Two figures stepped into the cave. They were dressed like the men who'd attacked us: ragged vests and tattered pants that cut off at the knees. The taller, a girl about my age, held out a serrated dagger at arm's length. Her hair was short and spiky, and her dark skin glistened with sweat. Her fierce stare told me that if I so much as looked at Maloch's ropes, she'd follow through on the threat she'd just made.

I smiled. "Happy to. That way, your knife can stay clean, my innards can stay... *in*, where they belong. Everyone wins."

Based on the strong resemblance, I guessed that the small boy with her, who looked to be around Aubrin's age, was her brother. His hair gathered in curls that gripped his head tightly. His eyes, big and wide, didn't blink. It was very creepy.

Instead of a weapon, the boy held a large clay bowl filled with clear liquid. At a nod from his sister, he stepped forward and laid the bowl at my feet, then scooped up a small cup full of the liquid and handed it to me.

"Now is not the time to think, now it is the time to drink!" he said in a remarkably low voice.

"Uh ... right," I said, taking the cup. I swirled the liquid around and gave it a sniff. It certainly seemed like water. I tried to forget everything the Lymmaris Creed—the ancient code by which all thieves lived—said about drinking with your enemies. It said a lot and none of it good. But why poison me if they could have killed me in my sleep? So I gulped it down. The water had a hint of sweetness.

Before I could thank him, the boy snatched the cup away, filled it up again, and knelt near Maloch.

My ex-friend sneered. "You're a complete naff-nut if you think I'm drinking even a drop of that!"

The girl rushed forward and stood directly over Maloch. "Everyone drinks at First Rise. It's our way. You will not insult our way." She poked the side of his head with the tip of her dagger, making Maloch yelp.

The boy held up his hand, as if to calm his sister. He closed his eyes and said, "Let the weapon go today, he will drink another way." With that, he stomped on Maloch's foot. Maloch yowled in pain. In that moment, the boy shoved the cup forward and poured the water into Maloch's mouth.

Maloch gagged and coughed. I caught the serious-faced girl smirking for just a moment. Then her face went hard again, and she started waving the dagger around.

I held up my hands. "So, yeah, thanks for the drink. It really hit the spot. I feel much better. I'm sure I'd feel better still if you put the dagger away and maybe told us what's going on."

"You're our prisoners," the girl said, signaling for her

brother to step back.

"*We know that!*" Maloch said, seething. "Now go get someone we can deal with."

The girl put a hand on her hip. "You'll deal with whoever you're sent, and this morning, that's us. If that's a problem, you won't see another drop of water or a lick of food until tomorrow morning. Got it?"

"Right, right," I said. "We're happy to deal with you. It might be easier, though, if you told us your names."

The boy looked up at his sister, who frowned uncertainly. Then she said, "I'm Reenakarutysor. And this is my brother, Holminjarlamaxin."

Maloch scoffed. "Those aren't names. Those are medications."

The girl's nostrils flared, but it was the boy who responded. "This is not a foolish game, you shall not insult my name!" With that, he kicked Maloch in the stomach, eliciting another squeal of pain.

"Does he," I said to the sister, "know that he speaks in rhyme?"

The girl's jaw hardened. "Of course he does!"

I blinked. "And . . . no one finds that odd?"

"If you must know, he's training to be a warrior-bard."

I blinked again. There hadn't been any warrior-bards for over a hundred years. The vocation had been quite popular in its day. Problem was: they were easily killed in battle. Given the choice between composing a rhyming couplet and parrying a lethal blow, too few chose to parry.

"Okay," I said. "Great. Erm, could I have your names again?"

The girl folded her arms. "Call me Reena. And he's Holm."

"Reena." I nodded, then smiled at her brother. "Holm. The warrior-bard. Got it. So, any chance you can explain why we're here?"

Holm picked up his bowl as Reena pointed her knife right at my chest. "Not for us to explain. We're taking you and Mighty Boy here to someone who can."

I held my hands up. "Okay. Let's go do some talking. Lead the way."

Reena shook her head. "No. After you."

I shuffled out of the chamber. Reena shoved the rag back in Maloch's mouth. Together with Holm, they each grabbed an end of Maloch and carried him behind me.

I considered bolting. If Maloch's theory was right, and it was him they wanted, they'd be more concerned with keeping him secure. I could get away and bring help back. But there was something about Reena that told me she could bury that dagger in my spine before I could run three steps. So, that most honorable Grimjinx tradition—running—was out.

When we came to an intersection, Reena barked directions. She guided me through an elaborate network of tunnels, glowing with the same unearthly purple light.

"Not that I'm, you know, objecting to violence against Maloch—sometimes it seems necessary, in fact—but I have to say that it's out of character for the Sarosans."

Holm gasped. Reena froze in place.

"Sorry, was I not supposed to know?" I smiled weakly. "You sort of gave yourselves away. Drinking at First Rise? That's a Sarosan custom, isn't it? To honor the world by taking a drink first thing in the morning."

Holm started to speak, but Reena shushed him.

"He'd have found out eventually," she said. Then she narrowed her eyes at me. "Move."

I continued forward. "It's okay, you know. I'm sympathetic. I know a lot of people who are upset about what the

High Laird is doing to you."

Before I realized what was happening, Reena had dropped Maloch and forced me up against the wall. The cold point of her dagger touched the underside of my chin.

"What do you know about it?" Reena said angrily. "Do you know what it's like to have your family arrested without a reason? Do you know what it's like to be regarded with suspicion wherever you go?"

Well, yes, I knew a lot about all that.

But I got the feeling it was all new and scary to her. And by family, I don't think she meant the Sarosans. Had Reena and Holm's parents been among those arrested?

Reena's eyes grew darker as her agitation rose. "Do you know what it's like to be forced to live like animals underground?"

"Ah, yes," I said, "speaking of animals . . . I'm not sure if you know this, but these tunnels are vessapede warrens. They're very dangerous."

"The tunnels suit our present needs, there are no signs of vessapedes," Holm said.

I looked at Reena, trying to make her understand how serious this was. "Maybe not now, but . . ." I swiped my hand across the dirt wall and moved the splinters of purple light to my fingertips. "When vessapedes burrow, they secrete this goo that crystallizes when it mixes with the earth. That's where the purple light comes from—these little crystals. The light can burn for up to two months after the tunnel's been dug. So the vessapedes who burrowed these tunnels have been here within that time."

Reena shook her head. "We've been living here for almost a month. If there were vessapedes, we'd have seen them by now."

I couldn't believe that the time I'd spent underground tracking these monsters with the Dowager was about to pay off. "Not necessarily. The vessapedes have a bimonthly hibernation period. They burrow for a month, then hibernate for a month. They never hibernate in their warrens, but they're also never far. If you've been here a month, then it's getting close to time—"

Reena threw her head back and laughed. "Lucky us, Holm. We kidnapped a vessapede expert. Next he'll be lecturing us on what they eat."

"Faces, mainly," I said matter-of-factly.

Suddenly, the dagger arched up and down through the

air, missing my nose by a hair. "You'll say anything to be set free. Keep moving. No one said I had to bring you back in one piece." She picked up her half of Maloch and waited for me.

I let the glowing dirt fall from my fingers, then turned and continued in the direction they prodded me.

The tunnel opened up into a cavern that shone brightly with indigo light from millions of crystals embedded everywhere. A motley assortment of tents, weatherworn and dirty, lined up in rows like streets before us. Sarosans, in their modest garb, went about their business: doing laundry, reading from books, and cooking over fires whose smoke rose and disappeared up a shaft in the ceiling high overhead.

Most likely, this shaft had been the route the vessapedes took to the surface to hunt in the forest at night.

Reena guided me through the maze of tents until we came to one that was just slightly bigger than the others. I pulled back the door flap, and Reena pushed me through. A large rock in the center served as a table. A couple of dilapidated cots stood to the left and to the right. A trio of burning candles filled the air with the scent of mokka trees in bloom.

An Aviard man with impressively large wings and an

older human woman seated at the rock table stood as we entered. Reena and Holm dropped Maloch at my feet, bowed, and left.

"Hi," I said. "Jaxter Grimjinx. Do you mind if I untie my friend? Well, he's not really my friend, but it looks like he's in pain and I've always had a soft spot for—"

The woman moved so fast I barely saw her. Before I knew it, she'd pinched a lock of my hair between two gnarled fingers and cut it off with a small knife.

"Hey!" I shouted. But they ignored me. The woman rolled my hair up into a parchment scroll, which she sealed into a glass tube and handed to the Aviard.

"I'll get this to the Dowager by morning," the man said, fluttering his wings.

The Dowager? What did she have to do with any of this?

Not giving either a chance to protest, I knelt next to Maloch and removed his gag.

"Where is he?" he demanded, straining at his bonds. "What have you done with my father?"

The two Sarosans looked confused. "Who is he, Warras?" the woman asked the Aviard.

"We had to take him too," Warras said. "He was a witness

when we kidnapped Grimjinx."

Maloch and I exchanged a look. This had nothing to do with him being the son of a Shadowhand. It was *me* they were after.

I nodded at the tube holding the parchment. "What is that? Why are you sending it to Dowager Soranna?"

Warras folded his arms. "By the order of our leader, you will remain here until the Dowager has persuaded her brother, the High Laird, to drop all charges against our people."

Of course. I was a hostage. A bargaining chip. No doubt the parchment in that tube was a note threatening my life if the Dowager didn't comply with their demands. And under any other circumstances, I would have let them deliver the note and then waited for the Dowager to arrange my release.

But I knew something they didn't.

"No," I said, softly but firmly. "I'm going to untie my friend. And then you're going to get someone to escort us back to Vengekeep. Do it my way and you might survive."

All I could hear was blood pounding in my ears as I fought to stay confident. I started to work on the ropes around Maloch's wrists. When the Aviard moved to stop me, I looked up sharply.

"One way or another, we're leaving here," I said. "You can let us go. Or . . . we wait."

The woman laughed. "Wait? Wait for what?"

That's when we all heard the first scream. Then the second. Next, a whole chorus of shrieks filled the cavern beyond the tent walls.

I looked the Sarosans right in the eye.

"For *that*."

6

Attack of the Vessapedes

"A sincere assurance is a lock pick for the heart."

—*The Lymmaris Creed*

Outside, it sounded like a slaughter. Which was probably exactly what was happening.

Without a second thought, Warras and the woman ran from the tent to investigate. I dug my thumbs into Maloch's bonds and twisted until the ropes fell to the floor.

"What is that?" he asked, clearly worried. The bloodcurdling screams were now joined with cries for help and the mad footfalls of people not knowing quite where to run.

"That," I said, my mind reeling back to my last vessapede

encounter, "is what happens when a family of vessapedes comes home to find a bunch of Sarosans in their living room. From the size of these caves, I'm guessing there's three or four. I tried to warn that Reena girl the vessapedes would be back soon. Say what you want about us Grimjinxes, Maloch, but we have *impeccable* timing."

I felt bad for the Sarosans. I really did. I meant it when I said I sympathized with them because of what the High Laird was doing to them. But I was nobody's bargaining chip. If they wanted the Dowager to help them, talking to her would work better than coercing her. But that was their problem. As were the vessapedes. My problem was to get us out of here alive.

Which was going to be harder than I thought. Angry Maloch was gone. *This* Maloch looked shaken. He'd gone pale. Beads of sweat dotted the furrows in his brow. "Vess . . . vessapedes?"

"Maloch," I said, suppressing a smile, "are you . . . afraid of vessapedes?" I wasn't, strictly speaking, an *admirer* of the beasts, but I wasn't feeling anything close to the terror I saw in Maloch's eyes.

He blanched. "You weren't there when they overran

Vengekeep. It was all we could do to fight them off." One of the many disasters the fateskein tapestry had sent to Vengekeep involved an infestation of vessapedes. Apparently, Maloch had fought on the front lines.

Bangers. The hardened fighter was scared of bugs. Granted, these bugs were as wide as Maloch was tall and they stretched for what would have been a city block in Vengekeep. And they'd just as soon eat your face off as look at you. Still, Maloch was picking a terrible time to jettison his tough-guy routine.

"Don't worry. I learned a few tricks for distracting vessapedes. We'll be fine."

Exiting the tent, we found chaos. Men and women ran around brandishing torches, pitchforks, and anything else they could use for weapons. Two massive vessapedes had entered the cavern and were thrashing about near the far side of the camp. Hundreds of spiky tendrils, which acted as hands, feet, and burrowing tools, lined their gray, sluglike bodies. The vessapedes emitted a high-pitched shriek that raised the hair on my arms.

"By the Seven!" Maloch froze, his wide eyes fixed on the vessapedes across the way. I clutched his arm and forced him forward, diving down behind a wagon.

Daring a look, I spotted two exits: the tunnel that led to the cave where we'd woken up—a dead end—and the tunnel from which the vessapedes had presumably entered. Which meant it was our exit.

"Get ready to run," I said, gripping his arm. "On the count of three . . ."

Before I could say another word, one of the vessapedes slithered forward, charging its way through the camp, destroying everything in its path. A crowd of Sarosan women and men leaped in front of it, waving torches, but the creature swatted most of them aside with its tendrils and continued onward. Headed right for us.

"Three!" I yelled, making a crazed dash from the vessapede's path. Maloch caught sight of the stampeding beast, screamed, and followed me. Entire tents flew over our heads as the vessapede made short work of the Sarosans' homes. We aimed for the perimeter of the camp, hoping to follow the wall around to the exit.

Just then, the second vessapede made its move. With a war cry, it lashed out at the Sarosans who had surrounded it and started ripping apart the other side of the camp.

We changed course, choosing a path between broken tents that brought us closer to the exit. As we cleared the camp, the exit tunnel loomed wide ahead of us. All we had to do was find our way to the surface and—

A bellow unlike anything uttered by the vessapedes in the cavern issued from the tunnel in front of us. The hairs on my arm stood at attention as a gelatinous gray face filled the tunnel entrance. A moment later, the biggest vessapede of the lot pushed its way into the cavern.

It was three times larger than the rest of the herd. The front of its wormy body reared up and its three mouths— each baring razor-sharp teeth—opened to shriek. The dozen or so spiky tendrils that were visible inside the cavern flailed about, searching for faces to eat.

The rest of the vessapede's body disappeared down the exit tunnel. There was no way past it.

Maloch stood limply in stunned horror. I hooked my arm around his and dragged him back behind one of the few tents that remained standing.

"We have to lure it farther into the cavern," I said.

"You want us to bring it *in*?" he asked.

"Once the tunnel's clear, we can—"

The air shot from my lungs as a blurry figure tackled me. Out of the corner of my eye, I saw the same thing happen to Maloch. Shaking my head, I found Reena crouched on my chest, dagger in hand, while Holm had Maloch pinned.

"Get back to your cell!" Reena said, her voice shaking.

"Have you gone completely naff-nut?" I yelled. "Your people are under attack and you're worried about us—"

"Get back to your cell!" she said again, this time without quivering.

A small group of Sarosans ran past us to attack the largest vessapede. The creature screamed louder than ever and began batting away the Sarosans like they were insects. As the vessapede shrieked, I noticed two bulbous yellow sacs throbbing just below its lowest mouth. That told me everything I needed to know about surviving this.

Reena pulled me to my feet. Maloch was wrestling with the much smaller Holm, but the boy proved surprisingly strong. And Maloch couldn't stop looking at the vessapede, inching its way into the room.

"I can help!" I said.

"You're trying to escape," Reena said, shoving me up against the tent.

"I know about vessapedes," I said. "You know I do. I predicted this would happen. I can put an end to this, but you have to help me."

Reena looked on as the adult Sarosans continued their increasingly futile battle. She bit her lip, then let me go. By now, Holm had managed to get Maloch on his stomach and was holding the bigger boy's arms behind his back.

"Bangers, Holm!" I said. "Now, let him up. We need him too. We have to find a pile of rocks."

"What?" Reena asked as Holm slid off Maloch.

"Somewhere in this cave, there's a pile of rocks," I said, looking wildly about. "They would have already been here when you set up camp. Small rocks. Lots of them. In a tall pile."

Reena looked dubious, but Holm stepped forward.

"I've explored the cave for weeks, I know of the rocks you seek!" the young boy declared.

I forgave the bad rhyme and said, "Show me!"

Holm turned and ran toward the heart of the camp. I followed as Reena prodded a still-aching Maloch along. We dodged our way through the debris, avoiding the vessapedes as they slithered by, until Holm brought us to a small nook along the far wall.

Tucked just inside was exactly what I was looking for: a cone-shaped pile of stones. Kneeling, I began tossing the stones aside. Soon, the others joined me.

"What," Reena said, tone laced with anger, "are we doing?"

"The vessapede that's blocking the entrance is the queen," I said, and I tapped under my chin. "Just under her lower mouth are feeding sacs. They only become visible when she's getting ready to nurse. The family came back to this cave not just because it's their home. They came back to get . . ."

We all stood and took a step back, having reached the bottom of the pile of stones. There, nestled in a shallow hole, sat four blood-red vessapede eggs, each the size of Holm's head.

Maloch picked up a rock. "So we smash them!"

I jumped between him and the nest. "Not if you want to live. Okay, everybody grab an egg, hold it over your head, and follow me. I have a plan."

Everyone did as they were told. I led our single-file line as we walked slowly through the decimated camp. The two vessapedes that had been tearing apart the camp stopped dead when they saw us. Each slithered aside, emitting a low growl-hiss.

Sweat poured from Maloch's forehead. "Jaxter . . ."

"We're fine," I whispered. "As long as we don't actually harm the eggs, we're fine."

The other Sarosans saw what we were doing and stepped aside, clearing a path as we marched toward the queen at the entrance. When the queen spotted us, she stopped her screeching and purred the same growl-hiss that the others had made. We stood before the queen for several seconds.

"All right," I said to the others. "Now back up. Slowly."

Everyone obeyed. We kept the eggs high above our heads in clear sight. And with every step back we took, the queen slid farther into the cavern. Once her entire body was inside, the exit tunnel was clear.

"Now what?" Reena asked.

"She'll give us a wide berth. She won't risk hurting the eggs. Holm, walk around and head down the tunnel. We'll get them to follow us out."

"And then what?" Reena asked.

"My ancestor Mirdella Grimjinx always said, 'When you don't want to hear the answer, don't ask the question.'"

"But I *do* want the answer."

"No, you don't. Trust me."

Holm led the way, followed by Reena, then Maloch, and finally me. The queen's large, slimy body coiled around itself as she continued to growl-hiss, her six pairs of eyes never once leaving her eggs. Holm moved slowly into the tunnel. The queen wiggled toward us, causing Maloch to whimper.

"She's going to follow us," I told him. "Don't worry. I keep telling you. As long as the eggs are safe—"

And that's when I tripped. And that's when the egg I was carrying shattered. All over Maloch's head, covering him in thick, gray fluid. The crowd of Sarosans gasped. Holm and Reena, frozen at the entrance of the tunnel, looked back in terror at the queen.

The monstrous vessapede reared up higher than ever. Her tendrils flailed at the cavern ceiling, and her scream made the earth shake.

Oh, zoc.

7

Tinderjack

"Trust is for those who forsake the solace
of suspicion."

—*Lyama Grimjinx, master thief of Jarron Province*

"Move!" I shouted, charging for the tunnel.

The four of us ran with only the dim purple light to guide us. At our backs, I could hear the queen burrowing her way into the mouth of the tunnel. I grabbed Maloch.

"When the queen's done killing you," he said tersely, "I'm going to kill whatever's left."

"Fair enough," I said, taking the egg from his hands and laying it carefully against the tunnel wall. "This will slow her down. She'll stop to make it safe. But then she'll come after us."

The shrieks of the vessapede grew louder, and we continued forward.

"You said you had a plan!" Reena said, tucking her egg under her arm.

"Running away from vessapedes *is* a plan," I said. "A pretty good one, too."

The tunnel forked off in three directions. Behind us, I could hear a growling-cooing sound as the queen found the first egg. It would take her only a moment to clear a niche in the tunnel wall, deposit the egg, and continue on her murderous rampage. No doubt the other two vessapedes would follow her.

"You must know these tunnels," I said to Reena and Holm, trying to catch my breath. "Which way to the surface?"

They looked at each other uncertainly. They knew as well as Maloch and I did that showing us the way out meant we'd save our own skins and leave them for the vessapedes.

"No. Let's just leave the rest of the eggs in another cave for the vessapedes to find," Reena said.

I shook my head. "Once they get the other eggs, they'll

head to the camp to finish everyone off. You're still in their home, remember? We have to lure them aboveground and then keep them from coming back." I had no idea how to keep the vessapedes out, but it was the best idea I had.

Maloch was still pulling fistfuls of raw egg from his face, slapping them to the ground in great heaps. "Show us the way out or we'll leave you here, dolly girl."

"You'll leave us either way!" Reena said.

A screech from behind announced that the queen was burrowing our way again. More shrieks followed, so loud that the tunnel shook, showering bits of earth down on us.

"We don't have time for this," I said, snatching the eggs from Reena and Holm. "You two take Maloch to the surface. If the vessapedes follow you, find a way to block the exit so they can't come back to the tunnels. But I don't think they'll follow you."

Reluctantly, Reena and Holm led Maloch down the left tunnel.

"Why?" Maloch called back to me.

I laid one egg down at the entrance of the right-hand tunnel. "Because they'll be following me." I tucked the remaining egg under my arm and scurried along the right-hand tunnel until the others were nothing more than faint silhouettes behind me. I called over my shoulder, "Get to the surface!"

The tunnel curved and widened. I wiped sweat from my eyes as I kept running. The purple crystals embedded in the walls gave off fainter light until finally I was in near darkness. Farther back, I could hear the distant growl-cooing of the queen as she found the egg at the tunnel's entrance. By now, the other two vessapedes would have caught up with her.

I leaned against the wall, trying to figure out what to do next. I couldn't outrun them. I couldn't threaten the egg or I'd be faceless in under a minute. All I could really do was outsmart them, but even that didn't seem like it would be enough. I closed my eyes to concentrate, hearing nothing but the queen's growl-cooing far away.

And that's when the smell hit me. Wafting from just ahead on a gentle, subterranean breeze: a sharp odor, musty and familiar. I thought back six months ago to when Callie, Edilman, and I were trying to escape from Redvalor Castle. I had taken my flashballs and made them into a makeshift explosive to blow a hole in the perimeter wall. I'd never forget that burning, musk-like odor.

I suddenly knew how I was going to get out of this.

If I was lucky.

A howl from behind me warned that the queen was on the warpath again. I moved back to where the tunnel was lined with purple crystals and gently rolled the egg around in the earth. Crystals clung to the shell, and soon the egg gave off its own glow. With a new source of light, I turned and ran toward that powerful odor. The question was: did the queen want her egg badly enough to follow?

Of course, I already knew the answer.

I pressed on, the stink in the darkness ahead guiding my way. To the rear, I heard the queen pause. Her shrieks quieted, and I knew she smelled what lay ahead too. Then I heard chattering. A metallic, clicking sound that I remembered from my time with the Dowager in the warrens. It was how the vessapedes communicated. First the queen clicked, then two distinct sets of clicks answered. It was clear they didn't want to proceed.

Come on, I thought. Crazy as it sounded, I *needed* them to follow me, if this was going to work. If they turned back now, they'd only finish off the Sarosans.

Taking a deep breath, I ran back toward the warrens until

I could just scarcely make out two of the queen's mouths at the head of her body. I held the glowing egg over my head.

"You're probably wondering if you picked the right tunnel," I shouted. "It's your lucky day!"

I turned and bolted into the darkness, managing to trip on my own feet only twice. The queen, ignoring the stink in the tunnel, shot forward. I'd forgotten exactly how fast they can move underground. I leaped over stone nubs, covering my mouth with one hand to fight off the pungent smell that threatened to gag me.

I stopped just short of stepping on a tinderjack plant.

I held up the glowing egg and found that I'd arrived in a large domed chamber, not unlike the one that housed the Sarosan camp. But instead of tents everywhere, I saw hundreds of tinderjack plants sprouting up from the ground. Part flower, part fungus, the tinderjack only grew underground. This crop was getting ready to bloom. A few had already blossomed, exposing three wide red-and-yellow petals on each plant. In the center of every set of petals, standing upright, was a leathery black pod. I swallowed, eyeing the exposed pods nervously. Gingerly, I moved between the plants and walked to the center of the room.

A chorus of roars trumpeted behind me. I turned to find all three vessapedes slithering into the chamber. But they stopped immediately upon seeing the field of tinderjack. Their screeching faded, replaced with a cautious growl-hiss.

I plugged my nose. "Oh good. I was hoping you knew what tinderjack is. Nasty stuff. Dangerous."

Near the edge of the chamber, one of the plants shook. As the colorful petals fell open, it belched a short plume of flame up into the air. I gritted my teeth and the vessapedes squealed. The newly blossomed tinderjack's petals curved back, exposing the pod within.

"Oh, yeah," I said, grinning. "Vessapedes aren't really fond of fire. You're smart. You knew enough to keep your distance from the tinderjack. We both know how volatile those pods are, right?"

I leaned forward to a plant that had blossomed, threatening to touch the pod within. The vessapedes fell silent and cowered.

"That's right. One wrong move and ka-boom." I pulled my hand back, and the vessapedes resumed their growl-hiss.

A burst of flame in the corner announced the blossoming of another plant. I eyed it nervously. "See, guys, the thing is: tinderjack isn't very stable. You never see this much of it so close together. Because when they bloom, the fire could ignite the entire field."

So exactly *why* was there so much tinderjack? Tinderjack was fairly rare, and nature made sure two plants didn't blossom near each other or they could both be destroyed during the bloom. This couldn't have occurred naturally.

Concentrate, Jaxter. You're facing down three vessapedes and standing in the biggest field of explosives in the Five Provinces. Now is not the time for scientific curiosity.

I looked around. A few more plants, some right in the thick of the field, were shaking, getting ready to bloom. It was only a matter of time before a fire burst ignited one of those pods, which would detonate everything around it and then . . .

"How does this sound?" I said, laying the egg gently down in an exposed spot near my feet. "Why don't I just put your egg right here? And you could maybe move away from the exit? Then we can all just walk—or slither, whatever you like—away and nobody has to get blown up. Deal?"

With exaggerated, careful steps, I moved sideways away from the egg. I trod carefully between plants, putting as much space between me and the egg as possible. Soon, I was up against the wall with nowhere to go.

The vessapedes looked to one another, clicking with their metallic teeth. Slowly, they moved to a small clearing opposite the wall where I stood. They each reared up and stretched their spiky tendrils out over the tinderjack field toward the egg.

My back to the wall, I walked along the edge toward the cave entrance. I gasped as a tinderjack bloomed at my feet, sending a jet of flame up past my face. Realizing there was little to stop the vessapedes from coming after me once they had their egg, I came up with a plan. Bending over, I gripped the newly exposed pod at the center of the flower firmly in both hands and gave it a quick, sharp tug.

It came loose from the stamen easily, and a trail of light-gray powder started to trickle from the hole at the pod's base. I continued my slow march to the entrance, letting the pod leave a trail of powder in my wake.

The vessapedes didn't know where to keep their multiple eyes: on me or their efforts to retrieve the egg. As I reached the mouth of the tunnel, I gave them a small salute. The queen had just managed to wrap a tendril around her egg when her two companions suddenly shot their own tendrils in my direction. With a yell, I slammed the nearly empty pod down at my feet. It erupted in a small ball of fire that raced along the trail of powder and back into the field of tinderjack.

I dashed down the tunnel as a deafening explosion rent the air and sent me flying. Flames shot from the tinderjack cavern. The vessapedes screamed. One by one, the plants detonated, shaking the tunnel until the entrance to the tinderjack chamber collapsed.

The ceiling quaked, sending more rocks and dirt on top of me. Soon, it would cave in. I picked myself up and plunged into the dark tunnel, running hard and not bothering to look back.

★

I emerged into the tunnel where the paths split off in three directions. There I found Reena and Holm standing guard over Maloch, who was once again tied with his arms behind his back. Reena waved her dagger and I fell in next to Maloch, hands raised. With a shove, the Sarosans led us back to their camp.

The effort to rebuild had already begun. Tents were being resurrected, debris was being recycled, and the wounded were being treated. But everything froze when Reena and Holm proudly offered up their hostages.

Throngs of Sarosans gathered around us. Warras, the feathers on his head matted down with blood, pushed through to the head of the crowd. I held up my hand.

"We just saved you," I said. "You owe us an explanation. We want to talk to your leader."

"That would be me."

A wizened, gaunt man stepped out from behind Warras. The long white hair that spilled down his back also framed his wrinkled and careworn face. Unlike the other Sarosans, he wore flowing robes that covered his arms and legs. Every move he made was slow and deliberate. He stood directly before me, and we stared at each other for several moments. Then he gently took Reena's dagger and slashed Maloch's bonds.

"That's not any way to treat our heroes, Reena," the leader said.

Reena scowled and Holm looked ashamed. I was a little stunned he was being so rational.

"That's right," I said. "Heroes. And heroes get rewards, right? So does that mean we're free to go?"

The leader clasped his hands together and smiled.

"Oh, I wouldn't say that."

Zoc. So much for being rational.

8

The Sarosan Plight

"Those who choose to see coincidence
fail to see conspiracy."

—*Ancient par-Goblin proverb*

"These caves are no longer safe!" the leader declared to his people. "We must leave at once."

Without question, the Sarosans began salvaging what they could and packing their meager belongings into wagons. I almost told him about how the vessapedes were dead so the tunnels really were safe. But it occurred to me that if the Sarosans were on the move and taking us with them, Maloch and I stood a better chance at escaping if we weren't underground. So I kept quiet.

As everyone worked, the leader pulled Warras aside and whispered in the Aviard's ear. Warras nodded, gripped the glass tube with the message for the Dowager, and exited through the tunnel. I didn't like that the Sarosans were manipulating her, but I knew the Dowager would do whatever it took to free me.

At least, I assumed so.

The leader guided Maloch and me through the carnage to one of the few tents untouched in the vessapede attack. The inside looked much like the place where Warras and his friend had taken my hair. A cot stood against one wall. A table with small bowls holding an assortment of herbs, spices, and plants I couldn't identify sat in the room's center.

I noticed for the first time just how tall the leader was. His head nearly touched the top of the tent. As old as he looked—and he looked *old*—his eyes danced, young and active. He moved slowly, wincing as his arms swayed at his sides. When he spoke, his voice was low and gravelly.

"Please make yourselves comfortable while I pack," he said, pointing to a couple of stools. I sat. Maloch remained standing. As the leader began to wrap the bowls from the table in swaths of burlap, he watched Maloch carefully. "You have something you'd like to say."

"I have *lots* I'd like to say," Maloch said, bobbing from foot to foot like he was ready for a fight. "Like: who are you? Why did you take us? Who are those naff-nut kids who keep attacking us?"

"You'll have to forgive Reena and Holm for behaving brusquely," the leader said with a sigh. "Their parents were among the first arrested when the High Laird declared the Sarosans outlaws. The rest of our tribe has been taking turns caring for Reena and Holm. But sometimes, Reena decides she can take care of herself."

So I was right about their parents.

"Otherwise, have you been treated well?" the man asked.

I shrugged. "Well—and remember that this is coming from a Grimjinx—as far as gaols go, this cave is one of the best I've seen. No bars, no locks. Almost like you didn't expect us to try to escape."

"Not all prisons have bars, Jaxter. Sometimes, the hardest prisons to escape are the ones we carry inside." He gave a single, soft laugh, as though he'd just said something funny.

I spotted Maloch's pack next to mine on the ground near the table. My belt and pouches sat on top of the packs. The man scooped up the small book tucked between the folds of my belt and handed it to me with a smile. "I believe this belongs to you."

I thumbed through my worn copy of the *Formulary*. The Sarosans hardly needed the book. They were the ones who'd made it in the first place.

"Forgive me," he said, "but I looked through your pouches. I see you carry the twelve essentials of nature."

I held up the *Formulary*. "I guess I should thank the Sarosans. This book has changed my life."

His eyebrows went up and his smile widened. "Very glad to hear that. Well, Jaxter, your friend is right. If we're to talk, I should introduce myself. My name is Kolohendriseenax."

"You Sarosans are fond of the alphabet," I said, reeling at yet another lengthy name.

He laughed. "Call me Kolo, if you wish. Everyone does."

"Okay, Kolo. You obviously know who I am, and Warras said you need me to—" I froze. A bell went off in my brain. "Hang on. . . ." I glanced at the cover of the book in my hands. *The Kolohendriseenax Formulary*.

"You're *that* Kolohendriseenax?" I asked, hardly able to breathe.

Kolo beamed. "The one and only."

I looked the gaunt man up and down. The book was so old, I'd always assumed the author was long dead. But if he really was the author . . . I scanned the room, my eyes coming to rest on a battered leather satchel, its shoulder strap slung over the edge of the cot. I couldn't help it. I gasped.

It was Tree Bag.

The Kolohendriseenax Formulary was much more than a collection of research on how to use the natural world to cure illness and negate magical energy. It was also a journal of Kolo's travels. It documented the years he'd spent wandering the Five Provinces, studying plant and animal life. The one constant during that time was the reliable satchel he took everywhere. He called it Tree Bag because of the giant whisperoak embroidered on the side. He spoke so fondly of the satchel that it almost became a character in the *Formulary*.

I know that sounds strange. But trust me, you couldn't read the *Formulary* without getting emotionally attached to Tree Bag.

I grinned like a demented gekbeak. "You have no idea what your book has done for me!" I gushed. "I didn't think I'd ever fit in with my family, but then your anti-magic paste showed me how to help my da pick magical locks. And Ma made some of her best document forgeries because the *Formulary* explained how to make everember parchment."

Kolo tilted his head. "It certainly sounds like you've put my research to . . . creative use. I'm glad I could help in some small way."

I had a thousand questions. *How did you discover the formula for the anti-magic paste? Did you ever figure out what combining waller root, presiberry juice, and oskahoney does?* I couldn't wait to tell the Dowager. She'd curse her luck to have missed the opportunity to meet the author of the book we'd spent hours dissecting.

Maloch tore the book from my hands and threw it against the tent wall. "I don't care about your zocing book. Every minute we're their prisoners is a minute I could be trying to find my father!"

I hated to admit it, but Maloch had a point. As much as I admired Kolo's work, he'd kidnapped us. And getting free had to be our first priority.

Kolo's brow furrowed with concern. "I'm sorry to hear your father is missing. What happened?"

"It's a long story," I said. "Maloch's da is . . . in danger."

No one knew Mr. Oxter was a Shadowhand, and I was bound by the Lymmaris Creed to keep the secret. "We were on our way to find him when your people . . . You know."

Kolo shook his head, clearly troubled by this. "My apologies, Maloch. It's clear our timing could have been better."

I wanted to say, *It's clear you shouldn't kidnap people*, but I didn't.

The Sarosan leader continued to pack the few belongings in the tent. "Perhaps it would help if I explained. I assume you have some idea of what's been happening to my people."

"The High Laird ordered all Sarosans arrested."

"And do you know why?"

"No clue," I said.

Kolo rubbed his chin. "Neither did we. We sent emissaries to the High Laird under a flag of truce, asking why we were being persecuted. Our emissaries were arrested without explanation. The remainder of us fled across the Provinces to avoid capture. Then we intercepted a message from the High Laird to the Palatinate that suggested we had stolen several ancient relics from the royal vaults."

Theft? The Sarosans weren't thieves. They *chose* to live simple lives. They had no reason to steal. And even if they *had* turned to a life of crime, trying to steal from the High Laird was a lousy first heist. The royal vaults were impregnable, a combination of locks, traps, and spells so dangerous the only one who'd ever attempt to steal from them would be—

"Then give back what you stole," Maloch said, breaking my chain of thought, "and let us go."

Kolo shook his head. "We are, I can proudly say, innocent."

"Innocent of theft," I said, "but guilty of kidnapping."

To his credit, Kolo looked genuinely ashamed. "We heard rumors that the Dowager was sympathetic to our cause. We considered seeking an audience with her, but when we tried the same thing with her brother . . . Well, we couldn't risk the rumors being false."

The Sarosan leader laid a hand on my shoulder. "You will not be harmed in our care. I'll see to that. But our people have been wrongfully imprisoned, and our only choice is to take drastic measures. The Dowager will have Warras's message tomorrow morning. Then she'll have two weeks to persuade the High Laird to release all imprisoned Sarosans."

"And what happens if she can't do that?" I asked.

"I have faith that the Dowager will do the right thing.

Until she does, we'll do our best to keep you comfortable."
He nodded to Maloch. "And when our people are free, we
will do all in our power to help search for your father. Now,
please excuse me a moment."

The second Kolo stepped from the tent, I leaped
straight up. "Kolohendriseenax! Can you *believe* it? *The*
Kolohendriseenax. It's just—I mean, I'm—I can't even—I
don't know what to ask him first."

Maloch grabbed me by the shoulders and shook me until
my vision blurred. "Would you get a grip on yourself? He's a
kidnapper. We're his victims. And they don't even want me!
This is all your fault. We'll never find my father."

I pulled myself free. "Are you kidding? We're closer than
ever to figuring it out."

"What do you mean?"

"Weren't you paying attention? The High Laird has
accused the Sarosans—who aren't thieves—of stealing from his impossible-to-enter vaults. Meanwhile, the
Shadowhands, the only thieves in the land who could *possibly*
enter those vaults unnoticed, have mysteriously vanished."

Maloch threw up his hands in disgust. "You're not making any sense."

"It's like par-Goblins say: *Serris torrna m'yurra, sholla ser ontoron*. 'Those who choose to see coincidence fail to see conspiracy.' It's a mite too convenient that the Sarosans were accused of theft around the time the Shadowhands started disappearing."

The blank expression on Maloch's face slowly gave way to understanding. "You think the Sarosans have something to do with my da's disappearance?"

"No," I said, peeking out through a gap in the tent. Nomadic by nature, they were used to pulling up stakes and moving on short notice. They very nearly had the entire camp ready to move. "But there's clearly a link between the Sarosans and the Shadowhands. As long as we're their hostages, we might as well make the most of it. Pay attention. Learn what we can. I don't know what's going to happen when the Dowager gets that ransom note, but one thing I know for sure: we find that link, we find your father."

9

A Sinister Message

"The purse of a fool buys the sweetest happiness."

—*Hulrick Grimjinx, coauthor of the Grimjinx/Aviard Peace Accords*

Emerging from the tunnels to the surface, we were met by a dissonant tune, like the sound of a hundred flutes each playing a different melody. As the fresh air—cold and biting—filled our lungs, Maloch and I trudged along in ankle-deep snow through a dense forest with the rest of the Sarosan convoy. Instead of tall and straight, the mist-colored tree trunks coiled up from the ground like thick wooden springs. A light breeze passed through the natural, fist-sized holes that perforated the trunks, causing the trees to "sing."

"Whistlebirch," I whispered to Maloch.

"Yeah?" he said. "So?"

"So, there are only two whistlebirch forests in the Provinces. Only one within a day or two of Vengekeep. At least now we've got a good idea where we are."

What we didn't know was where we were headed. Before leaving the caves, Kolo had said we were going somewhere he deemed safe that was no more than a day's journey. "We've created several safe havens across the Provinces," he'd told me. "These are secure places we can hide from the Provincial Guard and the Palatinate." I wondered what made these places "secure."

I looked up at the sun, dipping past its noon zenith. "We're heading northwest, so that means—"

I felt a sharp jab in my back. Glancing behind me, I found Reena wielding a long, thin reed—a blowgun—like a lance. Holm made a show of loading *his* blowgun with a small wooden dart.

"No talking," she said, threatening to poke me again.

Maloch and I walked at the heart of the long line of Sarosans, surrounded by the tallest, most muscled men and women in camp. You'd think that would be enough to ensure we weren't going anywhere. But Reena and Holm had taken it upon themselves to be our unofficial escorts. I like to think they knew just how wily a Grimjinx could be and couldn't trust me not to pull something crafty in an attempt to escape.

They clearly weren't taking my extreme desire not to be shot with a blowgun into account.

"You know," I said to Reena, "if you hadn't noticed, I *did* save the Sarosans from having their faces eaten by vessa-pedes. I'm not asking for thanks—although I wouldn't balk at any either—but maybe the least you could do is, I don't know, smile?"

Reena kept her chin up, her chilly gaze straightforward.

I tried again. "I'm really sorry about your parents. If it makes you feel better, the Dowager disagrees with what her brother is doing. I'm sure that, even if you hadn't kidnapped me, she would have eventually challenged him on his policies and gotten him to change his mind."

"'Eventually,'" she said. She didn't sound angry like usual. Now she was just sad. "Next week? Next month? Next year? I don't think my parents should suffer in Umbramore Tower even a minute for something they didn't do. Eventually isn't good enough."

I couldn't argue with that.

We traveled at a brisk pace the rest of the day, slowing only as dusk approached. As we crested a hill, I looked down to see a rocky cliff face not far ahead, just past a snow-covered clearing. The convoy banked hard to the left, taking us deeper into the forest.

"Now that's odd," I said softly to Maloch.

"What?"

"Well, I'm guessing we're headed for the cliff face. It's a natural camouflage and would give the Sarosans a tactical advantage in case of attack. We could head straight there through that clearing, but we're taking the long way around. What do you suppose that means?"

Maloch rolled his eyes. "You think too much, Jaxter. It doesn't mean anything."

Maybe. Maybe not.

As I predicted, after winding our way through more whistlebirch, we arrived at the cliff face just as the final rays of sunlight dwindled on the horizon. Maloch and I were tied to a tree while the Sarosans erected their portable homes by torchlight. Within an hour, it looked very much like the underground camp. As dinner was served, Maloch and I were brought to a campfire, where we joined the others.

As the Sarosans prayed, they passed around baskets of bread and cheese, the traditional evening meal. However, the food was sent around Maloch and me. Before Maloch could protest, the woman who'd cut my hair—who I'd learned was named Surral—arrived with plates of bread and cheese, which she handed to us.

"This is yours," she said.

Maloch was so hungry he dug right in. I was a little more cautious. Why did we merit special plates? Because we were guests? Outsiders? But I reminded myself that if they wanted to kill us, they could do it at any time, so I popped a hastily made cheese sandwich into my mouth. Both the bread and the cheese tasted bitter. I guessed when you lived like the Sarosans, you couldn't be picky about your food.

I felt a hand on my shoulder and looked up to find Kolo. "Jaxter, come with me."

Without another word, he moved away from the circle. I shrugged at Maloch, picked up my plate, and followed. Kolo led me back to his tent, butted up against the cliffs at the back of the camp. He'd wasted no time making himself at home. A long table on the far side was covered with familiar equipment: mortar and pestle, scales, small glass jars filled with exotic plants and unidentifiable fluids. It was like being back in the Dowager's laboratory. A black quill and a messy stack of parchment dangled half off the edge of the table. A small cauldron hung over a fire in the center of the room, its sweetly odorous contents bubbling gently.

Kolo dipped his finger into the cauldron, gave the liquid inside a taste, and nodded approvingly. "Just a moment," he said, stirring the kettle. "Need to finish this batch of tincture."

I looked at the top parchment page on the table. It was messy with notations: sentences underlined, words struck through, notes in the margins. My breath caught when I realized: I was witnessing the creation of a *new formula*!

Kolo took a jar labeled ICECLOVERS and dropped a few of the transparent, three-leafed weeds into the kettle. I knew little about iceclovers. They were rare, popping out of the ground only after a fresh snowfall. I couldn't wait to see what uses he'd found for them.

He submerged a cloth into the cauldron, then wrung out an excess of milky white liquid. Reaching up under his long sleeve, Kolo rubbed the damp cloth on his arm. At first, he winced, but after a moment, he clearly felt better. He put more tincture on his other arm, then sat across from me.

"Wonderful stuff, iceclovers," he said, holding up one of the clear-leafed plants. "Many medicinal purposes. Soothing for these weary bones."

He turned to the stack of parchment and made a notation with his quill. "How are you and young Mr. Oxter doing?"

"Bangers," I said. "Accommodations are cozy but clean, cuisine is imaginative, the staff"—I scowled in my best imitation of Reena—"surly but helpful. I'll be sure to recommend you for future kidnappings."

Kolo stifled a laugh as he ladled the remaining tincture from the kettle and sealed it into a small wooden jar. "For someone who's been kidnapped, you're being very reasonable."

"My ancestor Kardra Grimjinx always said, 'Reason is the mask of panic.'"

He nodded. "A mask or not, I appreciate you staying calm. My hope is that the Dowager will work to end our persecution, and then we can have you back studying with her before long."

Warras had returned just before dinner, which meant

the Dowager had received the ransom note. I had no idea what she would do. Offer to negotiate with the High Laird? Bring down the wrath of the entire Provincial Guard upon the Sarosans?

We hadn't exactly been getting along lately. Maybe she'd do nothing.

Kolo made another note on the parchment. "Until then, and I know I'm being presumptuous to even suggest this, I'm wondering if you would be interested in helping me with a small project."

He turned the top piece of parchment to face me. On the page, he'd described the texture, color, taste, and aroma of the iceclovers and had created a table listing the different ways he proposed combining them with other natural ingredients.

"I've been making some notes, you see. . . . Ideas I had for a new book. Sort of a follow-up to my *Formulary*."

My heart skipped a beat. A *new* book?

"Since I wrote the first book," Kolo said, thumbing through the pages of his work-in-progress, "I've come to discover so much more about the natural world. But at my age, conducting experiments has become difficult. I know it's a strange request for a kidnapper to ask his captive, but . . . would you be willing to assist me in my research for the duration of your stay? Which, again, I hope is not long."

On the outside, I stayed calm. On the inside, I was celebrating like it was the High Laird's Jubilee.

I reached out and touched the parchment. I skimmed the pages, trying to soak up all the new knowledge within. All from the man who had accidentally set the course of my life. I was being offered a chance to do the research *I* wanted to do.

True, it was only while we were captive. But nobody understood the natural world like Kolo. Even spending just a day learning from him would be amazing. And maybe, just maybe, it didn't have to end once the Sarosans set us free. I wondered: did Kolo need an apprentice . . . ?

This was absolutely crazy. On Kolo's orders, Maloch and I had been kidnapped. The High Laird was issuing insane decrees every day, and the Shadowhands were being methodically hunted. The world made no sense at all, and he wanted me to help him research a new book.

How could I say no?

"I'd be honored," I said, barely able to squeak the words

out. "As the par-Goblins say, *Terressa ovar nomloc harjina fal emlik*."

Kolo winked. "'Only a fool learns from less than a master.'"

My head spun. He even spoke par-Goblin. Clearly, this man was meant to be my mentor. As far as kidnappings went, I was guessing this ranked as one of the best.

"Excellent!" Kolo clapped his hands once and rubbed them excitedly. "We start in the morning."

★

The next three days were some of the best of my kidnapped life.

It wasn't all wonderful. Living as refugees didn't agree with Maloch or me. We woke every day feeling sore and sick to our stomachs. I noticed the sickness would vanish when we drank at First Rise, clearly a sign we were dehydrated. But I had no idea why we woke up dehydrated each day. I kept meaning to ask Kolo about it, but once we started work, it always slipped my mind.

Every day, Maloch was given small tasks—usually laundry or cleaning—which he did eagerly. He hadn't forgotten what I'd said about finding the link between the Sarosans and the Shadowhands. He firmly believed the Dowager would free us any day, and he wanted to gather as much information as he could to discover that link. Once we were free, I wouldn't see him for dust. He'd be off in search of his father.

After the First Rise ritual each day, I would report to Kolo's tent, where I helped him catalog a variety of plants, noting their many uses and testing the best ways to help them grow. He lectured at length on the medicinal uses of kasterban root and became childlike with glee when he discovered a new salve. I kept careful notes on the parchment pages, spelling out every unexpected side effect that came from combining new materials.

I loved it. *This* was what I wanted from life at Redvalor Castle. Research on the things that *I* enjoyed learning about. Too often, at Redvalor, we'd researched boring topics that only interested the Dowager. With Kolo, I never spent a single minute being bored. Or running down a tunnel to keep my face from being eaten by a hostile vessapede.

Well, not since that last time, anyway.

Sure, a part of me felt guilty. The Dowager could have

had me arrested. She could have had my family and me thrown into Umbramore Tower for fraud. Instead, she took me in as her apprentice and taught me as best she could. And I was grateful. But not every apprenticeship was a good match. I knew several kids my age who'd changed masters when things didn't work out with their original mentors. It's not like leaving the Dowager to study with Kolo would be unusual.

I had to stop thinking like that. Kolo hadn't even indicated he wanted an apprentice.

But if he did . . .

On the fifth day of our captivity, Kolo took me into the forest to collect iceclovers. We already had pages and pages of data on iceclovers, but Kolo was determined to make his soothing tincture even more potent.

We crawled around in the snow, plucking the clear weeds from the bases of the whistlebirch.

"I'm sorry we're spending so much time with iceclovers," Kolo said, depositing a handful into Tree Bag. "I find myself suddenly unable to continue my original field of research."

My face flushed with embarrassment. "Right," I said. "I'm sorry I destroyed your crop of tinderjack."

Kolo raised an eyebrow. "What makes you think it was mine?"

"You mean besides the fact that tinderjack doesn't grow so close together naturally? Or the fact that you're the most brilliant botanist in the Five Provinces and that field of tinderjack just happened to be close to your camp?" I asked. "Well, I noticed you also keep a supply of sablevine, which can be used to stabilize tinderjack pods for transportation."

"I envy your eye for detail," Kolo said with a smirk. "You are, of course, correct. But don't worry. There's more where that came from."

I grimaced. "Tinderjack's incredibly volatile. Even the Palatinate doesn't mess with it. Why would you want so much?"

"Let's just say it's an integral part of the research for my new book," he said.

Which I took to mean that, if I continued helping him with his research, we'd be experimenting with tinderjack someday. Suddenly, being chased by vessapedes with the Dowager seemed much more appealing.

Kolo continued, sighing wistfully. "However, if we receive good news from the Dowager, we may never have to worry about that avenue of research."

I shook my head. "The Dowager's sympathetic to your cause, but even if she speaks on your behalf, it might not work. From what she's told me, her brother can be very stubborn. There must be a *reason* the High Laird thinks the Sarosans are behind the thefts."

"I'm not convinced that the High Laird needs reasons for anything these days," he replied.

"What do you mean?"

"I think the High Laird relies on his advisers more than evidence to dictate his policies."

"So you think his advisers told him the Sarosans were responsible? Why would they do that?"

"Why indeed," Kolo muttered. Then he closed the flap on Tree Bag and said, "Jaxter, what do you know of the Great Uprisings?"

Suddenly, it was like being with the Dowager again. She was always changing topics in mid-conversation without any clear purpose.

"Not much," I said. "It's not exactly dinner-table conversation."

I knew what everybody knew about the Uprisings. They happened five hundred years ago, and it was illegal to discuss them. Just after the Uprisings, Mannis Soranna, the first High Laird, declared that the Great Uprisings were to be lost to history forever. Any book containing information about the Uprisings was burned. The theory was that if knowledge of those terrible times remained unknown, there was no risk of them ever happening again. And every High Laird since made enforcing that edict their top priority.

"What if I told you," Kolo said softly, "that what happened before could happen again? That maybe it *was* already happening."

I looked to Kolo. Misty eyes shone against his somber face. "What do you mean?"

For a moment, I wasn't sure if Kolo had heard me. He seemed lost in thought. Then he blinked and a smile parted his lips. "Forgive me. Just some musings from an old, old man. We should get back to camp."

He pushed himself up to standing, crying out in pain as he did. When I went to help, he held up a hand to decline. "My bones aren't getting any younger," he said. I felt bad.

Every move seemed to cause him pain. I suspected we'd be making more iceclover tincture soon to remedy that.

The sun was nearly down when we returned to camp. We joined the others for the evening meal, Maloch grousing for the millionth time about how terrible the food tasted. As everyone retired for the evening, I helped Kolo back to his tent. We found Warras waiting at Kolo's door, a folded sheet of parchment in his taloned hand.

"You need to see this," he told Kolo.

Kolo flashed a quick, cautious look at me before taking the parchment.

"Thank you, Jaxter," he said with a slight head bow. "I trust you can find your way back to your tent?"

Kolo and Warras entered the tent, leaving me to speculate on the parchment. A message from the Dowager? It seemed most likely. Once they'd disappeared inside, I crouched down and scuttled around to the back of the tent.

Lying on my belly, I gently slid my head under the tent's wall. Hidden by Kolo's cot, I could see Kolo, Warras, and the woman Surral at the table, their backs to me. I strained to hear their hushed tones.

"My team and I went to the village Orand as you instructed," Warras was saying, "looking for a message from the Dowager. We watched the Provincial Guard post this just hours ago."

Kolo held the parchment up to the lantern light. "'By the High Laird's decree . . . All Sarosan fugitives have until the end of the week to turn themselves in to the Provincial Guard. If every Sarosan is not accounted for, the Palatinate will release the bloodreavers.'"

A chill the size of a frozen silvernib slid down my spine. Bloodreavers. A fable left over from the Great Uprisings. Horrible monsters that had allegedly been used to hunt people down. Once they had the scent of your blood, they never gave up on finding you. Never. Legend said the first Palatinate Lordcourt had them all turned to stone five hundred years ago. This couldn't be real.

Although . . . I thought back to when Callie, Talian, and I encountered the rogue mage Xerrus in an Onyx Fortress at Splitscar Gorge. Supposedly, Mannis Soranna had ordered those dark citadels destroyed after the Uprisings. It was hard to believe we'd found one, because talk of the fortresses had only ever been a *story*.

But the Onyx Fortresses had proven to be more than legend. Maybe the bloodreavers were real too.

Surral threw her arms up in frustration. "With most of our people locked up in Umbramore Tower, they've got easy access to the blood of the relatives for everyone in this camp. If bloodreavers get a whiff of that, they'll find us in no time."

Kolo stiffened, his back going rigid as it often did when the pain in his arms became unbearable. "I need to think. We'll discuss this in the morning. Leave me."

Warras clicked his beak in protest. "Kolo, we don't have time—"

"Leave me." Kolo's voice was gentle but insistent. Warras and Surral bowed and exited the tent. I scrambled to extract my head and duck into the shadows as Warras and Surral stormed by.

"We can't wait for Kolo to make up his mind," Warras muttered, the red feathers on his head twitching with anger. "The Dowager must be persuaded to act more quickly. Meet me at my tent in two hours, once Kolo is asleep. We'll send our own message to Her Royal Highness."

"What sort of message?" Surral asked.

Warras pulled open his vest, revealing a large, gleaming knife inside. "The Grimjinx boy's little finger should do."

10

Escape

"Any heist you can run away from is a good one."

—*Shadra Grimjinx, master forger of Urik Province*

Something not a lot of people know about me: I like my little fingers. And what I like best about them is where they are: *on my hands.*

I thought about going straight to Kolo and telling him what Warras was planning. But as much as I admired Kolo, I didn't know him very well. For all I knew, he might agree with Warras. There was only one sure way out of this that allowed me to keep my digits: run.

I darted across the camp, stopping only to nod at the

guard who stood outside the tent I shared with Maloch. Once inside, I lit a lantern and started throwing everything I could into my pack.

Lying on his cot and half-asleep, Maloch moaned. "What are you doing?"

"We're leaving," I said, soft enough so the guard wouldn't hear. "Now."

He sat up, suddenly interested. "What about the link? You said we could find out what happened to my da if we . . ." He must have noticed the blind panic on my face, because he went from looking very tired to looking very concerned. I stopped as he clamped his meaty hand down on my shoulder.

"Jaxter," he said gruffly, "they've decided to kill us. Haven't they? You can tell me."

"Yes," I lied. "They'll be here in two hours. Everyone's in bed by now. If we're careful, we can slip past the sentries and—"

Maloch knelt and pulled a rumpled blanket from under his cot. Spreading it out, he revealed a collection of breads, cheeses, knives, forks, and other assorted items.

"I've been hoarding supplies," he said, gathering everything up and stuffing it in his pack. "I, uh, only got enough for myself. I always thought if I escaped, I'd leave you behind. But if we ration it, we should have enough to make it to the nearest town."

"You're all heart, Maloch," I said, extinguishing the lantern. "Let's go."

With a dull knife, Maloch slit a hole in the back wall large enough for us to escape. With our meager supplies, we dodged behind and around tents, inching toward the edge of the camp. All the while, I kept an eye out for Reena and Holm. These past few days, we could hardly go anywhere without those two watching us from afar. With each step, I half expected them to be waiting, blowguns in hand.

The moons, brilliant and full, shone down through the leafless trees. A thick blanket of new, fluffy snow glittered in the moonlight, giving the forest a dull white hue.

I whispered, "Right, the sentry checks on us every thirty minutes. We've got that much of a head start."

Maloch's eyes probed the black forest. "Any idea where to go?"

"We should head for the village of Orand." I pointed my thumb to several sets of footprints to our right. "It must be close. Warras just returned from there."

Maloch led the way while I cast nervous looks over my shoulder, wondering when our head start would run out. We trudged on silently.

The trees grew thicker the farther we went, and the moonlight became scarce. The growing darkness meant I spent almost as much time tripping and picking myself up as I did running. Possibly even more time.

When we hit a patch of bright moonlight, I looked down and realized we'd strayed from the path Warras and his team had laid. The footprints headed off to the right, curving around the large clearing we'd avoided on our way to the cliff face. Maloch was headed straight through the clearing.

"Stop!" I said, looking around. "The path is *this* way."

Maloch refused to stop. "This is faster. Look, we meet up with the path just ahead. It's more direct."

Then why had the Sarosans gone the long way . . . ?

"Maloch, freeze!"

He did as told, his leg suspended in mid-stomp. I ran up behind him and studied the smooth snow on the clearing. It seemed a little *too* smooth. I picked up three rocks. I tossed the first one just ahead of us. Nothing. I tossed the second rock farther. Still nothing.

When the third rock struck the ground just past the second, a large section of snow suddenly dropped away, revealing a square hole. A metallic *twang* rang out. An iron door with criss-cross bars dropped down from the trees above and slammed down over the hole. Looking down, we saw a cage buried deep in the ground. If Maloch had taken one more step, he would have fallen in.

Maloch stared at me with wide eyes, and I pointed to the Sarosans' trail. "That's what Kolo meant when he said this area was secure. They set these traps the last time they hid here. That's why they walked around."

"Right," he said, taking a step back. "Good eye. Let's . . . let's be careful."

We returned to the Sarosan trail and continued. Minutes passed into hours and I knew that, by now, the Sarosans were looking for us. But that wasn't even the worst of our problems.

My stomach began to cramp, my head ached, and when I stood perfectly still, my knees quivered. Both my feet suddenly felt like bricks. I would have complained to Maloch that I couldn't keep up, but I noticed he'd slowed down too.

"You feel it too, right?" I asked. "Sick."

Maloch pointed to our left. The horizon glowed red and purple, heralding the rising sun. With just a bit more light, it became easier to see our surroundings. The trees were growing thinner, and a rocky embankment had sprung up along our right.

"It's morning," he said. "We always feel awful in the morning. Ever since we were taken by the Sarosans."

"Yeah. Why is that?"

Maloch snorted. "You tell me. You're the one who studies nature."

I pulled out the wineskin containing the only water we had and took a swig. "It's because we're dehydrated. Think about it. The pain always goes away once we drink at First Rise." I offered him the water. "Drink up."

But half an hour later, the throbbing in my head was worse than ever. Why hadn't drinking worked this time?

We continued on the trail provided by Warras as it dipped south. Each step became harder and harder until I needed to help myself along by gripping each bush and boulder we passed. A stinging pain had set up shop directly behind my right eye. I clenched my teeth to ward off the headache.

"Can we maybe rest a minute?" I asked, rubbing my temples. "Just to catch—"

Maloch made a slashing motion across his throat and shoved me up against a tree.

"We're being followed!" he said.

He pointed behind us to where a distant pair of figures was stepping out from behind a grove of whistlebirch. Maloch scowled. "It's those two naff-nuts from the Sarosan camp."

I assumed he meant Reena and Holm. They'd probably noticed we were gone before the rest of the Sarosans. And Reena was so eager to prove herself, she probably hadn't told anyone that she and Holm were after us. She wanted the glory of capturing us for herself. Which meant we weren't in too much danger. As long as they were far away—

Shhkk! Something whizzed past my ear. A thin wooden needle with a small feather on the back buried itself in the trunk of the tree we'd hidden behind. Just inches from my face.

"Make that naff-nuts with blowguns!" I said.

We ran helter-skelter, darts whizzing by, each only

narrowly missing. Maloch expertly dodged back and forth, faking one direction while diving in the opposite. My strategy was far less graceful. It involved gripping my belt and pouches, whimpering, and keeping my head low.

As we ran, the trees, bushes, and boulders gave way to a wide, snow-covered clearing, stretching long from side to side for as far as I could see.

"I don't like the look of this," I said, remembering the traps near the Sarosan camp.

"We don't have a choice. Keep going." Maloch stumbled across the clearing toward the thicket of trees on the far side. It was the only place to hide.

Reluctantly, I followed, taking slower, more cautious steps. About halfway across the clearing, I heard a small cracking sound with each footfall. I paused, then took another step. Another crack, this one louder.

Looking down, I saw dark fissures under my feet, as though I'd opened up the earth simply by walking on it.

"Um, Maloch . . . ," I said, freezing to the spot.

"Jaxter," Maloch spun around, "we don't have time for this."

He stomped his foot. And the earth shattered.

Because it wasn't earth. We were standing on a frozen river. Cracks like black lightning shot out all around us. Great chunks of ice submerged into rushing water. Maloch and I fell to our knees, each clinging desperately to separate ice floes that now moved swiftly downstream, bits breaking away every time they crashed into another floe.

"There they are!"

Reena's voice sounded from the riverbank we'd just come from. I turned to see her and Holm, blowguns in hand. They stepped from the woods and raised the reeds to their lips.

Maloch was on his feet. Nimbly, he jumped from floe to floe, leapfrogging his way over the racing water until landing safely on the far bank. He walked along the river, motioning for me to follow.

"Jump, Jaxter!"

More and more chunks of ice disappeared into the water, making the slippery path across even harder to navigate. I stayed on all fours, gripping the ice with the knowledge that if I tried to follow Maloch, I'd end up drowning in the increasingly violent river.

Shhhk! A wooden blowgun dart stuck out in the ice, a hair's width from my little finger.

These people were *obsessed* with my little fingers!

With no choice, I sprang to my feet and tried to hop-scotch toward the far bank.

I deftly traversed two floes. The third splintered the instant I landed. Acting quickly, I blindly threw myself forward as the third floe disintegrated and sank. I fell face-first onto a sheet of ice that wobbled under my weight. Wearily, I stood and tried to spot a path to the far side.

There was now more river than ice between Maloch and me. He was jogging along the bank to keep up with me as the floe carried me faster and faster downstream. Unfortunately, Reena and Holm were also keeping pace.

"Rock!" Maloch shouted.

I followed his pointing finger and saw a large piece of stone sticking out of the river like a starshark fin. Before I could react, my ice floe smashed into the rock, flinging me backward into the river.

The freezing water engulfed me. Every limb went numb. My wobbly legs kicked against the raging current until my head emerged from the river and I could breathe again. I flailed about and managed to wrap my arms around the very rock that had just destroyed my makeshift raft. Feeling drained from my fingers. I wouldn't be able to hold on much longer.

Across the way, Maloch ran to a fallen tree trunk and tore off a large sheet of bark the size of his chest. Then he ran upstream, away from me.

"Don't leave me!" My words came out garbled as I swallowed mouthfuls of water. But once Maloch got farther away, he turned, studied the river, then jumped onto a passing floe. He zigzagged across bits of ice, heading for the middle of the river.

Shhk! Shhk! Reena and Holm fired dart after dart at Maloch. He held the chunk of bark up like a shield, deflecting the Sarosan missiles. When Maloch reached a large floe, he got down on all fours and used the bark as a paddle. The floe changed direction, moving closer to me. Maloch tossed the bark aside and held out his arm.

I let go my death grip on the rock, grasping at Maloch's outstretched hand. With a powerful heave, he pulled me onto the floe. I gasped and panted, barely able to move. Maloch spun around and kicked at the fin stone with both feet. The ice floe responded, floating across the river until we struck the far bank. We hardly had time to scramble onto the safety of the ground before the floe resumed its trek down the river.

I shivered uncontrollably. If Reena and Holm decided to brave the increasingly smaller ice trail across the river, we were done for. There was no way I could run, especially now that the chilly air had started to freeze my soaked clothes. Maloch winced as he pulled himself to his feet. He waved across the surging river at our pursuers.

"It's been fun," he said. "Enjoy Umbramore Tower. You're headed there soon."

"This is your last chance," Reena said, hands on her hips. "Come back with us now and you won't get hurt."

Maloch laughed. "In case you hadn't noticed, dolly girl, you can't hurt us from all the way over there."

Everything about the way she stood said that Reena believed otherwise. "You'll change your mind now that it's morning, Mighty Boy."

Maloch blew her off, waving his hand at her, then turned to walk into the forest. I stood, staring across at Reena.

"Jaxter, come on," Maloch said.

Morning? What did the morning have to do with anything? I looked to the horizon nervously. The sky burned red where, any minute now, the sun would pop up.

Reena and Holm stood their ground, like they were

waiting for me to work it out. *Morning* . . . It was when things got light. It was when the day began. It was when the Sarosans drank in honor of First Rise.

My fingers tingled as I wiped the sweat from my brow. Sundown, yesterday, was when the Sarosans had last fed us. I remembered what Kolo said: *Not all prisons have locks. Sometimes our prisons are within.*

And that's when I understood. It all added up. The pain. The weak knees. It wasn't dehydration. How could I have been so stupid?

Maloch shook me. I turned to find him glaring at me. "Are you coming or—?"

"We have to go with them, Maloch," I whispered, nodding at Reena and Holm, who waited patiently.

Maloch folded his arms. "And why's that?"

"Because," I said, looking him right in the eye, "they poisoned us."

11

The Smell of Blood

"Faith and bronzemerks will buy you a gannyloaf
from the breadsmith."

—*Ancient par-Goblin proverb*

Maloch shot a look at Reena and Holm, then turned
back to me and whispered, "What do you mean,
poisoned?"

"It's how they were making sure we wouldn't go anywhere,"
I said. "They poisoned our evening meal and gave us the antidote every morning in our water. That's why we felt horrible
whenever we woke up, and why they insisted we drink. If we
escaped during the night before taking the antidote, we'd get
sicker and sicker and slow down until they found us."

I stepped around Maloch and called over to Reena. "Essence of almaxa, is it?"

Reena nodded. Essence of almaxa was a slow-acting poison. It took a full day to hit its highest potency. It was a smart way to keep an escaped prisoner from getting no more than a day's journey away. That explained why the water tasted sweet each morning. It was laced with amberberry pollen, the cure for almaxa poisoning.

"Well," Maloch yelled across the river, "the joke's on you!" He slapped his arm around my shoulders and held me close. "My buddy Jaxter here has read your little book and already knows how to cure us. You lose!" He pointed to the pouches on my belt.

"Uh," I said, under my breath, "actually, being in the river just ruined everything in my pouches. The amberberry pollen will have washed away."

As if she'd heard me, Reena cupped her hands around her mouth and said, "We've got plenty of amberberry back in the camp. And you'll get some if you come back with us. Peacefully." She looked right at Maloch as she hit that last word.

Maloch, overcome by the poison, sank down on the

bank. I wiped my glasses off on his dry shirt, then waved our surrender.

Holm produced a small ax from the leather satchel on his back and went to work cutting down twin trees. When they fell, they spanned the width of the river. Maloch and I crawled across the crude bridge and raised our hands when we reached the other side. Reena shoved us roughly in the direction of the Sarosan camp.

By now, the morning sun was a half circle on the horizon, and Maloch and I had grown pale and even more sickly. Maloch plodded along, keeping his chin high to preserve a shred of dignity.

I didn't even bother. Between the poison tearing my insides up and the wet clothes numbing my outsides, it took all my effort to keep from collapsing, never mind trying to look rebellious. It wasn't long before I finally fell to the ground and curled up into a tight ball, shaking.

"I c-c-can't go on," I said, teeth chattering like a drummer gone mad.

"Get up!" Reena said, prodding me with her dagger.

I shook my head. "I can't f-f-feel my feet. Or my hands.

I'm going to freeze to death. I need a fire."

Reena shook her head. "We're near the perimeter defenses of the camp, which means we're not far. You can make it."

For once in my life, I wasn't acting even a little bit. Frostbite was setting in. I couldn't bend my fingers or my legs. She had to see that I wasn't going anywhere.

"Look," Maloch said, his eyelids drooping, "you've got us. We can't escape. We're only hurting ourselves by asking you to stop and start a fire. Just get Jaxter warm and we'll go back with you."

Reena and Holm studied each other, unsure. I played the one and only card I had left.

"I'm no use to you dead," I said. "Please. Build a fire."

The siblings conferred quietly. When they finished, Holm took out his ax and went in search of firewood while Reena dashed about, gathering kindling. Maloch dropped to one knee at my side.

"Th-thanks for the rescue," I said. "I th-thought I'd d-drown."

"You realize that they're taking us back so they can kill us, right?" he replied.

"Er . . . no. I lied. They weren't going to kill us. They

were going to chop off my little finger."

Maloch's fists clenched. Dense as he was, even he realized that everything we'd just been through was for nothing.

Well, not nothing. I still had my little fingers.

"When we get back to their camp," he said, with a low and dangerous tremor in his voice, "I'm personally going to hold you down when they swing the blade."

Reena and Holm built a decent-sized fire. My skin prickled as the heat slowly brought sensation back to my body. I peeled off as much wet clothing as I dared and laid it by the base of the fire to dry.

With an hour tops until Warras cut off my finger, I had this one chance to reason with Reena and Holm. I had to say *something* that would allow me to keep all my bits intact. There was only one thing I could think to say. And it was a huge risk.

"You know," I said to Reena, "we could help each other. No one has to coerce the Dowager. We can find the people who stole from the High Laird and clear the Sarosans' names."

"Jaxter . . ." The threat in Maloch's voice was palpable, but I ignored him. I knew very well I was defying the Lymmaris Creed. But if you read the copy of the Lymmaris

Creed as written in the Grimjinx family album, you'll find lots of annotations made by my ancestors. The most important note, written at the bottom of the creed in the hand of my great-great-great-grandmother, Syra Grimjinx, says, "If you can save your hide, ignore the Lymmaris Creed."

Reena and Holm looked at each other but remained silent, so I pressed on. "That's all you want, right? Let us help." A small lie, but it got Reena's attention.

"And why would you do that?" she asked, poking the fire with a stick but refusing to look at me. "What's in it for you?"

I clenched my fists and thought, *For a start, I'd get to keep all my fingers.* But I chose my words carefully and said, "Maloch's father is a Shadowhand. You must know them by reputation. Not only are they skilled thieves, but they're amazing trackers. Help us find Maloch's da and he can help us track the real thieves."

From the corner of my eye, I could see Maloch watching me carefully. I could tell that he suddenly understood what I'd suspected for some time: the Shadowhands had stolen from the High Laird and were letting the Sarosans take the blame.

"That's right, dolly girl," Maloch said, jumping in and

running with my lie. "My da's the best tracker there is. He can help."

Reena remained unconvinced. "Why do we have to find your da? Is he missing?"

"It's a long story," I said, hoping to avoid any more explanations. I held out my shivering hand. "A truce? What do you think?"

"I think," Reena said, leveling both Maloch and me with her nastiest look, "that you would say anything to get out of this."

"Yep," I said. "But have you noticed that a lot of what I've told you turned out to be true? Like how I told you the vessapedes would attack. And how taking the eggs would lead the vessapedes out of the camp. I was right about those, and I'm right about this."

Holm leaned back on his hands. "Not that we're believing you, but what is it you want to do?"

Maloch sat forward. He was interested in the answer too. Now I really had to improvise.

"You two go back to the camp, bring us the amberberry pollen, and then the four of us can set out to find Maloch's da." It was a ridiculous proposal. I hoped it would seem at least somewhat reasonable to them.

"You could really help," Maloch added. "You're . . . pretty good with that blowgun."

Reena looked confused by the unexpected compliment. For just a second, I thought she was going to take our offer. Then she threw her head back and laughed. She got to her feet. "Break's over. Let's move out."

I pointed to my still-damp clothes. "Just a bit longer? I'm almost dry." She'd hesitated, which meant the idea had *some* appeal. If I could just keep her talking about it . . .

But she'd already started kicking snow onto the fire, the flames disappearing with a smoky hiss. I looked to Maloch, hoping he'd help me try to talk her into going. But his eyelids were half-closed, and he'd grown much paler.

"Let's go," he said with a grunt. "All I care about now is getting that antidote." He struggled to stand, then gripped me under the arms to help me up.

Holm, who'd remained huddled by the smoldering embers to soak up every last bit of heat, looked up sharply. In one fluid action, he leaped to his feet and brandished a dagger, eyes darting around wildly.

"What's with him?" Maloch asked Reena.

"Silence is required now," Holm whispered. "We're all in mortal danger now."

"Not to criticize," I said, "but it's not a very good rhyme if you use the same word twice. No self-respecting bard would ever do that. Maybe you could have said, 'We're in danger, boy, and how!' Or maybe—"

My poetry lesson came to a crashing halt as a dark blur swooped down from above, collided with Reena, and sent her flying backward to the ground. Maloch and I jumped back. Holm crouched, dagger raised and ready to attack.

Reena cringed as the creature towered over her. The beast stood twice as tall as my da and had dark-red, leathery skin that shone like it was coated in oil. Its head was shaped like an arrowhead with jagged edges. Two glowing amber eyes were sunk deep into tiny holes. A double set of jaws, one atop the other, boasted crooked obsidian fangs. A glint of gold sparkled just under its chin. Its most notable feature was the two sets of sinewy arms. One pair hung off the shoulders where you'd expect to find them, and a longer pair protruded from the center of its scaly back, reaching up and over the shoulders. All four arms ended in vicious-looking claws.

The sight of those back arms brought a dozen nursery

rhymes and scary campfire stories to my mind. This was a creature that shouldn't exist. My whole life, I'd assumed it was made up, something to scare children. But every detail of the beast matched the bedtime story description, and a chill shot down my already frozen back.

Bloodreaver.

The bloodreaver's head twisted as it regarded Reena. One of its jaws dropped, and a horrible, warbling scream vibrated in my chest. Reena quickly rolled out from under the creature and scrambled away in a half crawl, half run.

Maloch scooped a still-smoking log from the remains of our fire and hurled it at the bloodreaver. The log exploded into ash as it struck the sharp ridges along the beast's side. The bloodreaver spun around, its glowing eyes landing on Maloch, Holm, and me. Holm let out a shout and charged, dagger held high. The bloodreaver leaped straight up, higher than anything should be able to jump, and used its multiple arms to swing back and forth from the tree branches.

The bloodreaver wove through the treetops at high speed, becoming a smudged silhouette against the pale morning sky. Suddenly, we heard a loud *pop*, and the blood-reaver disappeared in a cloud of gray smoke. A second later, another *pop,* and another burst of smoke appeared right next to Maloch. The bloodreaver leaped from inside the cloud and took Maloch to the ground. The two tumbled together until the bloodreaver came out on top, using its four arms to pin each of Maloch's limbs down.

A thin tendril covered in tiny spikes snaked its way out of a cavity near where its nose should have been. The tendril lashed out across Maloch's face, leaving several fine cuts that started to bleed. With no weapons, I quickly made a snow-ball, ran up, and threw it into the monster's face.

The nose tendril whipped through the air, slicing my forearm. Crying out, I fell back, clutching my arm to my chest.

The bloodreaver turned its attention back to Maloch. When it did, I got a closer look at the gold I'd spotted earlier under its chin. It looked like a small amulet on a chain.

Bloodreavers wore jewelry?

Maloch squirmed under its grip, but the poison in his body made retaliation nearly impossible.

I heard another cry from Holm, and before I knew it, he'd thrown himself onto the bloodreaver's back. He swung his dagger and sliced a tendon near one of the creature's back arms.

Both the bloodreaver's mouths dropped open and shrieked in pain. It lurched, sending Holm flying. He landed near Reena at the base of a tree. The creature focused on Holm, its injured arm hanging limply on its shoulder. Holm's eyes narrowed as the two squared off. Then the boy looked sharply to the right and took off into the woods. The bloodreaver followed, its powerful legs shaking the ground with each footfall.

"Holm, no!" Reena cried. She crawled around on the ground until she found her dagger, then ran off after the bloodreaver.

"C'mon," Maloch said weakly. "Can't lose them . . . Only way to get antidote."

Holm was small but fast and wiry. He stayed far ahead of the bloodreaver. To increase speed, the bloodreaver started to bounce off the trees, grabbing the trunks with its arms and throwing itself forward faster and faster. Holm looked back over his shoulder and then . . . slowed down.

"What's he doing?" I shouted. "Go, Holm, go! Faster!"

As the bloodreaver gained on the boy, it stopped using the trees to propel itself forward and took to the ground, running at top speed. It would disappear with a *pop* of smoke, only to reappear closer to Holm. The Sarosan slowed even more. Only when the bloodreaver had closed the distance between them to almost nothing did Holm add a new burst of speed, keeping him just out of the bloodreaver's claws.

My lungs burned. Maloch and I could barely keep up with Reena, who continued to shout for her brother. Finally, I tripped, and as I fell, I took Maloch with me. We pulled ourselves up on all fours. The bloodreaver was about to catch Holm, and when it was done with him . . . we'd be easy prey.

Holm howled again. I looked up to find that the blood-reaver was nearly on him. The boy's head moved side to side, as if he was searching for something. He darted to the left and made for a fallen tree. The bloodreaver changed course to pursue, and just as it did, Holm leaped up in the air, diving forward.

The bloodreaver bore down. Suddenly, the snow beneath its feet gave way. A hole in the earth opened up, swallowing the creature. A rusty pulley overhead whined as a giant metal door dropped, slamming shut over the hole.

Holm, who had landed safely near the base of the fallen tree, crawled over cautiously. A claw shot up and out between the bars, grasping at empty air. Holm got to his feet, smiling at the trapped creature.

Reena arrived, fell to her knees, and hugged her brother. Holding each other for support, Maloch and I joined them.

Maloch walked up to Holm. "You're a terrible bard," he said, looking away so as not to betray the admiration he had for the boy who'd saved his life. "But you've got hope as a warrior."

I nodded at the cage. "We know the bloodreaver can move magically. What's to stop it from popping out of the cage?"

Reena ran her finger across the bars. She held it up for me to see. Her fingertip was slathered in thick blue paste.

"The cages were made to hold any mages who came snooping around," she said. "They've been treated with Kolo's anti-magic paste. That thing is stuck in there."

The bloodreaver howled and pulled at the bars.

Reena stood and examined Maloch's face. "Does it hurt?"

Maloch looked surprised that she seemed to care. "What? This? Not . . . not really."

They shared an odd look for a few seconds. Suddenly, each coughed and the tension disappeared.

"Danger's passed, we're safe once more," Holm told his sister, "but what the zoc was that thing for?"

The four of us stood at the edge of the cage. The

bloodreaver was going wild, its arms flailing in an attempt to strike out and escape. But the heavy metal door wasn't going anywhere.

Maloch peered down at our captive. "That's not— It can't be a . . ."

I nodded. "A bloodreaver."

Reena laughed. "There's no such thing."

Maloch pointed to the cage. "Try telling him that."

"Imagined or not, the question's clear: what was that thing doing here?" Holm asked.

I took a deep breath. "I think it was looking for the two of you." I told everyone what I'd overheard in Kolo's tent, about how the High Laird had authorized the Palatinate to resurrect the bloodreavers by the end of the week if the Sarosans hadn't surrendered.

"But if the warning just went up yesterday," Maloch said, "why is the bloodreaver already here?"

Reena's eyes grew dark. "Someone at the Palatinate must've gotten eager. It wouldn't be the first time. You can't trust mages."

"But how did it find them?" Maloch asked, pointing with his thumb to Reena and Holm.

"Their parents are prisoners in Umbramore Tower," I said. "The bloodreavers must have been taken to the tower so they could get the scent of the Sarosans' blood, making it easy to track them down."

Holm reached out to Reena. Her back stiffened. "But that means . . ."

Suddenly, the pair turned and bolted, running deeper into the woods.

"What the—?" Maloch asked, bewildered. "Where are they going?"

I knew *exactly* where they were going. "The Sarosan camp."

The higher the sun rose in the sky, the weaker Maloch and I got. Pain shot through my legs like lightning, but leaning on each other, we followed the siblings back to the Sarosan camp.

Only there wasn't a camp anymore. The tents had been ripped to shreds. Wheelbarrows lay shattered, tools were now splinters. A few fires smoldered.

On the other side of the campsite, Reena and Holm scrambled around, calling out for anyone who might have been left behind.

"Help me," I said to Maloch, leading him toward the remains of Kolo's tent. It was a lumpy mass in the middle of the camp. I rummaged until I found a broken jar with a handful of amberberry pollen. Taking water from a nearby cistern, I dissolved the pollen and made enough antidote for Maloch and me. We sank to the ground and let the pollen do its work.

When Reena and Holm joined us, Reena's face was wet from crying. Holm remained stone-faced, his hand stroking the hilt of his dagger.

"There's no one left," Reena whispered. "We're all alone." For the first time since we'd met, she seemed vulnerable.

The pain from the poison slowly left my body. I sat up and looked around the devastated camp. "No signs of resistance. They were taken by surprise, no chance to fight back. No bodies. Which means the bloodreavers took everyone prisoner. They're probably in Umbramore Tower by now." Stiffly, I got to my feet and put my hands on my hips. "All right then. Let's get going."

Reena sat and hugged her knees to her chest. "Yeah. Just go. You're more trouble than you're worth."

Maloch stood. "Come on, Jaxter."

"No," I said. "I meant all four of us."

Maloch folded his arms. "You are *not* seriously suggesting we go to Umbramore Tower."

I shook my head. "I'm suggesting we do what I said before: we look for the Shadowhands."

All eyes were on me. "Look, Maloch, you need to find your father. The only way Reena and Holm can free the other Sarosans and find their parents is to prove the Sarosans are innocent."

"The only way to prove the Sarosans are innocent is to condemn the Shadowhands," Maloch said. Then he leaned in. "What you're suggesting goes against everything the Lymmaris Creed stands for. If the Shadowhands find out you betrayed them . . ."

"The Shadowhands are thieves-for-hire," I said, correcting him. "They get paid for what they do. Somebody *hired* *them* to steal from the High Laird. *That's* who we want to expose. All the High Laird wants are his relics back. If we can find who hired the Shadowhands—"

"—the High Laird will blame the employer, not the Shadowhands," Maloch finished. *"Queoras ziv orra dar?"*

I nodded. "'When in doubt, blame someone else.' We find who employed them, return the High Laird's loot, and everyone is cleared."

"But how do we find out who employed the Shadowhands?" Life had returned to Reena's voice. She was suddenly eager and interested in what we had to say.

"It would help if we knew exactly what was stolen from the High Laird's vaults," I said. "It might give us a clue as to who would want it. Or who would benefit most from having it. If the four of us were to—"

"We can't stay with them!" Maloch protested, pointing to Reena and Holm. "The bloodreavers have their scent. Those monsters won't stop until they have them."

"When the bloodreaver we captured doesn't return," I said, "you can bet they'll come back for him. And *that* bloodreaver has *our* scent." I held up my scratched arm. Maloch reached up and touched his face where the nose tendril had wounded him. "We're in just as much danger as they are. The only thing we can do now is stick together. This is the fastest way to find your father."

That took the fight out of Maloch. His shoulders drooped as his final argument vanished. We ransacked the remains of the camp for supplies. I went through Kolo's tent, filling up my pouches with the twelve essentials. Under Kolo's cot, I found Tree Bag and the parchments containing Kolo's new research. I slung the bag over my shoulder. The research inside was invaluable. And I hoped to return it to the Sarosan leader.

If he'd survived the attack.

Once we were ready, Reena unfurled a torn map of the Provinces and pointed out our location.

"Should only take us a couple days to get back to Vengekeep," Maloch said.

"We're not going to Vengekeep," I said, poking a point higher north on the map.

"Why not?" Maloch asked.

I smiled. "I know how to find out what the Shadowhands stole."

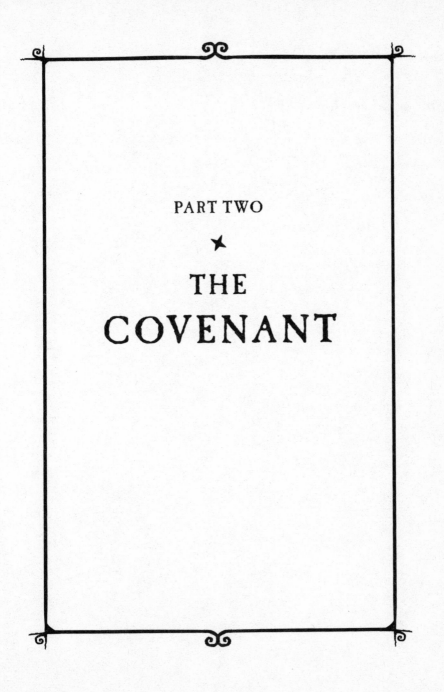

PART TWO

★

THE
COVENANT

12

Return to Redvalor

*"He who fights and runs away will find a wise
Grimjinx leading the retreat."*

—*Zepherax Grimjinx, Castellan of Blackfalchion*

I'd wager that, in all the years Oxric had worked as the
Dowager's majordomo, he'd seen many unusual things.
The Dowager's hobbies and interests alone attracted odd-
ness by the herd. But I'm not sure anything in all those years
could have prepared the Aviard for the sight of the four of
us, showing up on the doorstep of Redvalor Castle, covered
from head to toe in thick black mud.

"Oya, Oxric," I said, as though I often roamed the castle
like a pillar of sludge. My brown eyes stared out from behind

my glasses, the only clean item on my entire head. As I lifted my arm, a slurry of dirt and grass flew across the shiny marble floor of Redvalor's entryway. "Oops. I'll, uh, clean that later."

Oxric looked down his beak-mouth at us, his yellow eyes widening in shock. Not long ago, the castle's entryway had resembled a forest with grass and trees. Just before we left for Vengekeep, the Dowager had ordered the entry restored to its regular, opulent state. I was betting Oxric was wishing it still resembled a forest. Cleanup would have been *much* easier.

When I led our filthy group across the threshold, Oxric practically jumped aside to avoid being splattered by mud.

Reena smiled up at the majordomo as slime slid from her cheeks. "What a lovely . . . castle you have. Sorry about the mess."

Holm, barely able to move his tiny body under the weight of the mud, shuffled in behind her. "I am wet from head to shoes, parts of me are full of ooze."

Maloch brought up the rear. He pointed at Holm and said to Oxric, "Don't mind him. He's a warrior-bard."

The four of us sloshed into the pristine vestibule, which

was quickly becoming more mud than marble. Oxric looked at the grime, and a menacing, guttural coo escaped his beak.

"Could you let the Dowager know I'm back?" I asked Oxric. The Aviard remained frozen in disbelief. "If you're busy, I could go get her. . . ."

I took a single step toward the gleaming staircase, and Oxric nearly slid across the floor in his effort to block me.

"Don't . . . move!" he said curtly, pointing a taloned finger at me. Then he regarded the rest of the group. "Any of you!" With that, he turned and swept out a door to the side.

"I c-can't believe I let you bring us here," Reena said, her teeth chattering. "Holm and I might be the last free Sarosans, and you've delivered us right to the High Laird's sister."

"I told you, the Dowager is sympathetic to the Sarosans," I said. "She'll hear you out. One word from her to the High Laird and this could all be over. That's what Kolo was trying to achieve in the first place."

Maloch folded his arms. "Well, I can't believe we let you cover us all in this muck. It's disgusting. I've got mud in parts of me that should never have mud in them."

"Maloch can at times be dim," Holm said, "but this time I'll agree with him." To demonstrate, he lifted a leg, and a mud ball plopped to the ground.

I rolled my eyes. "Hey, we've been safe for the past couple of days, right? I told you this would throw the bloodreavers off."

Three days ago, after persuading Reena and Holm that we'd find a safe haven in Redvalor Castle, we started the long trip north. Our first stop was the hot springs of Otan Forest. We diverted water from the springs to make a mud bath, which I infused with the contents of three of my pouches. In theory, a coating of this mud with that mixture of magic-resistant plants would mask the scent of our blood from the bloodreavers. Apparently, it worked. We never spotted the bloodreavers. But it meant spending three days caked in the slime.

During the journey to Redvalor, Holm proved an excellent hunter, catching meals for us that Reena would skin and Maloch would cook. Maloch and Reena argued less and even spoke civilly to each other from time to time. But anytime I caught them being nice to each other, they'd quickly separate.

The door to the kitchen flew open, and a swarm of the Dowager's servants came through, their arms loaded down with huge towels. Another group followed with buckets of soapy water and mops. Some went to work on the floor, cleaning up the rivers of muck we'd tracked in. Others buried us in the towels, trying desperately to remove as much mud as they could.

"Is this a good idea?" Reena asked, her reasonably clean face finally showing. "What's to stop the bloodreavers from finding us now?"

I clicked my tongue. "I told you. Redvalor is protected by a number of enchantments. They'll hide us from the bloodreavers."

Reena glowered. Her Sarosan distaste for magic was powerful but she said nothing, because her desire to avoid the bloodreavers was stronger.

When the servants stepped away, we were still pretty hideous, but we were no longer dripping. Nothing a hot bath couldn't cure.

A high-pitched shriek echoed in the great hall. I looked to the top of the staircase to see the Dowager staring down at us. She wore a greasy work smock and had her long gray hair back in a ponytail, a sign she'd been working in the observatory. Reena and Holm exchanged glances. This obviously wasn't what they were expecting from royalty.

"Jaxter!" The Dowager hurried down the stairs and over to our group. She reached out to hug me, then thought better of it. She looked at everyone in that curious, childlike way of hers. "What . . . clever costumes. Is it Grundilus Day already? I love dressing up for Grundilus Day. Let me see if I can guess what you are. . . ."

I shook my head. "No, Dowager, it's more complicated than that. We need your help."

She nodded solemnly. "You know I'll always help you, Jaxter. What do you need?"

"I'm sorry to bring everyone here unannounced, but—"

"So, I was right then!" A knowing grin parted the Dowager's lips.

"Sorry?" I asked.

"You weren't really kidnapped. That note I got, threatening to hurt you if I didn't intervene with my brother on behalf of the Sarosans. It was one of your little tricks, wasn't it? Like pretending your grandmother had died. You sent me that ransom note to lure me away from the castle so your family could ransack it." She beamed proudly, happy she'd seen through the deception.

Only it hadn't been a deception. So *that* was why she

hadn't attempted to negotiate for my return. "No, that's not it. I really was—"

The Dowager raised her eyebrows. "You'll find I'm not quite as gullible as I appear."

I could practically feel the heat radiating off Reena as she stepped forward, fists clenched at her sides. "So, you *didn't* talk to the High Laird about releasing the Sarosans?"

I touched Reena's arm to keep her from exploding, but she pulled away. The Dowager appeared more confused than ever. "Jaxter, I have a feeling there's something I missed."

"There is," I said. "We need to talk."

The Dowager's wide, gleaming eyes became very serious. "Yes, of course. But you all look exhausted. Surely you won't object to a good night's rest?"

The four of us could barely stand. I wanted to tell her everything I knew right there and then. But there was a very real chance I'd fall asleep midsentence. Besides, the enchantments protecting Redvalor were hiding us from the bloodreavers. We were safe for now. One more night wouldn't hurt.

"Yes," I said, "sleep would be good." The others nodded with me.

"Might I also suggest," Oxric said, eyeing us distastefully, "a bath?"

The Dowager agreed. "Oxric, please take care of our guests. We can discuss everything that needs to be discussed once they're clean, well fed, and rested."

Holm moaned with delight at the mention of food. I smiled appreciatively at the Dowager. Even if things between us were a mite fragile, she hadn't hesitated to help.

She reached out and ran her fingers through my muck-filled hair. "I'm glad to see you again, Jaxter," she said in her singsong voice. "Now, if you'll excuse me, I need to wash whatever this is off my hand before it gives me nightmares."

★

The Dowager's servants acted swiftly. It wasn't long before Maloch and I were submersed in our own individual copper basins, up to our necks in steaming water. Reena and Holm had already finished bathing and were gorging themselves in the kitchen.

"I see why you gave up thieving to live here," Maloch said. He leaned back and closed his eyes, enjoying the first bit of comfort we'd seen since we were kidnapped. "When my da makes me a Shadowhand, the first thing I'm buying with my share of the thieving spoils is one of these things."

"It's called a bathtub," I said. "Most normal people already own them."

"I meant one made of copper, you bunknug," he said.

Oh. Really, if you knew how he smelled even when he *hadn't* been covered in mud for several days, you could understand why I thought he'd never seen a bathtub before.

"Hey, Maloch," I said, scrubbing my arms with a soft cloth, "you remember a few years ago when we snuck out of our houses late one night? We ran around to all the watering troughs in Vengekeep and spiked them with singespice so the water would boil."

Maloch's permanent pout dissolved. He laughed as the memory came back. "Then you touched raw singespice with your bare hand and started itching like crazy. So you dunked it into a trough—"

"—which I forgot was boiling—"

"—and then tried to tell your ma the next day that you'd scalded your hand making her a scorchcake for her birthday!"

By now, Maloch was laughing hard and loud. And I was too. This hadn't happened for a long, long time. I'd forgotten how good it felt.

"Yeah," I said, "as I recall, that was right before you told me we weren't friends anymore and started treating me like a half-baked garfluk."

Maloch's stony face returned. He closed his eyes and inhaled the steam. "Don't start with that again, Jaxter. I already told you that I had to. If Aronas or anyone on the town-state council had thought that me or Da were friends with the Grimjinxes, it might have looked suspicious. We couldn't let on that Da was a Shadowhand."

I *should* have understood. The Shadowhands did whatever it took to avoid detection. If our roles were reversed, I probably would have done the same. Although I can safely say I wouldn't have pounded Maloch the way he used to pound me.

"Besides," Maloch said, sinking deeper into the steamy basin, "you're the one who always used to talk about us being a team of thieves. Roaming the land, pulling heists. Can't get much closer than this."

I sat up suddenly. "Oh, please. You make it sound like

you planned all this."

"You're involved because I asked you to be involved."

"I'm involved because my parents were summoned—"

"And you."

I bit back a retort and instead said, "What?"

Maloch dipped a sponge into the basin and squeezed it over his head, allowing the hot water to drip down his face. "Your name was on that summons. I put it there. Didn't have to. Da told me to only bring your ma into this. But I put your name on that summons too. Haven't you wondered why?"

"Well, no . . ."

He looked away.

"Maloch, was it . . . an apology?" I leaned over. "That's it, isn't it? You felt bad for all the years you treated me rotten when we used to be friends. You wanted me to know you had no choice. Right?"

Maloch still wouldn't look at me. "Does it matter anymore? Once I find my da, we go back to the way it was. Hating each other's guts."

Maloch rose from the tub and wrapped himself in the yellow, fluffy robe Oxric had provided. He plodded barefoot across the marble floor of the bathroom.

"Did you . . . did you really hate my guts?" I asked, more confused then ever.

He paused. Then, without looking back, he said, "Like I said . . . does it matter?" Then he opened the door and walked out.

13

The Robberies

"Promises cost nothing and reap the key to a mark's vault."

—*The Lymmaris Creed*

I t didn't take much to forget the rigors of the past week. Awaking in my own bed at Redvalor Castle was remarkably restorative. When I went down for breakfast, I found Maloch, Reena, and Holm in fresh, new clothes that the Dowager had sent for in the middle of the night. We ate a massive breakfast, during which I told the Dowager everything that had happened to us once Maloch and I had been kidnapped by the Sarosans.

When I mentioned our encounter with the vessapedes,

she did an admirable job of not gloating that those three months we'd spent underground hadn't been wasted time after all.

Mostly, though, she was concerned about the link between the Sarosans, the Shadowhands, and the thefts that had upset the High Laird. She agreed that the quickest resolution to our problem was to learn who had hired the Shadowhands.

Midmorning, we retired to the garden behind the castle. The Dowager went to retrieve the missives sent by her brother. I relaxed in a padded chair, enjoying a hot cup of singetea under a warm summer sun. Though when I say warm summer sun, I really mean the thawglobe that floated over the garden. A gift from the Palatinate to the royal family, the brilliant yellow orb hovered above the garden, mimicking a summer day. The snow had all melted, and the plants were verdant and thriving once more. You had to look past the globe to see the sickly gray winter skies beyond.

On the lawn nearby, Maloch was teaching Holm the finer points of kioro. The pair wrestled on the grass, trading soft punches as each fought for the upper hand. He wouldn't admit it, but Maloch felt a debt to Holm for saving him from the bloodreaver. By helping the boy with the warrior part of his intended vocation, he was paying off that debt.

Now we just needed someone to work on Holm's awful poetry to help him with the bard part.

Reena was walking through the greenhouse, where the Dowager kept her collection of rare plants. She'd been quiet most of the day, speaking only to insist that she and Holm be allowed to drink at First Rise and again to request permission to tour the greenhouse. Other than that, she'd barely touched her breakfast and had become oddly distant. I guessed she was still uncomfortable accepting help from the Dowager after her brother had just arrested the last of the Sarosans.

I'd spread the papers I'd rescued from Kolo's tent across a wrought-iron table. Part of me didn't want to read any more than I already had. I wanted to wait until Kolo was finished and then read the new book from cover to cover.

But the part of me that was dying to read his new research won out. Kolo was probably locked up in Umbramore Tower. Who knew when he'd be able to finish writing the book?

Besides, I felt he'd *want* me to read it. It was like we understood each other.

I pored over the parchments, hardly knowing where to start. I selected a page with the heading *Mang Sweat: Experiment Number 010.*

Although unpleasant to procure, mang sweat

offers a variety of uses. Mixed with erris root,

the sweat becomes a cologne that Satyrans find

attractive. Boiled with the bark of a mokka tree,

mang sweat makes a sour tea that can cure headaches.

Well, *that* was disgusting.

The entry was unfinished, suggesting Kolo had still been searching for other uses for mang sweat. I felt sick, wondering if any of the tea he'd served me had been . . .

I decided to pretend I'd never read that particular passage and set it aside. I chose another parchment.

ICECLOVERS—Very rare. Only bloom after a fresh

snowfall. Remarkable at reducing pain. Can be made

into tincture that eases symptoms of Joldar's syndrome,

Mardem's Blight, firerickets, and an outbreak of silla
warts.

Note: Try infusing mang sweat with iceclovers.

I was beginning to suspect my hero spent way too much time around sweaty mangs.

I'd read over a few more pages when the Dowager joined me. Her arms were loaded down with papers, which she dropped onto the table with a thud before searching through the stacks.

When she thought I wasn't looking, she sent a rueful gaze my way. "It must have been harrowing," she said under her breath, tossing unwanted parchments aside. "Can you ever forgive me, Jaxter, for assuming the ransom letter was a joke?"

"It's okay," I said, assuring her for the fifth time. If she felt this bad now, I couldn't imagine what she'd have been like if she'd opened a parcel and found my little finger inside.

She stopped and tilted her head with a sad smile. "I'm glad to have you back. I admit I was worried that you were giving up your apprenticeship. I know things have been . . . strained between us. I'd really like to put all that behind us and talk about how we can make things better."

I focused on the edge of the table, unable to meet her eye. Since we'd left the Sarosan camp, I kept thinking about what things would be like if I could clear the Sarosans, free Kolo, and become his apprentice. The Dowager was smart, but most of her knowledge came from Kolo's *Formulary*. Studying with him would be so much easier.

"Something on your mind?" she asked.

"Hmm?" I asked, looking up sharply from Kolo's papers. "Erm, no. Not really."

I found myself wishing the Dowager would yell at me for disappearing. Then I wouldn't have felt so guilty that I was thinking about quitting as her apprentice.

The Dowager cried triumphantly and produced a parchment bearing the High Laird's wax seal. She laid it out in front of me.

"This is the most recent report my brother sent, the one I was so upset about when we were in Vengekeep." She pointed to a paragraph halfway down the page. "A number of relics were stolen from five royal vaults—one in each Province—in what is being described as a calculated attack."

I browsed the passage she'd indicated.

THE SCEPTER OF ARDRAM

—*Onyx shaft with gold rings*

—*3 rubies near head*

—*Protective glyphs along shaft*

—*Head of glass and emerald*

—*Taken from Vault #1 in Tarana Province*

THE GAUNTLETS OF HERROX

—*Iron back plates*

—*Gold palms*

—*Pointed onyx fingertips*

—*Protective glyphs along fingers*

—*Taken from Vault #2 in Jarron Province*

THE CORONET OF AELLIOS

—*Gold band*

—*Six points encrusted with onyx*

—*Protective glyphs engraved between points*

—*Taken from Vault #3 in Yonick Province*

THE ORB OF GOLLOS

—*Silver sphere with four gold bands*

—*Onyx discs embedded at the top and bottom*

—*Protective glyphs along each gold band*

—*Taken from Vault #4 in Urik Province*

Those four items were listed near the top of the page. Set apart, just below, the parchment read:

RELIC #5—THE VANGUARD

—*Taken from Vault #5 in Korrin Province*

I read the list over and over, looking for a clue that suggested the relics were unusual in some way. Or maybe had value beyond their apparent worth.

"Was there anything special about these things?" I asked. "Were they family heirlooms?" The vaults must be bursting with riches and wealth, piles and piles of precious coins and gems. "Why steal only these five things? And while we're at it, what is 'Relic Number Five—the Vanguard'?"

The Dowager shook her head. "Unfortunately, the vault records have no description of the Vanguard. All that's known for sure is that it's one of the very oldest artifacts in the vaults, stored long before they kept detailed records. In fact, everything that was stolen was kept in the farthest reaches of the vaults. They've been undisturbed for centuries, locked with some of the most powerful enchantments the Palatinate could devise. But somehow, the thieves got past all that."

I pointed to the list. "They're all made of gold and onyx." Gold and onyx were the two most magical substances in the Provinces. "If these were magical items, could we be looking for a rogue mage? Only a mage could use a magical item."

The Dowager considered. "Possibly. Or someone who thought they could sell the relics to a rogue mage."

"It doesn't make sense," I said. It would have been easier—and more profitable—to steal chests full of silvernibs. If you tried to sell ancient relics on the black market, they'd attract unwanted attention. I reread the High Laird's missive. "Now that's interesting. . . ."

The Dowager leaned in. "What?"

I pointed to the start of the paragraph. "The Provincial Guard believes that all five vaults were hit simultaneously— the same day and time. All about eight months ago . . ."

"So?"

I looked up. "It was eight months ago when the High Laird quarantined Vengekeep. He sent thousands of troops from all over the Provinces to surround the town-state. And when he did that, he weakened the defenses around the royal vaults."

The Dowager shook with frustration. "Oh, I told my brother that was a mistake! He should never have listened to his advisers. He's only got himself to blame for these thefts. It's like we left the door wide open for the thieves."

Yes. It was *exactly* like that. And the Shadowhands had pounced the moment the defenses were down. Almost as if they had known it was going to happen.

Reena returned from her visit to the greenhouse and sat sullenly next to me. I got the impression that she hated herself for enjoying the warmth of the magically created summer day.

The Dowager was oblivious to Reena's distress. "Did you see anything interesting in the greenhouse?" she asked cheerily.

Reena smiled weakly. "Yes, ma'am. Thank you, ma'am." She turned to me. "Listen, Jaxter, I've been thinking. I appreciate that you're trying to help. But I think Holm and I should turn ourselves in to the Provincial Guard."

I started to protest, but she cut me off. "You and Maloch are only in danger because of us. If the High Laird has all the Sarosans, the Palatinate will have to call off the blood-reavers. Maybe they'll send us to Umbramore Tower. We can see our parents again."

The Dowager straightened her back. Even in her work clothes, she could still project the very essence of regality. "Young lady," she said firmly, "do you realize that just by allowing you into my home, I am harboring an enemy of the state? An infraction compounded, not eased, by the fact that I am the High Laird's sister. The High Laird has declared that anyone assisting fugitive Sarosans will share in their punishment. And I don't risk going to Umbramore Tower for just anyone."

I could see Reena fighting not to blow up, as she might have if anyone else had spoken to her like that. She said evenly, "But you won't need to risk going to prison if Holm and I just leave."

"What the Dowager's trying to say, Reena," I said softly, "is that she believes the Sarosans are being treated unfairly and she wants to take a stand. If you surrender, she can't do that."

Reena's dark skin flushed, and she looked away. "Oh."

Sweaty and breathing heavily, Maloch and Holm joined us at the table, each grabbing a quaich of water to quench their thirsts. "Your brother's a tough little guy," Maloch said to Reena, who forgot she was angry and smiled to see Holm so happy.

Maloch looked at the Dowager's paperwork. "Got anything?"

"Not much," I said. "Five relics, possibly magical, but no idea why they're important."

"And we have no idea why the Shadowhands are disappearing," Maloch said, sinking into a chair next to Reena.

"Sure we do."

We all turned to Reena, who looked as if she didn't realize she was the one who'd spoken. She sat up straight.

"It's obvious. When you hire someone to secretly steal mysterious relics from the depths of the High Laird's vaults, you don't want any witnesses. So you remove the only people who might be able to identify you."

Reena was right. It *was* obvious. I couldn't believe I

hadn't thought of it. Like my ancestor Lorris Grimjinx once said, "Slashing your own throat and sharing a secret produce the same results." In other words, it's only really a secret if you're the only one who knows.

But Maloch remained unconvinced. "You're suggesting that whoever hired the Shadowhands is now eliminating them? That's not possible. The Shadowhands work in complete anonymity. There's no way whoever hired them could possibly find out their identities, unless . . ."

Maloch suddenly stopped as reality sank in for all of us. It was the Dowager who finally said it aloud.

"Unless one of the Shadowhands was a traitor."

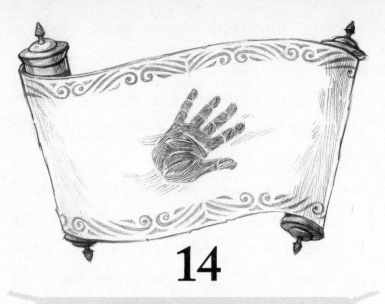

14

Finding the Traitor

"One man's treachery is another man's monthly
wage."

—*Minaeris Grimjinx, founder of the Tarana Thieves Alliance*

On the trip from the Sarosan camp to Redvalor Castle, I'd dreamed of sleeping peacefully in my own bed again. The previous night had been bliss. But this bliss was short-lived. Curled up in my nightclothes, under thick quilts, with warm embers glowing in the fireplace nearby . . . I should have been fast asleep but wasn't.

It may have had something to do with the crazy guy in my room.

At the foot of my bed, Maloch was pacing the floor,

throwing his arms up in the air and having a very loud argument with himself.

"This is completely naff-nut!" he said, shaking with rage. "The Shadowhands don't let just anyone join. They screen all candidates. If there's even a hint that you might turn on the Shadowhands, you'll never get in. It's impossible that there's a traitor. Impossible!"

Then he spun on his heel. "But that's the only explanation. Whoever hired the Shadowhands is trying to eliminate them. And the *only* way their employer could have learned the Shadowhands' true identities is if someone from within sold them out. That must be what my da figured out. He maybe even knew who the traitor was . . . and they got to him."

"Why are you even here?" I asked, snuggling up to my quilts. "You've got your own room. Go stomp and shake your fist in there. I'm trying to sleep."

"Jaxter!" Maloch said, whirling on me. "You should be just as worried as me. Your parents are trying to track down the remaining Shadowhands. I think whoever's hunting the Shadowhands will be just as happy to get anyone who's trying to warn them. Or even go after *former* Shadowhands as well."

I groaned and pulled the quilts up over my head. I just wanted to sleep. By my calculations, I needed at least a full week of restful nights to make up for all the sleep I'd lost in the Sarosan camp and on the trip here. But I clearly wasn't going to get any tonight.

Maloch had a point.

And I hated him for it.

A traitor who could reveal the identity of the Shadowhands probably also knew of any former Shadowhands. Ma was in just as much danger as the people she was trying to warn.

Maloch pulled the quilt back, exposing my face. "*We* have to find the traitor."

"I agree," I said, propping myself up on one elbow. "But we have no clue how to do that. Right now, we should focus on helping Reena and Holm and the Sarosans. You want to help Reena, right?"

That caught him off guard. He stared at me blankly for a long time. Then he lifted his jaw. "If we find the traitor, we *are* helping the Sarosans. The traitor can lead us to whoever hired the Shadowhands. We can turn that person in to the High Laird, and he'll be forced to let the Sarosans go."

My stomach churned. Why was it that I got physically ill

whenever Maloch made sense?

"Okay, fine," I said, "but that brings us back to the simple fact that we have no idea how to find the traitor."

Maloch got down on all fours and pulled my backpack from under the bed. "We *do* know how to find the traitor. In fact, the Shadowhands are going to lead us right to them."

"What are you doing?" I asked as he dropped the backpack on my bed.

"Start packing," he said, "and get dressed. We've got a long trip ahead of us, and we leave tonight."

Before I could ask him what he meant, he ran from the room. Reluctantly, I started packing. How was I going to explain to the Dowager that we were leaving again so soon? I had a feeling the idea wouldn't sit well with her.

Once I was ready, I met Maloch outside his room. He had his own pack and was ready to go.

"We should get Reena and Holm," I said, "and stop by the kitchen for some food. Oh, and I need to tell the Dowager—"

Maloch shook his head. "No. Just you and me. We're not Shadowhands, but right now, we're the next best thing. We don't get anyone else involved. It's too dangerous."

I wasn't convinced. Was this about being the sons of Shadowhands . . . or keeping Reena out of danger?

"C'mon," he said, tugging my elbow and leading me down the hall. When we got to the stairs, we found Reena and Holm, also packed and dressed for a long journey.

"My room shares a wall with you," Holm said, pointing at me. "I heard what Maloch wants to do."

"If you can clear our family's name," Reena said, turning to Maloch, "then we're coming with you. And don't even try to argue."

Maloch shot me a look. "Fine. But we're *not* telling the Dowager. She'll only try to stop us."

"Indeed, Mr. Oxter."

We turned to find the Dowager standing behind us, arms folded and looking very unhappy.

"For two sons of Shadowhands," I said under my breath, "we're really lousy at sneaking out."

"As Jaxter's mentor," the Dowager said, the singsong in her voice replaced with real authority, "I am responsible for his safety. I cannot claim that about the rest of you. But I promise that if any of you try to leave before we've discussed all options, you'll see just how much power the sister of the High Laird wields."

It sounded impressive, but I knew she was bluffing.

At least, I *hoped* she was bluffing.

We sat in the Dowager's study. Oxric served singetea all around. Maloch stood near the tall, slender windows that overlooked the moonlit garden. He hadn't said a word since the Dowager caught us trying to sneak out. He just did what Maloch did best: glared.

Reena and Holm shared a chair so large Holm's feet didn't even reach the floor. I sat across from them and watched Reena steal glimpses at Maloch. Holm noticed too. He gave a careful nod at his sister, then at Maloch, then rolled his eyes. I laughed.

The Dowager, who had been stoking the fire, turned sharply. "Did I do something funny, Jaxter?" I really hated it when she became all adultlike.

"Sorry," I said, looking down.

The Dowager strode over to the window near Maloch. "I gather you weren't just rallying your troops here to run off into the night without a purpose, Mr. Oxter. Perhaps you'd like to tell me what you were planning."

Maloch's lips fused shut. He leaned against the window frame and didn't say a word, stubborn as always.

So I volunteered. "Maloch thinks he knows a way to figure out who the Shadowhand traitor is."

Maloch didn't even bother trying to kill me with a look. His hand, curled into a fist at his hip, grew deep red and trembled the tighter he squeezed it. A message that I was going to pay for talking once he got me alone.

The Dowager gently took Maloch's shoulders and turned him to face her. The serious, stern Dowager gave way to the kind, gentle one I knew best. "Maloch," she said softly, "I know you're concerned about your father. There's a very real chance that he's still out there, hiding from whoever is hunting the Shadowhands. You have no idea where he is, and putting yourself in danger won't—"

"If he was in trouble, he would have gone to the Dagger!" Maloch blurted out, pulling away from the Dowager.

"The what?" I asked.

Maloch turned to look out the window again. He was silent for a long time. Then, he finally gave in and spoke.

"The Shadowhands have a hidden compound called the

Dagger. It's where they meet to plan their heists. It also doubles as a bunker they can hide in if things ever get too hot. I can't prove it, but I think my da was on his way there when he disappeared."

"But," I said carefully, "you don't know if he made it there."

He fell silent again. I pulled the Dowager aside. "Listen," I whispered, "I think Maloch knows more than he's saying. But he won't talk while you're here. He's afraid he'll betray the Shadowhands. Maybe if you left me to talk to him . . ."

The Dowager scanned the room. The windows were too narrow for us to fit through. The only way out of the study was through one door. She knew we couldn't leave. "I'll be right outside," she said.

Once she left, Reena, Holm, and I went to Maloch.

"Okay," I said, "so you were going to take us to the Dagger. Why?"

He took in a deep breath. "That's where the Shadowhands keep the Covenant. Every recruit has to sign it, and then they're magically bound to the Shadowhands. If you betray the group, all sorts of horrible things happen to you. It gets harder to breathe. You contract magical illnesses. You get terrible headaches . . . and your name starts to glow on the Covenant itself."

"So we go to the Dagger, get the Covenant, and expose the traitor," Reena said.

Maloch nodded at the door to the study. "But the Dowager can't help. If the Dagger is compromised by the Provincial Guard, then it doesn't matter if we find the Shadowhands or not. It's all over."

I guessed my own parents wouldn't approve of me leading the royal family to the secret Shadowhand bunker. Which meant I had to convince the Dowager to let us go on our own. "All right," I said, "let me take care of this."

I called for the Dowager, and she joined us in the study.

"I need you to trust me," I said carefully. The Dowager immediately stiffened, so I rushed to add, "I appreciate you taking us all in and making sure we're safe. We'd still be dodging bloodreavers if it weren't for the charms around Redvalor. We know you only want to help, but this is something we have to do ourselves."

"Jaxter, I have the resources to get you anywhere you need to go in the Provinces much faster than—" She stopped and tilted her head. She stared into space for several seconds as if trying to figure something out. "Wait a moment. What charms around Redvalor?"

"You know," I said. "When I started as your apprentice, you told me about the charms cast by the Palatinate to protect the castle from magical incursion."

The Dowager chuckled. "I forgot about that. Well, I wasn't exactly telling the truth. I told you that because I wasn't quite sure I could trust you. I didn't want you to get any sneaky ideas."

My arms went limp. "So . . . we're not protected here?"

Reena put her hand on Holm's shoulder. "But that means—"

And right on cue, we heard the unmistakable howl of a bloodreaver. We looked out the window and saw several of the creatures scaling the walls of the castle.

"Oh, zoc," I said.

A taloned fist smashed through the window, sending us all diving for cover. A bloodreaver reached into the study, snatching at empty air as we cowered from its grasp. It tipped its head back and screamed. A moment later, four distinct screams answered back.

As we jumped to our feet, the door to the study flew open,

and Neron, the captain of the Provincial Guard, charged in.

"Your Majesty," he said, sword drawn, "the castle is under siege."

"We figured that out," I said.

Pop! A cloud of smoke appeared in the study, and a bloodreaver leaped out at us.

Neron swung his sword at the creature, driving it back. "Everyone out!" he said, and we ran from the study, slamming the door shut behind us.

"Captain Neron," the Dowager said, "gather the guards and mount a defense!" The captain saluted and ran to the staircase to raise the alarm. The Dowager turned to us. "The rest of you will be safe if we go—"

"No," I said. "This is our chance. We have to go now."

The Dowager stood her ground. "You cannot go outside while those creatures—"

"If the guards distract them, we can escape unnoticed." I turned to the others. "Get our things." Reena, Holm, and Maloch ran to get the backpacks.

Before the Dowager could protest, I said, "You can't be seen harboring us. You said so yourself. If we're found here by the bloodreavers, there's nothing you can say to save yourself. We need you free to tell your brother what we've learned. Ask him to call off the bloodreavers. Tell him the Sarosans are innocent."

She shook her head. "He won't listen to me."

"Make him!" I said as the others returned. Reena handed me my backpack.

The Dowager looked unconvinced, but she finally nodded. "Come with me." She led us down the stairs to the foyer, where a dozen heavily armed members of the Provincial Guard, as well as Oxric and the Dowager's entire staff—bearing frying pans, brooms, and other makeshift weapons—waited to defend the castle.

She walked to a nearby table and retrieved Tree Bag. I had lent her the bag with Kolo's notes before we went to bed. "Read page fourteen. It's important."

I nodded and slung Tree Bag over my shoulder.

"Captain," the Dowager said to Neron, "you and your men are to engage the creatures. Keep them as far away from the main entrance as possible." Upstairs, we heard the study door smash and the pops of more bloodreavers appearing.

The Dowager ushered us to the main door as the guards ran upstairs. "You'll only have a few minutes at most to get away."

"We may not look like much," I said, referring to our motley group, "but we're fast."

The Dowager reached up to her throat and touched the pendant that hung around her neck. A small, star-shaped jewel sat inside a flat, silver triangle. She plucked the red gem from the triangle and placed it in my hand. "You and I will be able to communicate with this, in case you get in trouble. When you need to speak to me, just tap the gem three times."

I repeated, "Three times."

Above, we could hear the guards engage the bloodreavers. The creatures screamed as the soldiers swore and called them names that made Oxric blush.

"Let's move!" Maloch said, throwing open the main door. Reena, Holm, and I stormed out and the four of us ran into the freezing night.

15

The Dagger

"The knife you use to prick a Shadowhand will
double as the spade that digs your grave."

—*Baloras Grimjinx, architect of the First Aviard Nestvault Pillage*

We ran for a solid hour, heading east from Redvalor
Castle with Maloch leading the way. When we
came across a small valley sheltered by everleaf trees, we set
up camp for the night and collapsed, exhausted, next to a
modest fire.

"Not too big," Reena said as Maloch threw more branches
onto the flames. "The bloodreavers will find us."

"The size of the fire doesn't matter, dolly girl," Maloch
said, throwing an extra branch on, to emphasize his point.

"They can track us by the scent of our blood."

"And that's a problem," I said, pulling Kolo's parchments from Tree Bag.

Holm winced. "I know our blood betrays our group, but *no more mud*, I'm begging you!"

I shuffled through Kolo's unfinished book to page fourteen as the Dowager had instructed. There I found Kolo's notes that gave me the idea for the mud infusion that had hidden us from the bloodreavers in the first place. But now, in the margins, I found additional writing in the Dowager's hand. It read:

Perhaps the addition of jellyweed to these ingredients would make a good tea that produces the same scent-masking abilities.

I smiled. The Dowager was brilliant. No more mud baths for us. I couldn't believe I hadn't thought to make a tea. I quickly took out my flagon and the necessary ingredients, and soon we were all sipping a new elixir that would hide the smell of our blood.

"I've tasted worse," I said, gritting my teeth.

"Where, exactly?" Reena said, sticking her tongue out. "At the bottom of a latrine?"

"I think I'd rather let the bloodreavers get me," Maloch said.

"Jaxter's helping with his brining," Holm mused. "Drink the tea and stop your whining."

I beamed at the boy and forgave the terrible rhyme. Again.

Maloch nodded to the pouches on my belt. "How are your supplies?"

I patted the belt. "I stocked up before we left. Why?"

"According to my da, most of the Dagger's defenses are magical. We may need you to . . . you know, deal with them."

I couldn't help but smirk. He hated to admit that my skills in negating magic through nonmagical means were beyond his grasp. I enjoyed his envy while I could. Eventually, I'd have to admit that the spells protecting the Dagger were probably far beyond what I could handle.

"So are the Shadowhands mages?" Reena asked.

Maloch shook his head. "Shadowhands don't trust the Palatinate. Kind of like you Sarosans. They've never allowed a mage to join."

"Then where did they get all their defenses?"

Maloch leaned back. "The Dagger dates back to before the Great Uprisings, before there was a Palatinate to monitor the use of magic. Anyone could get any mage to cast any spell . . . for the right price. The first Shadowhands paid a bunch of mages to create the defenses long before there were laws against that."

This worried me more. Old magic was almost impossible to defeat. Spells that had endured for centuries were difficult even for an experienced mage to break. I hoped that Maloch's da had told him enough about the Dagger to get us through unharmed.

"And where are we headed?" I asked.

Maloch pulled Reena's map of the Provinces from his pack and spread it out. "The Amberlock Mountains."

Reena yawned. "We should get some sleep. It'll take days to get there."

"Well, the good news," I said with a smile, "is that I estimate we only have to drink one cup of tea a day to keep the bloodreavers away." As everyone groaned, I turned to Holm. "Hey, that rhymed! Think I've got a future as a warrior-bard?"

★

It took us four days to reach the Amberlock Mountains, and morale was vanishing quickly. Our food had run out, and water was dangerously low. Then a winter storm hit and slowed our progress through the mountain pass, nearly burying us under snowdrifts as high as the clock tower in Vengekeep.

"Are we getting closer?" I yelled over the roaring wind.

Maloch looked behind us to Reena and Holm, who were struggling to keep up. He leaned in so they couldn't hear him. "I don't know. I'm not sure where we are. The storm wiped out all the landmarks my da told me about."

We trudged on, fighting against the relentless wind, blind to everything but the cloak of white that surrounded us. As night came, we knew we needed to set up camp. But we hadn't planned on that. We thought we'd be at the entrance of the Dagger today. If we tried to set up camp outside, there was a very good chance we'd be buried by an avalanche or frozen solid in our sleep.

I heard a faint cry over the wind. Turning, I saw that Holm had fallen and Reena was kneeling at his side. I called out for Maloch, who was only a few steps ahead of me, but he'd already vanished into the wall of snow. Before I lost sight of Reena and Holm, I charged toward them.

"What's wrong?" I asked.

Holm had curled into a ball and was shaking so hard his teeth were chattering.

"He can't feel his legs," Reena said, massaging her brother's legs with her gloved hands.

I knelt down so the wind was at my back and I could shield Holm from the worst of it. Together, Reena and I rubbed his thin legs.

"Where's Maloch?" Reena asked, looking around.

"I lost him," I said.

Her face lit with alarm. "He's got the tent. What are we going to do?"

A layer of snow had already formed over Holm. Darkness crept in all around. Reena leaned forward and covered Holm with her body to protect him. I foraged through my pack, hoping to find something that could help us. But it seemed hopeless.

Just then, I felt a hand close around my shoulder. I turned to find Maloch holding a torch that burned with green-blue flames.

"I found it!" he said.

He handed me the torch, helped Reena to her feet, then slung Holm over his shoulder. Reena and I leaned on each other, struggling to follow Maloch into the snowy darkness.

Suddenly, the howl of the wind died down, and I realized that we'd walked into a cave. I immediately felt warmer. The torch flickered, illuminating a thick curtain of roots that dangled from the ceiling.

"You must feel right at home," I said, joking with Reena. She kicked my ankle.

Maloch laid Holm down on the cave floor and stood, looking around, quite pleased with himself.

"I'll admit," I said, "I was expecting a bit more from the fortress of the best thieves in the land."

"This isn't the Dagger," Maloch said. "It's the entrance. Or rather, it's the illusion that hides the entrance. *Harro dis garjoka!*"

Calling out in ancient par-Goblin, Maloch folded his

arms. The grimy earth walls began to melt. The roots in the ceiling dissolved as if made of ash. The illusion vanished and we found ourselves in a room of finely carved mordenstone. A row of green-blue flame torches lined the far wall. A large set of wooden double doors, engraved with columns of ancient par-Goblin text, sat in the center of the wall.

"So much for the magical defenses," Reena said, hugging herself to get warm.

"That was nothing," Maloch said. "Anyone who knows that bit of par-Goblin can shed the illusion." He pointed to the double doors. "Once we pass through there, though, we won't be able to trust anything we see, hear, or feel."

"Since you're the expert," Reena said, "why don't you tell us what we're up against?"

Maloch shrugged. "Hardglamours, mainly—illusions that can touch you. And a bunch of real traps. The trick is telling the difference. Beyond that, I don't know much. We have to be careful."

I walked over to the doors and studied the par-Goblin writing.

"Is it a warning?" Reena asked. "A big 'keep out' sign?"

"No," I said quickly. "It's nothing. Just a fable. A par-Goblin fable."

Not many non-thieves knew par-Goblin fables. Those familiar with the stories knew them to be particularly gruesome, every paragraph chock-full of bloodshed and dismemberment. To par-Goblins, the easiest way to teach children was to give them nightmares. Every single fable I knew ended with: "And then all the children died horribly."

The one on these doors was no exception.

I gave the doors a shove. Both were heavy, creaking as they slowly swung inward. Just beyond, we saw a small corridor with pale light at the end.

"They're not locked?" Reena asked. "I thought this was the ultimate thieving fortress."

"No need for locks," Maloch said in a low voice. "Not even magic ones. The par-Goblins always say, 'An unlocked vault tempts the fool and worries the wise thief.'"

Which, incidentally, was the title of the fable on the doors.

One by one, we followed Maloch through the doorway. The musty passage made my eyes water with each step. When we reached the halfway point, we heard stone grinding on stone overhead. We froze, looking up and around to see if we'd triggered any traps.

At the end of the corridor, a wall of rushing water spilled down over the entrance to the chamber beyond, disappearing into a crevasse in the floor. Getting into the next room meant passing through the small waterfall. We approached slowly. Maloch was the first to gag, followed by Holm, then Reena. The mold in the corridor had plugged my nose, but the powerful odor of the water hit me once we got close.

"It's awful," Reena said with a gasp, covering her mouth and nose with her hand. "It smells like something died."

To be more specific, it smelled like cadaverweed, a plant whose blossoms stank of rotting flesh. The water had clearly been infused with the plant.

I moved to the front of the group, grabbed a handful of blackdrupe pit powder and crushed benna leaves from my satchels, and mixed them together in my palm. Daring to take a deep breath, I blew the gray powder into the waterfall. The powder dissolved instantly and vanished.

"If it was acid," I said, "the powder would have turned blue. I think it's safe. It's just water. Stinky, fetid water. We don't have a choice. We have to go through."

Grumbling, everyone ran through the wall of water. We emerged out the far side, drenched and smelling like dead bodies. Once we were all through, the shower of water instantly stopped.

We stood back to back, wringing as much of the disgusting water from our clothes as possible. But no matter how hard we tried, the pungent odor lingered.

"An easily broken illusion," Reena said, "and a stinky shower. If these are what the Shadowhands consider traps, it's no wonder they're so easily hunted."

Maloch and I ignored the jibe. We'd both noticed the same thing: a soft whirring sound, like clockwork buried in the walls. I had a feeling Reena would regret her taunts. Instinct told me the water was just the beginning. The *real* trap was about to be sprung.

16

The Horror in the Walls

"A silvernib is quickly spent. A secret pays out over
and over again."

—*Vaster Grimjinx, creator of the Ghostfire Proxy*

Maloch pressed his ear to the arch of the doorway
through which we'd just passed. "Where's it coming
from?"

I shrugged. "Best guess? Everywhere."

"Are we just going to stand here?" Reena asked, one hand
on her hip. She and Holm still hadn't noticed the sound
behind the walls.

"Forget it," I said to Maloch. "We'll figure it out. Soon
enough."

We stepped away from the doorway. The room we were in was perfectly circular. Magical green-blue flames from a chandelier above offered a dim, eerie light. Dusty cobwebs hung like palls from ceiling to floor, forcing us to push them aside as we walked deeper into the room. In the exact center, we found a tall stone table with another par-Goblin fable engraved across the surface.

Along the far wall, perfectly spaced, stood twelve stone sarcophagi, each twice as tall as Maloch. They were painted with skeletal images—skull-like faces contorted in fear. Or pain. The only visible door was the one we'd just come through. Clearly, the stone caskets hid the entrance to the Dagger.

"It's a hardglamour," Maloch said. "A solid illusion. None of it's real. If we were Shadowhands, the illusion would disappear. But we're not, so we have to figure out which one has the door that leads to the next chamber." He studied the writing on the stone table. "I wonder if there's a clue here."

"Nope," I said, having read the fable quickly. "More bloodshed, more severed limbs, more dead children."

"What?" Reena and Holm asked together.

"Nothing," Maloch and I replied.

Reena coughed and made a retching sound. "We can't stay in here much longer. We stink. The room is filling with that smell. We have to keep moving." She walked up to a sarcophagus on the left.

"Reena," I said, "be careful. You don't know what—"

Ignoring me, she wrapped her fingers around the sarcophagus lid, gave it a yank, and jumped back, thinking she'd outsmart any trap. But the trap outsmarted her. As her feet touched down on the stones behind her, a small hole in the floor fired a column of thick, greenish gas straight up, surrounding her. Reena collapsed to the floor.

Maloch and Holm ran to her. When they got close to the gas, they stopped and wobbled back and forth. Holding my breath, I ran over and pulled them away.

"Give the gas a minute to dissipate," I said. I turned to Holm, whose eyes were filled with fear, and said more gently, "I'm sure she's fine. If the gas was lethal, we'd all be dead."

Once we could no longer smell the gas, we knelt near Reena. She was alive but unconscious.

"What do we do now?" Maloch asked. "If we try more of the caskets, we could trigger more gas."

I studied Reena's sleeping form. Something stirred in my

memory. Something I'd read about poisonous gases . . .

"Check her eyes," I said, tugging back her eyelids. Even in the soft light, I could see that the whites of her eyes had gone dark yellow. "Tarsa gas. It's produced by decomposing tarsa plants. Now, where was I reading about some kind of counteragent . . ."

"Shhh!" Holm held his finger to his lips. We all fell quiet. "While we crouch near Reena, boys, I hear something like a noise."

Maloch shook his head. "Seriously? You can't just say, 'Hey, I hear something'? Do we have to listen to your terrible poetry every time—"

"Maloch, shut up," I said, because I'd heard something too. Not the clockwork whirring from earlier. This was louder. Closer.

We all sat quietly, with only the sound of Reena's labored breathing.

—*tickittatickitta*—

There it was again. A fast, rhythmic tapping, like metal on stone.

—*tickittatickittatickitta*—

It echoed softly off the circular walls, making it seem as

if it was coming from everywhere.

—tickittatickittatickitta—

When I closed my eyes and concentrated, I could tell that it was coming from behind us. Whirling around, I held the torch at arm's length.

—tickittatickittatickitta—

The tapping was louder and constant now. I peered down at the uneven stone floor, and for just a second, it looked like the floor was moving. Like it was crawling toward us.

—TICKITTATICKITTATICKITTA—

The taps erupted into a loud chattering that filled the small chamber. I held the torch closer to the moving floor. But it wasn't the floor that was moving. It was the army of bugs marching at us.

"Scythebeetles!" I said. "Bangers!"

The bugs had perfectly round shells as big as the palm of my hand. A dozen armored legs stuck out from all sides, making the *tickittatickittatickitta* sound as they scuttled forward. A pair of long, curved pincers that gave the bugs their name protruded from their faces. Those pincers could cut an iron blade in half.

When I looked up, it seemed as if the wall behind us was

moving too. Until I realized it was thousands and thousands more scythebeetles pouring from the cracks into the room. The clockwork we'd heard had clearly been a mechanism in the walls that released the bugs.

I got down on one knee. "You usually only see scythe-beetles in the southwest. The Dowager and I were planning a trip to find some next summer. She wants to study their saliva. It's supposed to help plants grow."

—*TICKITTATICKITTATICKITTA*—

"Uh, Jaxter," Maloch said slowly, eyes darting every-where. Scythebeetles were now crawling along the ceiling.

"Relax," I said, "they're harmless. They only eat carrion." I leaned forward to get a closer look at the ones approaching my feet. Behind me, I heard fast shuffling. I turned to find that Holm and Maloch had dragged Reena onto the top of the table with them.

"What?" I asked.

"In case you've forgotten," Maloch said, gripping a hand-ful of his wet, reeking tunic, "we smell like carrion."

Oh. Right.

I leaped back as the closest scythebeetle took a swipe at my boot, cutting open the side. Scrambling, I joined the others atop the table, just steps ahead of the advancing insect horde.

I groped for my water flagon. "Water!" I said. "Scythebeetles hate water. Get the table legs wet."

The three of us knelt on the tabletop, dousing the stone legs to keep the scythebeetles from climbing up. When they came in contact with the water, the bugs would hiss and scurry back. But they'd keep trying to reach us, and soon the legs would be dry. And given that we didn't have much water, that wouldn't be long.

"Can we wash the smell away?" Maloch asked, holding his flagon above his head.

"Don't waste the water," I said. "It's our only weapon."

"Then I'm open to ideas," he said, sending another trickle down the stone legs to keep the scythebeetles at bay.

I closed my eyes and blocked out the sound of the scythe-beetle feet tapping furiously all around. I had to think. They were blocking the doorway we'd come through, so leaving that way wasn't an option. We could only escape through one of the sarcophagi . . . but we still didn't know which was the right one. Opening more might fill the room with tarsa gas, and then we'd be—

Suddenly, the memory slammed into the front of my brain. Kolo had been writing about tarsa gas in his new manuscript. I pulled Kolo's pages from Tree Bag and scanned each piece of parchment until I found what I needed:

. . . the effects of tarsa gas can be countermanded with an infusion of amberberry pollen, winkroot, and embermoss.

"Give me one of your shirts!" I said to Maloch, as I rifled through my pouches for the right ingredients. Without a second thought, he pulled off the shirt he was wearing and tossed it to me. I glowered. "You just did that to impress Reena when she wakes up."

"Just do what you're going to do!" he howled.

"Fine!" I ripped the shirt in half. When his jaw dropped, I said, "I told you to give me *one* of your shirts. You didn't have to give me the one you were wearing."

"But you ripped it!"

"Which is why I asked for one of *yours!*" I continued ripping the shirt until I had four long strips. I dumped the ingredients into my water flagon, gave it a vigorous shake, then poured it over the shirt strips. I tied one around my mouth and nose like a mask. The sweet smell of the amber-berry pollen mixed with the nauseating stench of the cadaverweed water from Maloch's shirt. I could only hope that Kolo knew what he was talking about.

But then, when didn't he?

"Put these on," I told Maloch and Holm. Holm tied the fourth strip around his sister's face. "It will protect us from the gas."

I looked to the far wall where the sarcophagi stood. The scythebeetles had gathered on the floor behind me. The floor between the table and the caskets, however, was practi-cally bare. I noticed a thin ledge on the wall just above the sarcophagi that ran around the entire room. This was not going to be easy.

"Keep the legs wet," I said to Maloch, "and get ready to run when I tell you."

"What are you going to—?"

Before he could finish, I jumped off the table and hit the ground running toward the sarcophagi. A second later, the scythebeetles picked up my scent, and half of them followed me. With the scythebeetles snapping at my heels, I pounced up and forward, wrapping my arms and legs as tightly as I could around the nearest casket. Digging in, I shimmied up the sarcophagus to the ledge just above.

A legion of scythebeetles crawled up the bottom of the sarcophagus. I reached down and yanked the lid open. A jet of tarsa gas spat from within the casket, blasting the bugs to the floor. Apparently immune to the gas, the scythebeetles waited near the edge of the casket for my natural clumsiness to kick in and send me falling into their waiting pincers.

I crawled quickly along the ledge to the next sarcophagus and threw the lid open. Columns of gas shot up from holes in the floor. The vapors hung like a greenish cloak in the air. They weren't disappearing as quickly as the dose that had knocked Reena out. Soon, the chamber would be full, and I doubted the masks could protect us from that much gas.

I moved to the next sarcophagus and flung open the lid. No gas this time. But thousands more scythebeetles spilled out.

"Good news, guys. I found more bugs!" I said cheerfully. Maloch bared his teeth at me. Holm made a rude gesture that I was pretty sure he was too young to know.

I continued along the ledge, opening casket lids and

filling the room with alternating gas and scythebeetles. The gas in the air had grown so thick that it was hard to see Maloch and Holm through the haze. And even with Kolo's infusion, I was growing dizzy. If I released more gas, it would probably knock us out. I had to get it right this time. But how?

Only two sarcophagi remained . . . on opposite sides of the room. I looked down at the caskets. The one to the left was covered in dust. The one to the right looked just as dirty, with cobwebs that stretched from its base down the length of the long shadow it cast.

The shadow . . .

None of the hardglamour caskets cast shadows. So the one with the shadow had to be real!

Maloch, whose flagon was now empty, had taken to batting scythebeetles away from the table legs with the torch. "Jaxter, do something!"

I crawled to the real sarcophagus and bent over to pull at the lid, when the thin ledge beneath me gave way. I fell headfirst, barely able to catch myself. I hit the floor at the feet of the sarcophagus and cried out as my wrists bent backward.

In a blink, the scythebeetles charged, pincers snapping. I

grasped at the sarcophagus, trying to pull myself to my feet, but my injured wrists didn't have the strength.

"Aaaaahhh!"

I jumped at hearing Holm shout from the center of the room. He stood with one hand on his hip, the other holding his sister's full wineskin above his head.

"To this fate I won't be bound! Now these bugs are *going down!*" He shot a stream of water from the wineskin. It hit the floor, creating a wet path between the table and me. Scythebeetles hissed and clattered away from the water.

Holm jumped and ran down the clearing he'd created, shooting more bursts of water to keep the bugs away. He helped me to my feet, and together we threw open the sarcophagus lid.

No gas. No bugs. Just a corridor.

Holm turned and knelt, spraying more water to keep the path clear for Maloch. The wineskin wheezed, nearly empty.

"Last one in is beetle bait!" I said to Maloch before disappearing into the hall beyond.

Maloch tossed the torch into the scythebeetles, sending them hissing away. Mumbling, he picked Reena up in his arms. "Wait up! She's heavier than she looks." He jumped from the table and ran. The scythebeetles charged as we disappeared into the sarcophagus and shut the lid behind us.

We collapsed in the corridor, the sounds of the advancing scythebeetles now muffled behind the door. The only light came from the other end of the hall. Here, we were mere outlines in the dark.

Maloch's breathing was the heaviest of all. "You know . . . ," he said, his shoulders rising and falling with his chest, ". . . bound . . . doesn't rhyme . . . with down."

Holm leaned back against the wall, holding his stomach. "Oh . . . shut up . . ."

As my eyes adjusted to the low light, I spotted a fist swing through the air and connect with Maloch's face, sending him backward.

Reena sat up, flexing her fist, and pulled the infusion mask from her face. "Who's heavier than she looks?"

Maloch leaned back, rubbing his jaw with a smirk. Reena rolled her eyes. "Oh, put a shirt on," she said, then got to her feet and led us to the other end of the corridor.

17

A Deadly Oasis

"Innocence is relative, but relatives are rarely innocent."

—*Thollin Grimjinx, mastermind of the Great Icesepulchre Plunder*

Maybe it was because the journey to and through the mountains had left us without food. Maybe it was because we'd used the last of our water fighting off the scythebeetles. Maybe it was because everything we'd been though had driven us completely naff-nut. Whatever the reason, when the next room appeared to be a kitchen with a well and a generous supply of food, it never occurred to me that everything might be laced with deadly doses of poison.

Actually, it *did* occur to me. But I was so hungry I didn't care.

As the others stepped gingerly around the room, poking stones that they thought might set off traps, I went through the tall wooden pantries and made myself a sandwich bigger than my head. The pantries sparkled with a faint golden light, indicating that the meats, vegetables, and breads inside were magically preserved from spoiling. I filled my flagon with well water, sat on a small stool, and shoved my face into the sandwich.

"You're going to die," Maloch said as he followed the curve of the circular room, inspecting the wall for anything suspicious. "And when you do, I'll probably laugh."

"He's got a point, Jaxter," Reena said, trying to sound disapproving, though she was eyeing my sandwich enviously.

"And what reason do we have to think this is anything but what it appears to be: one big kitchen?" I said.

"You mean aside from the fact that we *know* every room is protected by traps?" Maloch said. "Gee, I don't know. Enjoy your last meal."

"You said yourself the Dagger was designed as a bunker," I said, and maybe a few chunks of sandwich fell out of my mouth as I said it. "And that in case of danger, the Shadowhands could hide here for months and be perfectly safe. It stands to reason they would keep a kitchen with magically preserved foods."

"Maybe so," Reena said, "but how can you be sure this is it? It could be another hardglamour."

I took a torch from the wall and held it near my sandwich. It cast a long shadow on the equally long wooden table. "Hardglamours don't cast shadows."

Reena and Holm looked at each other, then dove for the well, drinking until I thought they'd burst. Maloch remained unconvinced, jeering as the siblings raided the pantries and began feasting.

"It could still be poisoned," Maloch said.

"Just shut up and eat," I said. "You get cranky when you're hungry."

Before Maloch could argue, Holm tossed him a blackdrupe, and Maloch grudgingly bit into it. We sat around the table, alternately eating and stuffing food into our packs for the trip out of the mountains. We heated well water in giant cauldrons and took turns bathing to get the cadaver-weed smell out. Clean again, we sat down to strategize.

There were two other doorways in the room besides the one we'd entered through. "So, any guesses on where we go from here?" I asked.

"We could split up," Reena said. "Two pairs, each picking a different door. We'd cover more ground and find the Covenant faster."

"And we'd be in twice as much danger," Maloch said. "I think we should stick together."

While Reena and Maloch argued, I considered our situation. As Maloch suggested, the kitchen *should* have been filled with traps. So why wasn't it? It didn't seem like the Shadowhands to provide an oasis for intruders.

"Maloch," I said slowly, "what was that you said earlier? About Shadowhands getting safe passage through the Dagger?"

"The Dagger is linked to the Covenant," he said. "The defenses automatically deactivate in the presence of anyone listed on the Covenant, any Shadowhand."

I squinted at the wall past Maloch's shoulder. I could have sworn I saw the stone shimmer.

"Uh-huh," I said, my eyes never leaving the wall. "Any idea how long before the defenses reactivate once a Shadowhand leaves the room?"

Maloch looked to Reena quizzically and shrugged. "No. I don't think it would be too long, because—"

He stopped. By now, everyone had noticed. The walls were shifting. The dark stone rippled and changed. Bricks turned into long metal spikes that slowly stretched across the length of the room.

Maloch and I, hitting on the same thought, looked at each other.

"A Shadowhand was in this room just before we got here," he said.

"And the defenses are turning back on," I concluded.

"Look!" Reena shouted. We watched as the pantries transformed into great, jagged, iron blades that started to spin, slicing the air with a high-pitched whine.

The two doors that led out were slowly disappearing, being filled in with hardglamour stones.

"Move!"

I grabbed a torch as we scooped up our packs and dove for the closest door. With the doorway collapsing, we fell to all fours and crawled through into the next corridor. The kitchen disappeared just as we pulled Holm through the small hole.

Gasping, we stood in the hall and looked back at where the door to the kitchen had once been.

"Is this enough of a fortress for you now, dolly girl?" Maloch asked.

"More than enough, thanks," Reena said.

I caught Maloch's eye and he nodded. His hand slipped to his belt, and he drew his dagger.

Reena stiffened. "What is it?" she asked.

"The kitchen was safe because a Shadowhand had been there shortly before us," Maloch said softly.

"Which means," I said, "we're not alone here."

The four of us sat there, staring at one another as the distant spinning blades hummed.

"But . . . ," Reena said, ". . . but that's good, right? We came here hoping to find the Shadowhands. To prove the

Sarosans didn't steal from the High Laird."

"We came here to find the *Covenant*," Maloch said firmly, "because the Shadowhands were betrayed by one of their own. And if the Shadowhands are disappearing . . ."

Holm swallowed. "Here among the spiky walls, the traitor walks these very halls."

"Uh . . . yeah," I said.

Reena took the torch from me. "Even better. We don't need the Covenant. We just find the traitor, bring them to the High Laird—"

Maloch and I shared another look. Reena rolled her eyes.

"What?" she asked. "There are four of us. Holm and I have blowguns. This will be easy."

"You really don't understand the Shadowhands," Maloch said, shaking his head.

"We're not exaggerating when we say they're the best of the best," I said. "They are masters at hiding, stalking, and taking out their adversaries. I heard they were trained by the assassin-monks of Blackvesper Abbey."

"We have the advantage, that is clear," Holm said, "if they do not know we're here."

"Maybe," I said. "But hear that?" I pointed to where the kitchen door had been. The sound of the whirling blades continued. "I bet our Shadowhand friend can hear it, too. They know that a trap has been sprung. They could be looking for us right this very minute."

I'd been raised on stories of the Shadowhands. Their tracking skills were as legendary as their distaste for mercy toward intruders. "If they find us before we find them," I said, "we won't get out of here alive."

18

The Nursery

"The greater the guilt, the richer the reward."

—*The Lymmaris Creed*

Reena, who'd been deprived of a thief's upbringing filled with stories of the Shadowhands' prowess and cunning, seemed unimpressed. She turned and continued down the hall to the open doorway at the far end. "We need to keep moving. Come on."

We all followed, Maloch and I watching the rear. The hall led to another perfectly circular room. This time, the walls were pink. On the far side, a giant toy chest sat in the corner. A colossal stuffed Satyran doll with crocheted wool horns on its head and fuzzy hooves at the end of its overstuffed legs lay slumped on the floor. A jack-in-the-box that came up to my chin stood just inside the doorway, so that we had to bend over to go under the massive crank on its side.

"I'm guessing," Reena said, "the Shadowhands don't really need a nursery in their bunker."

Maloch scrutinized the walls. "Another hardglamour. It's hiding the way to the next chamber. Find the exit but be careful."

We spread out, stepping gingerly around the life-size toys that littered the floor. I stopped, standing over a rag doll that looked like a little girl. It was as big as Aubrin. One of its button eyes was missing, replaced with an X stitch of twine. It grinned up at me with a jagged smile.

Holm made his way to the center of the room, where a gorgeously decorated table displayed a tall and beautiful dollhouse. It was the only toy in the room that wasn't over-sized. Which made it suspect.

Holm seemed fascinated by the minihouse. He circled the table, eyeing the house from every angle. Reena came up next to me and whispered.

"Holm's always wanted to live in a real house," she said.

"We've only ever lived in tents."

The boy leaned in and peeked through the tiny windows. Suddenly, his eyes grew wide. He reached out.

"Holm, no!" I said. But it was too late. The second he touched the house, a shower of blue sparks exploded around him, and Holm was gone.

The three of us ran toward the house.

"Where is he?" Reena cried, looking around frantically.

"Down there." Maloch pointed to the main door of the house. Standing next to the door was a miniaturized Holm, no bigger than my thumb—the perfect size to go into the dollhouse.

"Ah," I said, "so this dollhouse makes its own dolls. Clever."

"Holm, are you okay?" Reena asked.

We leaned in as close we could. It looked like he was talking, but we couldn't hear him. He kept pointing to the house and waving his arms.

Maloch chuckled. "I'm pretty sure there's a minimum height requirement for warrior-bards." He reached out to give the diminutive Holm a poke.

"Maloch!" I said. A flash of blue sparks later, a tiny

Maloch stood next to Holm at the dollhouse's front door. Holm gave Maloch a kick in the shins.

"The house is cursed," I said to them. "And curses are contagious. Holm got it when he touched the house, you got it when you touched Holm, you naff-nut."

"How do we help them?" Reena said, nudging me in the ribs. "Can't you do something with your pouches?"

Unfortunately, curses were too powerful to be counteracted by the magic-resistant plants in my pouches. Maloch and Holm could be stuck that way a long, long time.

Reena bent over and squinted at our small friends. They were waving their arms over their heads and pointing behind us.

"Oh, that can't be good," I said as Reena and I slowly turned around.

The stuffed Satyran doll loomed over us, its woolen hooves making no sound as it stomped across the floor.

"Somebody wants to play," I said. Silently, the doll raised an arm and swung.

Reena and I each dove in a different direction. As I hit the ground, I saw the other toys in the room stirring. The one-eyed rag doll pulled itself to its feet. The crank on the jack-in-the-box churned sluggishly, and an eerie, dirgelike tune rose up out of the box. The toy chest lid creaked open, and a legion of marionettes painted like harlequins crawled up over the edge, dragging their thin strings behind.

"When Holm touched the house, it set off the trap," I said, backing away from the Satyran, which had bent over to attack Reena with its crocheted horns.

"Yeah," she said, "I got that." She rolled out of the doll's way, then spun and hit it with the torch. The Satyran ignited but didn't slow down. Its flaming arms flailed, trying to hit whichever of us was closer.

"I think you made it mad," I said as we regrouped under the table that held the dollhouse.

The other toys, much slower than the Satyran, were crawling or walking toward us, arms outstretched. Suddenly, the rag doll sprang, wrapping its cloth arms around Reena's leg. Reena cried out as the arms squeezed tighter and tighter. I pulled a dirk from my boot and swung it at the rag doll. That's when the harlequin marionettes leaped forward, darting all around and wrapping me in their thin but powerful strings.

Reena thrust the torch forward, but a toy par-Goblin

hobbled across the floor and snatched it from her hand. I twisted and turned to free myself. But every time I jerked, my limbs were pulled in tighter to my body, and soon it was hard to breathe. The marionettes cackled.

Shhk!

I looked around to see a thin dart sticking out of the nearest marionette's painted face. *Shhk! Shhk!* Two more darts in two more marionettes. Reena had managed to grab her blowgun and was sending out poisoned darts everywhere she could. The poison had no effect, but the toys were clearly not expecting the assault.

They paused. My hand uselessly pinned to my side, I dropped the dirk and used my shoulder to nudge it over to Reena. She abandoned her blowgun and grabbed my weapon. With one powerful swipe of her arm, she freed herself from the rag doll's clutches and me from the marionettes' strings.

Together, we crawled out from under the table. I pointed to the hall that led to the saw-blade kitchen. It was the only visible exit.

"We can't leave them," she said, nodding at the dollhouse. But Maloch and Holm were nowhere to be seen. I could only guess that they'd gone into the house for shelter once the toys had come to life.

"We can't help them if we're dead," I said, pulling her arm toward the doorway.

Just as we ran for the exit, the jack-in-the-box lid shot open with a *sproing!* A massive toy spiderbat on a spring bounded from the box and landed at our feet. With the dollhouse to our backs, we were completely surrounded by the army of toys.

A flit of motion near the dollhouse caught my eye. I saw tiny Holm jumping up and down on the roof. He was pointing to Maloch, who was smearing something dark on the white shingles to spell TOUCH THE HOUSE.

At this point, spending the rest of my life as a tiny doll seemed better than being killed by the world's most vicious toys. I grabbed Reena's hand and yanked her toward the dollhouse. We fought off the toys as they tried to drag us to the ground. With a final jump, I reached out and touched the roof of the dollhouse.

My vision filled with blue sparks and the next thing I knew, I was dangling with one hand from the edge of the roof. Reena, holding tightly to my other hand, squirmed precariously below me. I felt two strong hands clamp around my wrist. Slowly, Reena and I were pulled up to safety.

Lungs heaving, squatting on all fours, I looked up to thank Maloch for saving us. Instead, I met the eyes of my father.

"Bet it's a long time before you play with toys again," Da said, a glint in his eye.

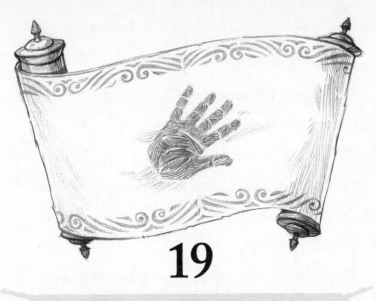

19

The Last Shadowhand

"The enemy of my enemy is my next likely target."

—Ancient par-Goblin proverb

We scaled down the side of the dollhouse. Well, Da and Reena scaled. I made it halfway before I slipped and fell. Da was ready, though, and caught me before I hit the tabletop. Now that I was shrunken, the house seemed normal in size. The larger-than-life toys, on the other hand, were now monstrous. They circled the table menacingly. Clearly, they knew they couldn't attack without getting miniaturized.

"Da, what are you doing here?" I asked as he led Reena

and me inside the house.

The second I stepped inside, I was yanked into the vestibule and nearly choked by Ma's hug.

"We should be asking you the same thing," Ma said. She sounded both worried about me and angry about my disobedience. "By the Seven! You're supposed to be with the Dowager."

"Yes," I said, as soon as I could breathe again. "Well, things got complicated."

We all walked into the living room. Holm and Reena hugged while Maloch reclined in an overstuffed chair, hands behind his head.

"We tried to get your attention," Maloch said to me. "Holm saw your parents in the window of the house—that's why he touched it. Your da had the idea to smear the food from our packs on the roof to spell out that message."

Da sighed. "What a waste of perfectly good beetloaf," he said. "But it worked."

"Why are you here in the first place?" I asked. "You're supposed to be off finding the remaining Shadowhands."

Ma and Da shared a look of deep concern. "That's what we did," Ma said, sitting on a footstool. "We used the information Maloch's da left for me to search for the last three Shadowhands. Both Alvar and Bennis were nowhere to be found. No one had seen them for days."

"What about"—I searched my memory for the name of the third Shadowhand—"Dylis? Dylis Jareen? Did you find her?"

"And not a moment too soon."

I jumped to hear a raspy voice behind me. Turning, I saw a Satyran woman sitting in a high-backed chair in the corner. She looked about Ma's age, with a few wisps of silver hair among the curls on her head and the whiskers of her beard. The mottled gray horns protruding from her forehead matched the cloven hooves that poked out from underneath the long, flowing mage robes. Her arms, hidden beneath the robes, were wrapped around her chest.

"I didn't think the Shadowhands allowed mages in," I said.

Dylis Jareen smiled at me. It really wasn't a pleasant smile. It seemed pained and distant. She nodded down at the robes. "A disguise. I'd figured out what was happening to the Shadowhands and had gone into hiding. It was sheer luck your parents found me when they did. Lucky for me.

Otherwise, I might not be here."

Da cleared his throat. "Yes, well, that's a story for another time. Maloch had just started to tell us why you're here, but he didn't get very far before the toys started attacking. So out with it."

I took a deep breath, and between myself and Maloch and Reena and Holm—in his own peculiar way—we recounted the story of the past couple of weeks, from the kidnapping in Vengekeep to our fleeing Redvalor Castle in search of the Covenant. Ma's and Da's faces went from concern to fear to laughter and back to concern again. The whole time, the expression on Dylis's face barely changed. She showed no surprise, no emotion whatsoever. And sometimes when I looked over to her, I could almost feel her tiny black eyes peering through me.

When we finished our story, Da folded his hands behind his back and started pacing. "Well, it looks like we all hit upon the same idea: find the Covenant, find the traitor."

"But why don't you have it yet?" Reena blurted out. She immediately looked down, realizing she'd been rude.

"It's a fair question," I said playfully, trying to cover for the awkwardness. "Three skilled thieves. Two Shadowhands who can deactivate the Dagger's defenses. You should have been in and out in no time."

Ma agreed. "Yes, it should have been simple enough. But when we got here, we found we weren't alone."

"We were attacked," Da said. "Tall brutes in heavy coats. We never saw their faces. They just came at us, swords waving. It was all we could do to keep ahead of them."

Ma gestured at Dylis. "It was Dylis's idea to come to this room. She activated the nursery hardglamour, and we touched the house so we could hide. We've been here for two days, hoping that whoever infiltrated the Dagger thinks we've left."

That didn't bode well. If the three of them had been hiding in the dollhouse for the past two days, then they couldn't have switched off the hardglamour in the kitchen. Which meant that whoever had attacked them was still at large.

"Speaking of which," Da said, reaching for my pack, "we ran out of food yesterday. Do you mind?"

I quickly unpacked my supply of food, and Ma and Da dug in. I offered a slab of sanguibeast ribs to Dylis. The Satyran declined, pulling her robed arms closer to her body with a wince.

"So I'm just going to ask the obvious question," Maloch said, folding his arms and looking right at Dylis. "If all the Shadowhands are gone except one, and we know that one of them was a traitor—"

"Choose your next words very carefully, Maloch Oxter," Dylis said, her black eyes raking over Maloch. I caught a glint of light and looked down to see the tip of a dagger poking out the end of Dylis's long sleeve.

"Dylis isn't the traitor," Ma said firmly. "We think the traitor may have faked his disappearance to throw off suspicion."

"And that person would have gone to great lengths to throw everyone off the track," Dylis said, her eyes never leaving Maloch. "They might even, say, leave behind evidence suggesting they'd uncovered a plot and were going in search of the missing Shadowhands themselves. . . ."

Maloch, face flushed, leaped to his feet. "My father is no traitor!"

"Enough!" Da said, hands raised. "We're here to help each other, and pointing fingers won't accomplish anything."

Maloch slowly sat. He and Dylis continued to size each other up.

I tried to ease the tension. "Finding the traitor is one thing. We also need to find out who hired the Shadowhands in the first place." I said to Dylis, "Do you have any ideas who it was?"

The Satyran gave a black look. "If I knew, I'd already be spitting on their corpse."

Lovely.

"Dylis," Ma said, placing her arm around my shoulders. "Would you mind telling your story to Jaxter? He's quite bright. He might see something that we've all missed."

Dylis sat up and grimaced, pulling her arms in closer to her chest. She eyed me warily, then shot an untrusting look at Reena and Holm, both of whom immediately bristled.

I smiled weakly at the Sarosans. "Would you mind heading upstairs for a bit? This is strictly between thieves." When both took deep breaths, I quickly added, "The faster we get things sorted, the faster we can get your parents out of Umbramore."

That shut them up. The siblings collected their things, stormed out of the room, and stomped loudly upstairs. Dylis began.

"The Shadowhands," she said in her raspy voice, "were

contacted several months ago through the usual means. . . ."

Contacting a cadre of highly secret thieves is about as hard as you'd imagine. It's not like they have a shop set up that you can just pop into. You have to know people. And those people have to know people. And if you're lucky, those people know people who know how to contact the Shadowhands. The Shadowhands had spies everywhere. It wouldn't be long before word got to them that someone was seeking their services and they made contact.

"I went to the meeting personally. Yab Oxter came along to watch my back, hiding in the shadows while I made the deal. . . ." She leered at Maloch, who stiffened at the mention of his father. "Our employer supplied us with detailed maps of all the royal vaults, a list of the items to be procured, and instructions on the precise day and time that the vaults would be at their most vulnerable."

I thought about what the Dowager and I had discussed, and it still bothered me. How had the contact known exactly when the Provincial Guard would be called away from the duties of protecting the vaults? I kept thinking the answer to all our problems had something to do with that. But I shrugged it off as Dylis continued her story.

"He paid us handsomely—six thousand silvernibs in advance, with a promise of another four thousand upon delivery of the items. I made the deal, then gathered the other Shadowhands to discuss the job. We quickly divided into teams of three and made off for the vaults. Just as our contact indicated, the Provincial Guard had left their posts on orders. A job that would have otherwise been nearly impossible, even for a Shadowhand, became one of the easiest ever. We all reunited at the Dagger with the four stolen items."

I blinked. "I'm sorry?"

Dylis ignored my interruption. "We came back here with the four stolen items, then proceeded to Firesilk Falls. We found a large chest with the balance of our payment buried near the riverbank. We took the silvernibs and put the stolen relics—the orb, the gauntlets, the coronet, and the scepter—into the chest and buried it exactly where our employer instructed us. And that was that."

Then the Satyran's face darkened, and she gave a snort. "Or that *should have been* that. Months later, I began to realize that my fellow Shadowhands were vanishing. I got an urgent message from Yab to meet him at the Dagger. On my way, I was attacked, so I went into hiding until your parents found me."

I watched her, trying to look sympathetic. Every gesture seemed to cause her pain, especially when she moved her arms. When she finished speaking, her eyes fell.

Ma looked at me brightly. "Any thoughts?"

I rubbed my hands together. "Maybe. I need to think it over a bit. Sleep on it."

Da yawned. "Good idea. We could all do with some rest. Then we can get up early and plan a way to get to the Covenant."

We gathered our belongings. Dylis grunted as she got to her feet. She leaned over slowly, her furry left hand snaking carefully from under her robe as she reached for the bag at her feet.

I stepped forward with a smile. "Here, let me get that for you."

But before I could touch her bag, she scooped it up with a wince and held it tight to her body. "Thank you," she said with a pained smile, "but I prefer to carry it myself."

We all went upstairs. Reena and Holm had already

collapsed from exhaustion in one of the bedrooms. Dylis took one room, Ma and Da another, which left Maloch and me in the final bedroom. The walls were decorated with bright flowers. Frilly lace framed the canopy bed.

Once the door was closed, Maloch threw his bag in the corner and started pacing. "I can't believe she thinks my da is the traitor. I should have cut her just for suggesting it. I don't trust her."

I sat on the edge of the bed, polishing the lenses of my glasses. "You've got good reason."

Maloch stopped in his tracks. "What do you mean?"

"Dylis is the traitor," I said plainly, "and I can prove it."

20

Shimmerhex

"Anger the mage twice, the thief once, and the fool
as often as you like."

—*Lorris Grimjinx, inventor of the rubyeye*

Ma was right. I saw something that everyone else had missed.

Maloch sat next to me on the bed. "What do you mean?"

"Didn't you hear what she said?" I asked. "She said they returned to the Dagger with the four stolen items. *Four.* We know from the Dowager that *five* relics were stolen that night."

Maloch's eyes lit up. "You're right. So maybe . . . maybe . . ."

It was funny to watch him try his hand at thinking. Every now and then, his eyes would soften, as if he was about to collide with an actual thought. Then they'd go dark again. I decided to help him along.

"So maybe," I said, "whoever hired the Shadowhands gave a list of five relics to Dylis. But when she went back to the Shadowhands, she only mentioned four of them. Then she went and stole the fifth item for herself. When their employer dug up the chest and found one of the items missing, he assumed the Shadowhands had betrayed him. So he set out to eliminate them all and get his missing relic back."

By now, Maloch was practically bursting with energy. He was up again, pacing furiously, pounding his fist into his hand. "Makes sense to me. Can you convince your parents?"

I shook my head. "Probably not. But then there's the matter of her arms. Have you noticed how she always keeps them in her robes? And how she winces whenever she moves them?" Maloch stared blankly at me, and I sighed. "You said anyone who betrays the Covenant contracts a magical illness. Well, Mardem's Blight is a magical disease that gives you bleeding lesions up and down your arms. *That's* how we expose her. Well, that and—"

"What?"

"She mentioned burying the orb, the coronet, the gauntlets, and the scepter. That means the fifth relic—the Vanguard—is still missing. Did you see how quick she was to make sure I didn't touch her bag? Now what do you suppose is in there that's so valuable?"

Maloch pulled out his dagger. "Then we march in there and—"

"If we go into her room, weapons raised . . . She's a Shadowhand, Maloch. We'll both be dead before we can cry for help. We come from thieving stock, you and me. There are subtler ways to do this."

✦

By subtler ways, I meant for Maloch to sneak into Dylis's room and poke around. But he had other ideas.

"I'll stand guard," he whispered, dagger brandished, as we stood outside Dylis's door. "You go in and find the Vanguard."

"We don't even know what the Vanguard looks like," I

said. "I doubt it's something mounted on a plaque that reads, 'Hello, I'm the Vanguard, and don't I have a silly name?'"

"It's an ancient relic," he said. "It's the thing in her bag of supplies and clothes and food that *looks like an ancient relic.*"

I placed my hand on the doorknob. "And remind me, why am *I* doing this? As you keep telling me over and over and over, I'm not the best thief in the world."

He shrugged. "Remember when you let me believe the Sarosans were going to kill us and we nearly died of almaxa poisoning? Well, do this and we're even."

What he really meant was "do this or I'll pound you." And even though we'd have had a much better chance of succeeding if Maloch tried this, he wasn't a complete naff-nut. He wasn't about to risk accidentally waking a sleeping Shadowhand.

Taking a long, deep breath, I gave the lightweight door a gentle push. A faint green-blue light, spilling in through the window from the torches in the nursery outside, filled Dylis's room. I got down on all fours and crawled quietly inside.

The Satyran snored loudly, her horned head barely

peeking up out of the blankets. I crept across the floor to Dylis's bag in the far corner. As she emitted a rumbling snore, I reached out and gingerly pulled the bag toward me.

I opened the drawstring that cinched the top and felt around inside. The first thing I found was a loaf of moldy bread. I stuck out my tongue. Satyrans loved moldy food. The smell alone nearly made me retch. I set the bread aside and dove in again.

My search yielded a map, two changes of clothes, a whetstone that I guessed was for keeping her horns and hooves sharp, a tinderbox, a flagon, a set of burglar tools, and a small satchel filled with silvernibs. I felt around in the nearly empty bag and came across the last item. Pulling it out, I found a wad of soft cloth. Gripping tighter, I could feel something hard and round in the center. I moved to the window for as much light as I could get.

Palming the cloth, I peeled back the top layer, exposing a glint of polished light-brown metal: a large coin, the size of my palm. Raised symbols in par-Goblin dotted the exposed surface, and a sparkling green jewel sat embedded in the center.

It was a par-Goblin tingroat. The currency hadn't been used since the Great Uprisings, when the High Laird's silvernibs, copperbits, and bronzemerks came into use throughout the Five Provinces. While it couldn't be used to buy bread from the baker, it was valuable as an extremely rare artifact.

Could this be the mysterious Vanguard?

As I reached out to touch it, I was suddenly yanked backward, sending the tingroat to the floor with a thud. I cried out when a cold metal blade was pressed firmly against my throat.

"What do you think you're doing?" Dylis growled in my ear. Her left arm hooked around my shoulder, keeping me in place.

My cry alerted Maloch, who charged into the room, dagger drawn.

"Let him go!" he said with a snarl, pointing his weapon threateningly at Dylis.

"The Vanguard! The Vanguard!" I squealed, pointing to where the tarnished coin had fallen near the edge of the bed. Dylis's grip on me tightened, and her blade dug into my neck.

Maloch dove for the coin, but before he reached it, a blur flew into the room and tackled him. When the pair rolled into the light, I found Da pinning Maloch's arms down at his side.

"Don't touch it!" Da said.

A moment later, Ma, Reena, and Holm stood in the doorway, Reena holding the small lantern from her pack. The room filled with warm yellow light.

"Dylis," Ma said, sounding tired, "let Jaxter go."

The Satyran pulled the blade away from my neck but held me tight. "He was trying to steal from me."

Ma rolled her eyes. "I raised my boy right, Dylis. He knows better than to try to steal from a Shadowhand. Don't you, Jaxter?"

I grinned with a more-than-slightly-guilty look on my face.

Da stood, pulled Maloch to his feet, and guided him over to Ma. Then he took the cloth from my hand and gently picked up the tingroat. With great care, he folded it back up into the cloth until it was completely covered.

With a rough shove, Dylis sent me across the room toward my parents. Her left arm hung out of her robes.

Despite being a bit furry, there wasn't a single lesion or wound to be found.

"I should have let him touch it," the Satyran said, sheathing her dirk. "It's a lesson he'd never forget."

Ma's hands went to her hips, and she looked disapprovingly at Maloch and me. "Explain."

Maloch and I took turns, and somehow we managed to get the whole story out. My theory about Dylis's arms. The Vanguard.

I could see rage building behind the Shadowhand's eyes as all the details of our foiled heist unfolded. "I made the deal with our employer myself!" she said. "There were *four* relics on the list and only four." She reached into a side pocket on her bag, produced a piece of parchment, and tossed it at me. I unfolded it to find a detailed description of the orb, the gauntlets, the scepter, and the coronet, along with diagrams of the vaults and instructions on how to get past a variety of magical defenses that guarded them. There was no mention of the Vanguard.

"This is what I got from our employer," Dylis continued. "You're lying about a fifth relic."

"They're not." It was Reena who interjected. "The

Dowager showed us the report from the High Laird. Five vaults were broken into that night. Not just four."

We all sat silently for a moment. The Shadowhands had been hired to steal only four relics. So what happened to the fifth?

"If you don't have Mardem's Blight," Maloch said, glaring at Dylis, "why do you hide your arms?"

Dylis drew herself up to her full height, towering over Maloch. She waved her left arm, which was already fully exposed. Then, with great effort, she pulled back her right sleeve.

Reena gasped. Holm gaped. Maloch groaned. From her fingertips to just past her elbow, Dylis's right arm was made of clear, sparkling glass.

Da held up the tingroat, shrouded in cloth. "This is how whoever is hunting the Shadowhands got them all. Each was sent a package containing a tingroat cursed with a shimmerhex. One touch and they were turned to glass. This vallix-skin cloth is the only thing protecting me from the curse." Vallix skin was the only known material that could protect from a curse. "We're thinking if we study the tingroat, we might learn who sent it."

Dylis pulled her right sleeve back down, covering the glass arm again. "I suspected something was strange and didn't touch the coin when it arrived. But in trying to wrap it up, I just barely grazed the tingroat's edge with my finger and . . ." She looked down sadly. "And yes, it's quite painful where the glass meets flesh."

Maloch leaned against the wall. "I—I remember the day a package was delivered to our house. I think Da must have already figured out that the Shadowhands were disappearing at that point. He took the package with him when he went to look for the remaining Shadowhands. Just before he vanished."

Ma let out a long sigh. "All right, then. Do we finally believe there are no traitors among us? We're all friends now, yes?" Maloch and Dylis cast each other a final suspicious look before nodding to Ma. "Wonderful. Then let's get some sleep. Someone is still searching for us in the Dagger. We need to be alert to make it to the Covenant chamber before they find us. Right? Back to bed, everyone."

We all went back to our rooms. Maloch and I lay side by side on the canopy bed. "So . . . we're even now. Right?" I asked sleepily.

Eyes closed, Maloch said, "Even. Well. Almost."

With a shove of his beefy arm, I flew from the bed onto the floor. He wrapped himself up in all the blankets and turned away. "G'night, Jaxter."

I climbed back onto the side of the bed without any blankets. "Yeah. Good night."

21

The Final Trap

"Honor bought is honor owned."

—*Corenus Grimjinx, founder of the Grimjinx clan*

The next morning, we had a hearty breakfast, gathered our stuff, and exited the house. Little had changed overnight. The killer toys surrounded the table, as if daring us to escape. Dylis led us to the edge of the tabletop.

"And how," I asked, looking around at the gigantic nursery, "do we break the curse?"

Da waved his hand. "The shrinking curse is part of the Dagger's defenses. And Shadowhands can activate and deactivate the defenses at will. Dylis?"

The Satyran cleared her throat and raised her left arm. *"Shedekk!"* she cried in par-Goblin.

The walls and toys of the nursery began to melt into shimmering streams of light that spun into a whirlpool at the room's center, like water down a drain. The dollhouse and table vanished, but before we could fall, a flash of blue sparks restored us to our normal size. When the magical light show subsided, we found ourselves in a room filled with beds and bureaus.

Reena's lip curled. "If it was that easy, why didn't you do that when the toys were attacking us?"

Well, I wasn't going to say it. But she had a fair point.

"It was safer to bring you into the house with us," Ma said. "For all we knew, the traitor was watching. If we'd destroyed the hardglamours, it could have exposed you."

Maloch examined the beds. "Where are we? Is it another illusion?"

"This is the women's dormitory," Dylis said. "We have a ways to go before we reach the Covenant chamber."

With the hardglamour gone, we could now see two doors leading from the room. Dylis led us through the door that went back to the kitchen. The moment we entered, spikes began to appear from the walls as the whirling blades emerged from the ceiling.

"*Shedekk!*" Dylis called out, and the magical defenses disintegrated. We took a moment to restock our food supplies. When we were ready, Ma gathered us all close.

"Dylis, Ona, and I will lead the way," she said. "You four hang back just a bit so Dylis has a chance to deactivate the defenses. Stay close to one another. Maloch, keep an eye on the rear. Don't want anyone sneaking up on you."

Maloch nodded. I felt a twinge of jealousy that Ma had given him the job of guarding the rear. Then I realized that if we were attacked from behind, Maloch's screams would give Reena, Holm, and me time to escape. Suddenly, I felt better.

Dylis led us from the kitchen down an unfamiliar corridor. As the adults made their way cautiously ahead, Reena poked me in the side.

"So what did you find out last night?" she said in a whisper. "After Holm and I left."

"Not much, really," I said. She looked skeptical, so I

repeated everything Dylis had told us.

"Jaxter," she said slowly, "you believe we're innocent, right? The Sarosans?"

"Of course," I said. "That's why we're here: to prove it."

"I've been thinking," she said, "about the stolen relics. What if you *did* believe we stole them? Let's say you're the High Laird. Let's say you don't have any proof the Sarosans stole them. Why accuse us?"

I considered what she said. The High Laird had refused to say why he blamed the Sarosans. Why would suspicion fall on them?

"Well," I said, "if I were the High Laird, I would notice that the relics were made from gold and onyx. That suggests they're magical. Since the Sarosans hate magic, I'd think you stole them to destroy them."

"But there are magical artifacts all over the Provinces. Why would we choose the five that were the hardest to get, the ones in your vault?"

"Maybe because you found out they were really powerful."

Reena grew more excited as she pieced things together. "The Dowager told you the relics had been in the vaults for hundreds of years, since the Great Uprisings. And all information about the Uprisings is gone. So how would we even know about them?"

I remembered my discussion with Kolo about the past and how details of the Great Uprisings had been destroyed. If someone *had* sought the relics because they were powerful, they must somehow know something about the Uprisings. But the knowledge didn't exist. And if it did, it was unlikely the Sarosans had it.

"Fair point. Which brings us back to: the Sarosans couldn't have done it. So who else would want to destroy the relics?"

"I think whoever employed the Shadowhands doesn't want to destroy them. I think they might want to use them."

"A rogue mage?" I said. The Dowager and I had considered it. It was rare for a mage to go rogue. When one did, the Palatinate Sentinels were specially trained to track that mage down.

"Maybe," Reena said, but I could tell by her tone that she didn't believe it. "Or maybe higher up . . ."

I knew immediately what she was implying. "You think the Palatinate . . ."

"I don't know. I'm a Sarosan. We're naturally suspicious

of all mages, and the Palatinate aren't exactly our friends. But if those relics were locked away, they *must* be incredibly powerful. And only the Palatinate—"

I held up my hand. "If the Palatinate wanted magical relics from the vaults, all they'd have to do is ask. The High Laird trusts them. They wouldn't have to stage a break-in."

Reena's eyes fell. "You're right. We're not any closer to figuring this out, are we?"

"Let's see what happens when we get to the Covenant chamber and find out who the traitor is. It's all we've got right now."

We stepped from the corridor into a massive dining room with a large table and twelve chairs. Dylis yelled out in par-Goblin, turning away an army of hardglamour warriors in armor who had just started descending on us from the rafters above. We marched across the room.

"Well, this is a good sign, isn't it?" Da said brightly.

"What do you mean?" I asked.

"All the defenses are active. Which means no one has been here for a while. I think whoever was looking for us gave up and left. Should be a breeze."

We finally came to an armory where a lethal assortment of swords, halberds, and maces hung from wooden racks on the walls. Dylis pointed across the room to a short hall that led into the Covenant chamber. Maloch positioned himself in the archway that led back to the dining room. Reena, Holm, and I stood in the center of the armory. Ma, Da, and Dylis approached the Covenant chamber.

"I'll go on alone," Dylis said.

"Can't we see the chamber?" I asked. To be here in the Shadowhands' hidden lair was thrilling enough. I'd been burning to see the innermost sanctum—the Covenant chamber—since I knew that was where we were headed.

Ma shook her head. "This isn't a defense Dylis can deactivate. Only a Shadowhand can enter the chamber. Anyone else who tries . . . Well, it's not pretty."

Dylis took a torch, walked into the archway, and disappeared behind a sharp right curve. The rest of us waited.

And waited.

And waited.

"What's taking so long?" Maloch asked.

I looked at Ma, whose face was marked with concern.

"Maybe it takes a while to get to the chamber itself?" I replied.

Ma shook her head. "As soon as she rounded that corner, she was in the chamber."

"Maybe she left through another door?" Reena said. It was clear that she didn't trust Dylis.

Again, Ma disagreed. "This doorway is the only way in or out of the chamber."

We looked at one another, the same thought forming in our heads. Had Dylis gone in and come face-to-face with the traitor—a Shadowhand who'd faked their disappearance and was now just waiting to dispatch us all in the most grisly manner possible?

Ma brushed her hands together. "All right then. We've got no choice."

She held out her hand to Da. He frowned, then reluctantly handed her a thin, long dirk. Ma turned and moved to the doorway.

"What are you doing?" I asked.

Ma shushed me with a look. "I'm still bound to the Covenant," she said softly. "Which means I can enter unharmed. Now listen. If I don't come out, you won't be able to help me. You have to get out of here as quickly as possible. You won't have anyone to deactivate the defenses, so your best bet is to run as fast as you can to the exit. Understood?"

Da was clearly not happy with this, but he nodded. The rest of us joined him. Ma smiled brightly. "Won't be a moment. Carry on."

She walked through the archway and rounded the corner.

Behind me, I heard a thud. I turned to find Maloch, unconscious on the floor, his hand gripping his neck.

"Maloch!" Reena called out, running to him.

"We have to go!"

I spun around and saw Ma, already returned from the chamber, face white as a sheet.

Da gripped her by the arms. "Dylis?"

"She's a glass statue. Had the Covenant in her hand . . . but it wasn't the Covenant. It was a duplicate with a shimmerhex."

Shhk!

The sound came from the hall leading to the dining room. Now Reena was unconscious, lying over Maloch. Just past them, hooded figures entered from the corridor, blow-guns raised to their lips. S*hhk! Shhk! Shkk!*

Holm crumpled over, followed by Da. The last thing I heard was Ma cry, "It's a trap!" before a dart sank deep into my skin, just below my ear, and the world went black.

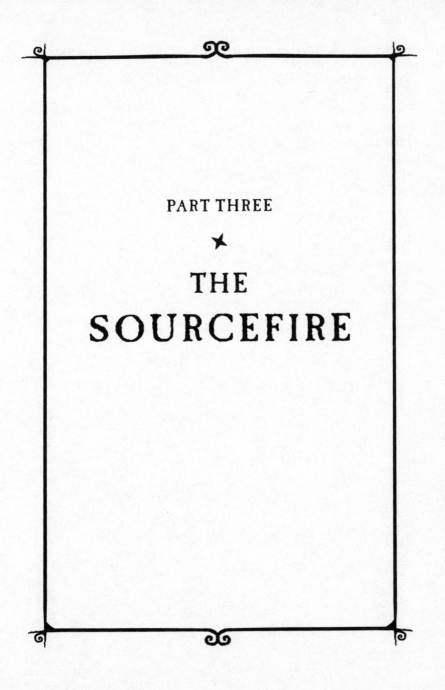

PART THREE

★

THE
SOURCEFIRE

22

Underground. Again.

"In the end, a skilled thief dresses as well as a
castellan."

—*Ancient par-Goblin proverb*

The Kolohendriseenax Formulary lists 168 different
combinations of plants that can render someone
unconscious when ingested, injected, or inhaled. I'd been
subject to two in as many weeks. I didn't like what that suggested for the days ahead.

When I awoke, a headache volleyed back and forth
between my eyes. The spot on my neck where the dart had
entered felt like it was on fire. My legs tingled. All these
symptoms pointed to one cause: our assailants had used

yerrani to subdue us. A tricky poison. You had to use just the right amount if you wanted to render someone unconscious. Even a fraction too much and the result could be deadly.

Our captors knew their herbs.

I lifted my head and looked around. Terrific. Another cave. I was tired of caves. Just once I wanted to be held captive somewhere less dank. A dungeon, maybe. An island in a river of lava, perhaps. I made a note to avoid caves for quite some time when we got out of this.

If we got out of this.

Reena's lantern burned bright, hanging from a hook dug into the earthen walls. Ma and Da were still unconscious, lying on the cave floor near a collection of stalagmites. Turning, I found that Maloch was awake, leaning with his back to the wall and struggling hopelessly with the manacle and chain around his ankle. I looked down and found a similar chain around my leg, the other end fused to a stalagmite. We were all wearing them. All except—

"Where are Reena and Holm?" I asked, scanning the area.

Maloch tugged at the manacle. "No idea. They were gone when I woke up." He picked up a rock and began bashing the chain. When he missed and hit his shin, he howled.

This woke Da. He propped himself up on one elbow, squeezing his eyes shut in pain. He shook his head. "Funny, I don't remember indulging in ashwine."

"Better," I said. "It's yerrani."

Da wiped his nose. "Oh, lovely. That explains the pins and needles in my legs." He looked at Ma. "Should we let her sleep it off?"

"No way anyone could sleep with you three nearby," Ma grumbled, stirring. Da helped her sit up.

I looked around. "Doesn't look like the Dagger. Unless it's another hardglamour."

Da shrugged. "If they used yerrani, we've been unconscious at least a couple of days. They've had time to move us. No telling where we are."

"Who were they?" Maloch asked.

As if in answer, three cloaked figures in hoods stepped into the cave from a nearby tunnel. One held a torch, while the other two laid pitchers filled with water at our feet.

"Drink," they said as one. Parched, we weren't about to argue. Da handed the pitcher to Maloch, who drank greedily. Just as Maloch passed the pitcher to me, one of our captors unlocked the manacle on my leg and pulled me to my feet with a single, strong yank. He shoved me in the direction of the tunnel. With weak legs, I stumbled from the cave. The hooded figures followed, ignoring Ma's and Da's protests.

Yes, I was definitely giving up caves for a very, very long time.

The hooded figures led me into an egg-shaped cavern where stalactites hung like massive teeth. I looked around, and a wave of recognition nearly knocked me off my feet.

Half a dozen tents huddled in the center of the chamber. A circle of torches marked the boundaries of the site. It reminded me of the Sarosan camp, only much, much smaller. As if to confirm my suspicions, the hooded figures threw off their cloaks to reveal three very tall, lean men. Their sleeveless shirts, torn breeches, and long hair told me they were, in fact, Sarosans.

"Jaxter!"

Reena emerged from one of the tents and ran to me, smiling.

"Are you okay?" I asked. "Where's Holm?"

"He's fine," she assured me. "We're all fine. Everything's great. You'll see."

She gave me a quick hug, then turned and disappeared back into the tent. My escorts took me to the tent at the very center of the camp. They pulled back the flap and pushed me inside.

The interior was nearly bare. A small table. A chair. And in that chair sat Kolo.

The old man smiled widely, while I could only return what I imagined to be a look of total shock. He stood slowly, grimacing in pain as he did. His hand emerged from his long, billowing sleeve as he reached to shake. I took his hand, dumbfounded.

"We've been worried about you," he said in his gravelly voice.

"*You've* been worried about *me*?" I asked incredulously. "Kolo, we thought you'd been taken by the bloodreavers! We thought you were rotting away in Umbramore Tower. What are you doing here?"

Kolo went to the table and poured us both cups of singe-tea. I drank gratefully, and he filled my cup twice more before I felt sated. When I slowed down, he spoke.

"It was sheer luck that a handful of us managed to escape when the bloodreavers attacked," he said, rubbing his finger along the rim of his teacup thoughtfully. "Eight of them struck without any warning. They would grab several people in their arms and then vanish in a puff of smoke, only to return empty-handed moments later. I can only imagine that the bloodreavers magically transported anyone they caught to Umbramore.

"Only nine of us managed to evade the bloodreavers." Kolo's face grew dark and his voice dropped. "*Nine* of us, Jaxter. The Sarosans once numbered over two hundred. When the High Laird first ordered our arrest, we lost over half that as our people were taken into custody. Now . . . we're only nine."

"I'm sorry," I said, looking into his pained eyes. He fought so hard to keep his people free. I couldn't imagine what he was going through.

He cleared his throat. "It doesn't matter. Nine is all we need. Very soon, all the Sarosans will be free again." He turned and picked up Tree Bag. "I want to thank you for bringing me my book. I knew I'd found a kindred spirit in you."

Kolo motioned for me to follow. Together, we walked out into the camp. He took a torch from the perimeter and whispered in the ear of the camp guard. Then he led me down a tunnel on the far side of the chamber.

"My parents," I said as we stepped into the darkness. "And Maloch. You can't just leave them there—"

He raised a hand. "They're being brought back to camp as we speak. You have my word they're safe. I apologize. I wanted to have a quick chat with you first. I admit, I'm curious. How is it that you and Maloch weren't in the camp when the bloodreavers attacked?"

"We, uh, were trying to escape. Reena and Holm saw us leave and came after us."

Kolo raised his eyebrows thoughtfully. "Then it may be a small blessing that you got out. It spared Reena and Holm what came next. Although I'm sad you decided our hospitality was no longer to your liking."

"My nanni always said that guests should never overstay their welcome . . . especially when the host is planning to chop their finger off and send it to the Dowager."

"Ah," he said, not even a little bit guiltily. "Yes. Warras told me of his plan. Well, I'm sure we can agree that it's a good thing it never came to that."

That wasn't what I wanted to hear. *I never would have let him do that, Jaxter* would have been better. What he said made it sound like he agreed with the Aviard's plan.

"Like I said, Jaxter, I see you as a kindred spirit. Someone who appreciates knowledge, reveres the natural world . . ."

Well, he had me there.

". . . and hates magic and all those who practice it."

And that's where he lost me.

I didn't hate mages. Or magic. I didn't particularly love them, but I also didn't share the Sarosans' hatred. But based on his tone, I didn't think contradicting him was wise.

"I was incredibly lucky to find these caves," he said. "Of all the Sarosan safe houses, this is, in many ways, our best. I couldn't ask for a better location."

"Why? Where are we?"

He nodded upward. "These tunnels run directly below the Palatinate Palace. Right now, not so far above us, every mage in the Provinces is plotting and planning."

The tunnel we took split into a fork. To the left, I could hear the roar of rushing water. We took the path to the right.

"So," I said slowly, "why is this the perfect place for you? I would think you'd want to be as far away from mages as possible." The Palatinate had, at the High Laird's command, unleashed the bloodreavers. In fact, being here seemed completely naff-nut. Wouldn't the bloodreavers find it easier to track the remaining Sarosans if they were hiding directly below the Palatinate Palace?

"The Palatinate aren't the only ones who can plan," Kolo said angrily. "We have our own plans, and they're about to come to fruition. Now that we have the Covenant, we can finally make our move."

My jaw dropped. The Sarosans had the Covenant? How was that even possible? And then it occurred to me that I was asking the wrong questions.

"Kolo, why were your people at the Dagger? And how could they get past—"

I stopped as a familiar scent hit my nose. I blanched at the thick, musty odor. A moment later, we stepped from the tunnel into a massive cavern. Bigger than any I'd ever seen before. So big, I couldn't see the far side in our meager torch-light. The light was just enough to show me what filled the room.

The entire floor was covered with tinderjack plants. At least five times as many as I'd found back at the Sarosans' old camp. I sealed my mouth shut, afraid to so much as breathe in the presence of so many explosive plants.

Kolo beamed proudly, staring out over the field of tin-derjack. "We've dedicated our lives to convincing people that magic is evil. That those who practice it seek only to suppress the rest of us. The people of the Five Provinces wouldn't listen. We have to protect them from their own shortsight-edness, Jaxter. Finally, we alone have the power to put an end to this.

"In their paranoia, the Palatinate recalled every mage in the land, afraid that the 'Sarosan menace' might try to exact revenge if the mages were unprotected. They're all living up there in the palace, every single one of them. They've made it too easy."

Kolo looked down at me, his eyes disappearing into shadow. "You see, I'm going to blow up the Palatinate."

★

When we returned to Kolo's tent, I found Ma, Da, and Maloch there, as Kolo had promised. Granted, they were all tied to chairs and Maloch was gagged with what looked like a dirty stocking, but otherwise they were fine.

Reena and Holm stood near Warras, who held a sword. As we entered, Reena ran to Kolo.

"Kolo," she said, "these are good people." She pointed to Maloch. "He's irritating but . . . basically good. Do we need to tie them up?"

Kolo gave her black hair a pat. "There is a reason for everything, Reena. We're so glad to have you back in the fold. Why don't you and your brother leave us now? We have things to discuss."

Holm stepped forward. "But—"

Before he or his sister could utter another word, Warras guided them from the tent. It was just the five of us.

"Reena has a point," I said. "Do they need to be tied up?"

"Really, we're no threat," Ma said. She and Da leaned their heads in together and flashed their cheesiest smiles.

"We'll see," Kolo said.

"He wants to blow up the Palatinate," I said plainly. Ma's and Da's eyes widened. Kolo's lips curled disapprovingly. Then he shook his head, deciding there was nothing he could do now that it was out in the open.

After a bit of gagging, a red-faced Maloch managed to eject the filthy stocking from his mouth. He spat and coughed. "If you're angry at the Palatinate, you've got no reason to keep us as prisoners. We have nothing to do with them."

"Perhaps not," Kolo said, "but you have, quite by accident, helped me overcome a rather large hole in my plan."

Kolo went to his table and poured himself a cup of singetea. He took a small jar and began adding iceclovers in great heaping spoonfuls. He stirred, each turn of his wrist causing a grimace of pain. He lifted the cup to his lips, took a large swallow, then smiled at me in contentment.

The iceclovers.

I had to steady myself to keep from falling over. Of course. The answer *had* been staring me in the face the whole time.

I was about to speak when a small movement out of the corner of my eye distracted me. The far edge of the tent behind Kolo had risen slightly, and two dark-skinned ears pressed in, listening. Ah, Reena and Holm. Taking my own sneaky lead.

"I don't know what you've heard about the Grimjinx clan," Da said gently, "although I imagine you've heard quite a bit. Thieves? I'll gladly take that. Cutpurses? Well, I'll frown but I'll accept it. Liars? And proud of it. But I think you'll find that no one can ever call us murderers."

Ma agreed. "Right. I don't think we'll be able to help you

blow up the Palatinate. So, if you could just untie us—"

"Forgive me," Kolo said, taking another sip of tea. "I haven't been clear. I don't need *your* help. I need Jaxter's."

Everyone looked to me, incredulous.

"Er, like Da said, the Grimjinxes aren't killers," I said. "Can't help you, I'm afraid."

Kolo shook his head. "You won't be killing anyone. I need you to sneak into the Palatinate and retrieve the Sourcefire."

Everyone knew of the Sourcefire. Legend had it that the Sourcefire was the magical fire spewed by the volcanoes that had formed the Five Provinces millennia ago. The green-blue flame torches that would burn until extinguished were made from it. Rumor was there was very little of the original Sourcefire left. What remained burned forever in the heart of the Palatinate Palace.

Kolo pointed upward. "We can get you into the palace. You just have to find the Sourcefire and bring it to me."

Ma and Da, who usually faced danger with a sense of playful abandon, were growing more concerned.

Da started struggling with his bonds. "You're not sending my son into that. Send me. I'm a master burglar. I can be in and out in no time. Just tell me where to find the Sourcefire—"

"You're a master thief, Mr. Grimjinx," Kolo said calmly. "Given time and the right resources, I've no doubt you could return with the Sourcefire and leave the Palatinate none the wiser. But time is short." He took a pocket watch from the table and wound it. "Right now, the Palace is filled with young apprentices. Jaxter's age gives him natural camouflage."

Kolo handed me the pocket watch. If the time was correct, it was midafternoon. "You have until sunset to bring me the Sourcefire."

"That's just a few hours!" I protested.

Kolo ignored the interruption. "At the end of the day, I'm igniting the tinderjack. I assure you there's more than enough in that cave to destroy the palace and all those in it five times over. If you return with the Sourcefire, you'll all go free. If you don't return, your parents and Maloch will be in the room with the tinderjack."

My jaw clenched as I tried to contain my anger. I couldn't believe I had been ready to give up my apprenticeship with the Dowager to study with Kolo. Sure, he was brilliant. But he was also completely insane.

"If you try to warn the Palatinate," Kolo said, raising a cautionary finger, "I'll ignite the tinderjack right away with your family and friend in the room. I have people watching the exits of the palace to make sure there are no evacuations. Understood?"

I met his eyes with my own steely glare. "And when I bring you the Sourcefire and you've used it to destroy the Covenant, then what?"

Kolo's eye twitched. He hadn't been expecting that.

Ma leaned in. "Destroy the Covenant? What are you talking about?"

"The Covenant is magical and can only be destroyed by magic, right?" I asked. Ma nodded. "That's why he needs the Sourcefire. For all the ways Kolo has found to thwart magic with natural means, not even the most magic-resistant plant is enough to negate the power of the Covenant. The Sourcefire's the only thing powerful enough."

"But why?" Maloch said, teetering in his chair as he yanked at the ropes that held his hands.

"Haven't you guessed, Maloch?" I asked, cocking an eyebrow at the Sarosan leader. "Kolo is the traitor."

23

The Traitor's Story

"Believe deeds, not words, but use words to forge
deeds."

—*Ancient par-Goblin proverb*

Kolo's back went rigid. The others stared at me,
dumbfounded.

I rolled my eyes. "I'm just mad at myself for not figuring it out sooner. My first clue was the iceclovers. He
made a tincture that he used to stop the pain in his arms.
Just now, he put them in his tea. In his new book, he talks
about how iceclovers can soothe the symptoms of Mardem's
Blight . . . which he got from the Covenant by betraying the
Shadowhands."

I walked over to Kolo and yanked on his sleeve. He hissed in pain. There, up and down the arms that he hid from view at all times, were a series of bloody lesions from Mardem's Blight.

"He's a . . . *Shadowhand*?" Maloch could barely spit out the word.

"I should have realized it sooner. He speaks par-Goblin," I said. "My guess is he's actually a former Shadowhand, like Ma. That's how he was able to lead his people through the Dagger. He went there knowing any Shadowhands who hadn't fallen victim to the tingroat trap would head to the Dagger to find out who the traitor was. He got there first and switched the Covenant with a fake that had a shimmerhex."

"But he's not a mage," Maloch said. "How did he put a shimmerhex on the fake Covenant that Dylis grabbed?"

I took a guess. "A shimmerhex is a curse. It's contagious. All he had to do was use one of the cursed tingroats and touch it to the fake Covenant."

Kolo turned around, a curious smile stretched across his wrinkled face. He reached into his robes and produced the real Covenant. The gray parchment had a faint blue aura around it. He pulled it open, revealing a long list of names. The twelve names at the very bottom were clear and untouched; Yab Oxter was one of them. All the names above it were crossed off. When I found Ma's name, I realized that the crossed-off names must all be former Shadowhands, either dead or retired. Halfway up the list, a fiery orange glow burned around the name Kolohendriseenax.

"It's been a very long time since I was a Shadowhand," Kolo said, rerolling the scroll. "One of the youngest ever inducted. About five years older than you are now, Jaxter. I was a master burglar. But like most thieves, I couldn't beat magical traps. Then, one day, I was running from some Palatinate Sentinels, and I hid under a phillanis bush. They used their magic to sweep the forest looking for me . . . but phillanis is magic-resistant and they couldn't find me. That began my fascination with magic-resistant plants.

"I started studying them, trying to figure out how to use them in my burglaries. Some of my fellow Shadowhands said I was becoming obsessed with my studies. I'll admit, I became sloppy in my thieving, even tripping magical traps on purpose during a heist in an effort to try out my countermeasures. Eventually, the other Shadowhands gave me an ultimatum: stop my experiments or be drummed out of the group."

"They forced you out?" I asked.

"Hardly. Anyone who chooses to leave the Shadowhands may. They're still bound by the Covenant and can never betray the group. But anyone *forced* to leave is a danger. It's only ever happened twice in Shadowhand history. Those who were kicked out were knocked unconscious, only to wake up days later on a ship leaving the Provinces. So I faked my death before they could vote me out. I hid by going on a journey. The one you read about in the *Formulary*."

Kolo sat in his chair. "I learned everything I could about beating magic the natural way. I joined the Sarosans and adopted their ways. By the time they made me their leader, I'd grown to hate magic as much as they did. In all that time, I never forgot what the Shadowhands had done to me.

"Then several months ago, through sheer dumb luck, I was presented with a chance to get revenge on the Shadowhands. It was too good to pass up. I disguised myself, hired the Shadowhands to pillage the royal vaults, and . . . well, you know the rest."

"But in the process," Da said quietly, "you've endangered your own people. They've been hunted, harassed. Most of them are in misery, wasting away in Umbramore Tower."

Kolo nodded. "And I will atone for that. It was a calculated risk I had to take. Once the Palatinate is gone, I'll be
able to free them, and they'll see that their incarceration was
a small price to pay for the utter annihilation of magic in our
world. You'll see. They'll understand."

My mouth went dry. Kolo had been willing to sacri-
fice the people who'd made him their leader just to get his
revenge. The man was *clearly* not mentor material.

"So you want to destroy the Covenant to get rid of
the evidence that shows you betrayed the Shadowhands?"
Maloch asked.

"That's part of it, I'm sure," I said to Maloch. I pointed
to Kolo's arms. "The lesions are just the first symptom of
Mardem's Blight. It's incurable, and it'll eventually kill him.
But it's a disease with a magical origin, and—"

"—and if I can destroy the magic responsible for the
disease," Kolo finished, holding up the Covenant, "I'll be
cured."

The Covenant was old and powerful magic. Normally,
he'd need a high-ranking mage to destroy it. But since he
couldn't exactly ask the Palatinate to help . . . "The Sourcefire
is one of the few things powerful enough to destroy the

Covenant. Once that happens, the Mardem's Blight goes away," I said.

Maloch fired off a single, short laugh. "In case you forgot, Jaxter nearly got us all killed with the vessapedes. He's a klutz. You should send me."

I looked at Maloch. What did he have in mind? True, his thieving skills may have been ever-so-slightly better than my own, but I couldn't imagine him offering to take my place just to save me.

Kolo was about to object when Maloch continued. "Send both of us. Increases the chances of finding it. We can split up and get to it faster."

Well, so much for wanting to save me.

Kolo considered. Then he walked behind Maloch's chair and untied the ropes.

"I can't fault your logic," Kolo said. "But Maloch, just in case you had any ideas about running for help while Jaxter finds the Sourcefire, let me tell you something: I know where your father is. Even if the threat of me killing the Grimjinxes means nothing to you, keep in mind that I'm the only one who can tell you how to find him."

Maloch's pursed lips suggested he was holding back a

retort. Instead, he bowed his head in compliance. Kolo clapped his hands and Warras entered. "Take Jaxter and Maloch to the Palatinate," Kolo told the Aviard. Then he turned and gave us his final instructions. "Sunset, boys. You have until then to return with the Sourcefire. Otherwise—"

"We get it," I said tersely, walking from the tent before Warras could push us out.

We were about to infiltrate the most heavily guarded stronghold in the land, next to the High Laird's palace. We didn't need to be reminded what was at stake.

We needed a miracle.

24

The Palatinate Palace

"The bad thief acts. The wise thief listens . . . and
then blames the bad thief."

—*The Lymmaris Creed*

Warras escorted us to a small alcove near the camp.
A rickety ladder disappeared into the rocky ceiling,
ending at a smooth square stone.

"Push up on the stone," the Aviard instructed, his wings
fluttering, "and you'll be inside the palace."

"Since you were so eager to come . . . ," I said to Maloch,
stepping aside so he could ascend first. Maloch pushed Warras
aside and climbed. Gripping the ladder with one hand, he
used the other to shove the stone. It made a harsh grinding

noise as it slid out of the way. Warm, golden light streamed down into the cave, the scent of bleach not far behind. Maloch continued the rest of the way up, and I followed.

The secret entrance brought us into a small room filled with great wooden tubs containing soapy water. Mounds of robes sat in baskets against the far wall. Large hooks, glowing gold with magic, hovered near the ceiling. Every so often, a hook would dip down, pick up a robe, and dunk it into one of the tubs. Wooden paddles moved on their own, churning the water in the tubs. A moment later, the hook would retrieve the newly washed robe and deposit it on a rope strung across the room, leaving it to dry.

"The laundry room?" Maloch asked.

"What were you expecting?" I said. "The chambers of the Lordcourt?"

I walked down to the laundry basket and chose two gray robes. "Bangers!" I said, slipping one over my head. "This should make disguising ourselves as apprentices easier."

Maloch took the other robe from me and put it on. He sniffed and grimaced. "It smells."

I took a whiff. "Yeah, but it still smells better than you normally do."

Maloch raised a fist, but I left the room before he could swing. Together, we moved cautiously down a corridor made of smooth gray mordenstone. The hall ended in a juncture that looked like a wheel spoke. Seven other halls shot out around us, none offering any clue as to where to go next.

"This place is huge," I said. "How are we going to find the Sourcefire?" I pulled out the watch Kolo had given me. We didn't have much time.

We chose a corridor at random and walked until we came to a door on the left. "We have to start somewhere," Maloch said, yanking on the door handle.

A blast of heat met us as we entered the room beyond. Columns of fire rose from great circular pits that covered the floor. The sound of metal pounding metal echoed throughout the room. Sparkling mounds of tiny rocks lined the walls, nearly reaching the ceiling. We quickly took cover behind one of the rock piles. I reached out, grabbed a sparkly handful, and studied it.

"It's gold ore," I said, tossing the raw stones aside. "This is some kind of forge."

In the center of the room, four mages—the spellspheres in their palms pulsing with magical energy—were manipulating the operations. With a gesture, the first mage would lift a massive chunk of the gold ore up into the air and deposit it lightly into one of the fiery pits. As a smooth stream of glowing, molten gold oozed from the pit down a shaft, the second mage would direct pools of liquid ore into circular molds as wide and deep as a hand. The third mage, manipulating an arsenal of giant, floating hammers, would pound the molten metal, sending sparks flying into the air. As the golden disks took shape, the fourth mage would magically marry the disks with gold chains and send the finished products flying across the room to hang from pegs in the walls.

"Maloch?" I asked. "Every mage in the land is hiding here because they think the Sarosans are trying to kill them. Why is this lot making jewelry?"

Maloch discovered a rack of finished medallions nearby and snagged one. "There's writing on them. Magical symbols. Hey, weren't the bloodreavers wearing those?"

He was right. I recalled the bloodreavers wearing identical medallions around their necks. "Hey, you know what those look like? Those are—"

"What are you doing here?"

The voice from behind made us both jump. We turned to find a tall mage with spiky white hair, wearing azure and black robes, towering over us. His left eye had been replaced with a multifaceted ruby that seemed to wink at us a hundred times whenever it caught the light.

"We're . . . lost?" I said. My hand slid to the pouches under my robes. I grabbed a handful of smoke pellets, preparing for a quick exit.

"Your work here is done," the one-eyed mage said angrily. "Didn't you hear the bell? Why do you think the other apprentices left?"

Maloch and I looked around innocently.

"Oh!" I finally said, smacking myself on the forehead. "That was the bell telling us to *leave*. Sorry, we thought it was the bell telling us to . . . cower behind a pile of ore."

While the ruby stared impassively, the mage's remaining eye regarded us like we were complete idiots. Which was actually what I was going for. He stepped aside and pointed to the door we'd just come in.

"Report to the training room!" he said. "Return here at the next bell to continue work."

"Next bell. Right." Maloch gave a short bow, and I

followed suit. We scampered past the mage, back out into the hall. The mage followed us, watching carefully. When I took a cautious step to the right, he raised an eyebrow into a point so sharp I was afraid he'd scratch his forehead. I took a step to the left and the eyebrow lowered.

"Come along, Tevrok," I said, tugging at Maloch's arm and leading him down the left passageway. "We'll be late for training. In the training room. Where we train."

When we rounded the corner, out of the one-eyed mage's sight, Maloch whirled around and sank his fist into my stomach. I doubled over, gasping for air.

"What . . . was that . . . for?" I asked.

"You called me Tevrok," he said with a sneer.

"Right," I said. "I thought I was doing you a favor, giving you a false name. You wanted me to call you Maloch?"

He pushed me up against the wall. "Tevrok is par-Goblin for sanguibeast excrement."

Oh, right. I kept forgetting he spoke par-Goblin.

I coughed. "Er, sorry. Force of habit."

He grabbed me by the shoulder and pulled me down the corridor.

★

In the end, I used my superior powers of deduction to locate the training hall. Basically, we followed the sounds of explosions and screams.

The trail of thunderous mayhem led us to a massive room, several stories high. Circular wooden platforms hovered at different levels over the stone floor. On each dais stood a trio of gray-robed apprentices, each brandishing a glowing spellsphere. They seemed to be taking turns casting spells at one another, with great streaks of energy flying across the room. Some succeeded, others failed. It was the failures that typically led to the explosions and screams that had guided us here.

As we stood gawping, a pair of strong hands gripped us by the nape of our necks and yanked us back. A Satyran woman in mage robes, who looked like a younger and meaner version of Dylis, regarded us coolly.

"Where is your third partner?" she asked.

"Well," I said, "you see, it's like this. We were late. We're not usually late, but it's been quite a day. You wouldn't even *believe* me if I tried to tell you—"

The mage dragged us both across the room to where an apprentice sat on a bench, cowled head facing down.

"I found you some partners," the mage said with a roar.

When the apprentice looked up, I found myself staring into the face of Callie Strom.

Her eyes lit up with a mixture of happiness and confusion. Before she could say a word, I leaped forward and started shaking her hand.

"Hi there! My name is Tyrius," I said, eyes wide in a "please play along" sort of way, "and this is"—oh, zoc, I couldn't think of anything better—"Tevrok."

"I'm going to kill you," Maloch said, low enough so only I could hear.

"Thank you, Madam Zaia," Callie said to the dour mage.

"Begin your drills," Madam Zaia said. She waited until the three of us moved.

"Over here," Callie said confidently, leading us to a wooden platform nearby. She pulled a spellsphere from her robes, cleared her throat, and said, *Boshoren!*"

Nothing happened.

"Boshoren!" Callie insisted again.

The Satyran mage looked ready to eat us all alive. She

marched over, and Callie stood at attention.

"Sorry," Callie said quietly, "I only just got my spell-sphere. I'm still learning—"

"Again!" the mage said. "And concentrate."

Callie gulped. She closed her eyes and took a deep breath through her nose. Then she said forcefully, *"Boshoren!"*

This time, the spellsphere flickered to life. A cascade of purple and orange sparks spilled out of the sphere and danced along the surface of the wooden platform. A moment later, the platform rose up into the air.

Callie kept her eyes closed, and the platform rose until we were higher than any of the other groups, almost to the ceiling. As the platform came to a halt, Callie opened her eyes and nearly killed me with a hug.

"What are you doing here?" she asked. She looked over to Maloch and frowned. "And why is *he* with you?"

"Hey, you're no prize either, Strom," Maloch said, folding his arms.

I had completely forgotten that Callie was here. When I imagined Kolo going through with his plans to destroy the palace, I hadn't even realized that Callie would be among those . . .

I shrugged off the thought. "Callie, what's going on here?"

I looked over the edge. Below us, the other trios of apprentices continued their mini war games, dodging one another's spells and improvising defensive maneuvers.

"Pretty intense, huh?" Callie asked, rolling her spellsphere between her fingers.

"I thought apprentices weren't allowed to have spellspheres until they were sixteen," I said, eyeing the dark gray marble.

Callie shrugged. "That used to be the rule. But it got thrown out the window when we were evacuated. Not only do we all have spellspheres, but we spend half our days learning the magical language. It's supposed to take years to master, but they expect us to learn it *now*. Let me tell you: it's not easy."

"Yeah," Maloch said with a laugh, "that much is obvious."

Callie grabbed a fistful of his robe. "You want to give it a try? It's exhausting. Half of our training is to build up stamina. Every time you use magic, it drains you. Use too much and it can knock you out. So give it a try, Maloch. I'd really love to see that."

Maloch looked away, and Callie turned back to me. "It's crazy here, Jaxter. When it was just me and Talian, we moved at a slow pace, learning all about the history of magic. But now we never stop learning. We spend mornings learning how to speak magic, afternoons training in here, and evenings working our assigned jobs—in the forge, in the gardens. . . ."

She sat cross-legged on the platform. "It's like they can't teach us fast enough. People keep getting hurt. Everyone's trying to please their teachers, and when they try too hard, they get sloppy. The Palatinate is convinced the Sarosans are out to get them. But most of them are locked up in Umbramore Tower. I can't imagine the few left are any threat."

Maloch cleared his throat. Callie's face fell. "What?"

I pulled out the pocket watch and eyed the fast-moving second hand. "You might want to rethink that."

25

An Impossible Menagerie

"When you sell the impossible, you are a master thief."

—*Kaelis Grimjinx, architect of the Dagger*

By the time Maloch and I had finished recounting everything that had happened to us since Vengekeep, I thought Callie was going to fall off the floating platform. Her eyes got big when we described being kidnapped by the Sarosans. Her jaw dropped when we told her about being hunted by the bloodreavers. And her hands shook when we talked about dodging traps in the Dagger. I didn't think she'd have any reactions left by the time we got to Kolo's plot to blow up the Palatinate.

I was wrong.

"We have to warn everyone!" she said, leaping to her feet and pulling out her spellsphere. She barked a command, and nothing happened. "Come on, you stupid thing. Go down! Down!"

"Whoa!" Maloch said, holding his hands up. "You can't tell anyone."

Callie pointed over the side of the platform. "There are two hundred mages in this building and almost as many apprentices. Most of them are our age. And they're my friends. Of course I have to warn them!"

This was going to be hard.

"Callie . . . ," I said gently, and got the same deadly look she'd just given Maloch.

"Talian's here, Jaxter," she said, seething. "Remember him? He's your friend."

"I know," I said to her. "Really, I know. But Kolo's got spies watching for an evacuation or attack. He'll ignite the tinderjack if he suspects the Palatinate has been alerted."

We locked eyes for what felt like an eternity. She didn't seem entirely convinced. "We have to do *something*," she insisted.

I kept my tone even. "I don't know what we can do. It's not like we can have Kolo and his men arrested and taken—"

Or could we . . . ?

"The Dowager!" I said. I drew my hand back into my robe, rummaged around in my pouches, and pulled out the star-shaped gem from the Dowager's pendant. "I can talk to her with this. All we have to do is have her send the Provincial Guard to arrest everyone in the Sarosan camp, and it's all over."

"Would she do that?" Maloch asked.

"If it means saving hundreds of lives, she will," I said. "Here goes."

I tapped the gem three times as instructed. Nothing happened. I waited a moment, then tried again. Still nothing.

Callie shook her head. "It won't work in here. While we're on lockdown, the Palatinate is fortified so that no magic gets in or out. You'll need to go outside to use it." She tilted her head as she considered. "Although it might work if you went to the North Tower. The top is open air."

It was as good a plan as any. "There's no telling how long it will take the Dowager's guards to arrive."

"Then we get the Sourcefire and give it to Kolo," Maloch

said. "We can stall him until the troops come."

"You contact the Dowager," Callie said, taking charge the way she often did. "Me and the Armpit here will find the Sourcefire."

"'Armpit?'" Maloch asked.

Callie grinned. "Didn't you know that's what everyone in Vengekeep calls you behind your back?"

I nodded. "A couple more baths a year wouldn't kill you, Maloch."

Maloch's jaw tightened. I took that to mean I would pay for that remark later. I'd lost count of how much I had to pay for later.

"The Sourcefire is heavily guarded with magical defenses," Callie said. "But I think I've learned enough magic to get us past them."

"You *think*?" Maloch asked.

Callie ignored him and held out her spellsphere again, trying to coax the platform to go down. Instead, we just continued to float. I tried not to sneak any nervous peeks at the pocket watch. Callie was already under enough stress. But at this rate, we could be stuck up here right until the moment when Kolo ignited the tinderjack.

A few more tries and suddenly the platform lurched downward. Thrown to the surface of the dais, we dug our fingers in and cried out.

Our free fall dropped us past the other training platforms. The other apprentices gaped in stunned silence as we plummeted, the floor rising to pulverize us. As we were seconds from death, a green glow surrounded our platform. For a moment, I felt weightless. The dais gently slowed until we touched the floor with a tap. Madam Zaia stood there with her spellsphere, clearly unhappy.

"It's a simple spell," she said to Callie, whose face had gone so red she looked a bit like a bloodreaver. "If you can't even—"

A deep, sonorous bell rang out, echoing off the walls. It sounded loud enough to be heard throughout the entire Palatinate. As it faded away, a strong woman's voice took the bell's place.

"All apprentices will report back to their workstations," the voice said.

One by one, the other floating platforms descended. The apprentices stepped off and began filing out of the room. With the Satyran distracted, we quickly mixed in with the departing crowd and exited.

We followed the other apprentices until we got to a wheel-spoke juncture. There, people peeled off in groups, each heading down whichever corridor led to their workstation. We waited in the hub of the spoke until it was just the three of us.

"Won't you be missed at your 'workstation'?" Maloch asked. We were both thinking back to the ruby-eyed forge master. He seemed the sort to send bloodreavers out to retrieve any apprentice who was even a minute late reporting for duty.

Callie blew it off with a wave of her hand. "They were in such a hurry to get everyone safe in the Palatinate that they didn't take any time to . . . well, organize it. I've skipped plenty of work sessions and classes."

"Says the girl who's going to get us past the magical defenses of the Sourcefire," Maloch said.

Callie elbowed him and turned to me. "Okay, Jaxter, here's how you get to the North Tower—"

"Down that hall, take two lefts, up the stairs all the way to the top," I said.

Callie and Maloch pursed their lips as one. Maloch

tapped his foot impatiently. Finally, Callie said, "You know we're going to ask how you could possibly know that, so stop showing off and tell us."

I pretended to pout. "You used to like it when I did that, Cal." I pointed to the flickering torches on the wall. "There's a breeze wafting through the corridors. Faint scent of jewelpine trees. This palace lies just south of the largest jewelpine forest in the Provinces. Since we can smell the forest and we know the wind comes in from the north, *that* way must be north. When the defense classes let out, I could hear students head down that hall. From the angle their voices echoed back off the walls, I knew they—"

"Let's go," Maloch said, pulling Callie away. "By the time he finishes, Kolo will have blown us up a dozen times over."

Sometimes, I really think my deductive skills are woefully unappreciated.

★

When I arrived at the stairway to the North Tower, I found myself wishing I'd let Callie give me directions, instead of just deducing it all. She probably would have mentioned the 1,543 spiral steps that led to the very top.

Oh, yes. I counted.

The stone stairs wound in a tight spiral through the tower's core. By the time I reached the last step, my jelly-like legs could barely support me and my lungs ached from all the heavy breathing. The top of the tower was completely flat and open. A blast of freezing wind hit me as I moved to the center. I spotted the jewelpine forest to the north, and to the west, I watched the sun sink closer to the horizon. Time was running out. I could only hope the Dowager could get here fast enough. Fingers shaking, I took out the star-shaped gem and tapped it three times.

It started to glow dark orange. Red dots of light danced beneath the gem's surface, and a moment later, they shot up out of the gem and hovered above my palm. The pinpricks of light swam around and chased one another, going faster and faster until they suddenly stopped and formed a fuzzy picture of the Dowager's face.

"Jaxter?" The Dowager's voice, distorted and wobbly, sounded from the red dot image.

"It's me, Dowager," I said, staring into the image's eyes. Even this replica of her face had the same dreamy quality to it.

"There you are!" she exclaimed. "I've been worried about you. Listen, things are not going well here. My brother is being as stubborn as a ganchmule. Won't listen to a word of reason. I keep telling him and telling him—"

"Dowager," I interrupted gently, "I need your help."

I quickly explained the situation and stressed that the Provincial Guards she sent needed to be stealthy, because if Kolo knew they were coming, he'd kill Ma and Da and blow up the Palatinate.

"How do the guards find the caves?" she asked.

We'd been unconscious when Kolo's men brought us to the safe house. I had no idea how to get there from the outside.

I scanned the surrounding area, my eyes resting on a river to the east that ended with a waterfall. I remembered my walk with Kolo and the sound of rushing water . . .

"There's a waterfall to the east of the Palatinate Palace," I said. "The entrance to the cave is there. Please, Dowager, hurry."

The Dowager's head tilted to one side. "You and your friends should get out of there. It's much too dangerous."

"I can't," I said. "Not until I know Ma and Da are safe. Besides, we have a plan."

We didn't really. We hoped that once we had the Sourcefire, we could bargain with Kolo. Maybe stall. But stalling would only last so long.

"I'll be there soon!" the Dowager said. Her face vanished, and I slipped the gem back into one of my pouches. In the distance, the sun continued to vanish. My shoulders slumped. It might take me until sundown to go back down all those stairs again.

Turned out that the way down was much faster. I took five steps, tripped on my robe, and fell down the remaining stairs.

A fall like that would have killed most people. But then, most people hadn't spent a good portion of their lives falling from trees, off rooftops, and over their own two feet like I had. I knew just how to tumble to protect myself from major damage.

A dubious talent, yes, but one I was fiercely proud of.

It's too bad my talent gave out before I reached the bottom. Just as the final steps spun into view, I struck my head against the wall and was knocked out cold.

★

Somewhere in the distance, a warbling howl pierced the air.

I awoke bruised, nauseated, and seeing little white lights before my eyes. I stood groggily and tried out all my limbs. Everything worked. Ma and Da would be impressed to hear I hadn't broken any bones this time.

The green-blue torches in the hall had turned dark purple, painting the walls with thick shadows. Between the distant howling and the throbbing in my head, I found it hard to concentrate. What was going on? Why was it suddenly dark? What was that sound?

The whats and whys vanished as a new question occurred: how long had I been out? Obviously, it wasn't sundown, or I'd have been in bits and pieces. But I'd lost precious time. I searched my robes for Kolo's pocket watch, then noticed it smashed on the floor. For all I knew, it could be minutes to sundown.

Maybe that's what the howling was: an evacuation notice. But no. Kolo had promised to blow up the palace if he saw the Palatinate trying to leave. That meant the sound was . . .

A warn charm. Someone had triggered an alarm. And I had a pretty good idea who.

I had to leave.

The upside of Maloch and Callie triggering the warn charm meant it would be easier for me to find them. All I had to do was follow the horrible, horrible, earsplitting wailing to its source and try not to go crazy in the process.

Bangers.

I ran down the hall toward the warn charm. The closer I got, the more my skin crawled. Fear coursed through my body. It felt like stickworms burrowing in my brain, urging me to turn back. Oh, zoc. This wasn't an ordinary warn charm. This one was enchanted to cause intense fear meant to send thieves into a blind panic. Inevitably, that fear would drive the thief toward waiting captors.

And it appeared to be working. Distracted, I'd lost track of where I was going. Just ahead, a line of four mages was moving toward me. Beams of light from their spellspheres swept the corridor walls. Trying to stay calm—hard to do when magic is *forcing* you to panic—I disappeared behind the nearest door.

Like everywhere in the palace, the room was very dark,

save for the purple torches. But even still, I could tell this was the largest room I'd seen yet. Easily the size of several city blocks in Vengekeep, the room was so long I couldn't see the far end. And everywhere I looked, I saw cages. Hundreds and hundreds of cages filled with more exotic beasts than I could count.

My mind reeled back months ago to when Callie, Talian, and I discovered the rogue mage Xerrus in his hidden Onyx Fortress. Xerrus had been doing horrible, illegal experiments, using magic to combine different types of animals. But there was no evidence of that cruelty here. The creatures in these cages all seemed perfectly normal: healthy, well-fed, even docile. A marked difference from Xerrus's experiments, which were crammed into cages too small for them and abused terribly.

I watched as a pair of mages moved from cage to cage. The first mage examined the creatures and murmured instructions that the second mage hastily scribbled into a large book.

"This is naff-nut," the second mage said. "You hear the warn charm. We could be under attack. We're here, doing our job like always, when we should be out there defending the palace."

"Relax," the first mage said. "The Sentinels are investigating. Nalia told us we're not to leave this room. She wants a complete catalog of the menagerie by nightfall."

As my eyes adjusted to the lighting and I got a better look around, I realized I didn't recognize any of the creatures. No sanguibeasts. No garfluks. But while I didn't recognize them, they seemed familiar.

The hulking pair of black-furred, trihorned animals in the corner looked like nightmanx. The monstrous, spiky-skinned reptiles—two stories high—resembled torranthars. And the gelatinous, childlike creatures that swung on the bars of their cage were the spitting image of skeelapes. Every beast that I could see wore a small gold amulet around its neck.

Nightmanx, torranthars, and skeelapes.

Which was impossible, because none of these things existed.

They were legends. Stories.

Weren't they?

My curiosity got the better of me, and I tiptoed closer for a better look. Just then, I heard an unearthly howl that made my blood run cold.

Looking up, I saw a row of cages hanging from chains in the ceiling. Each was home to a bloodreaver. They still wore the golden amulets I'd seen on the one in the forest. The many-armed creatures batted against the bars lightly. My breath caught in my throat. One of them met my eyes and suddenly went wild, howling and thrashing at its cage. Soon, all were doing the same. The cages smashed into one another as they swung like pendulums.

The menagerie keepers looked up at the bloodreavers. "I hate those things," the mage with the book said.

His partner shook his head. "You worry too much. Remember, they're under our control."

He pointed to a medallion that hung around his neck. So I was right. The forge was making control medallions like the ones Xerrus had used to control the balanx in the Onyx Fortress. Had the Palatinate stolen the idea from him? And why?

"Why do we bother with the cages?" the mage with the book asked. "They can disappear and appear at will."

"They only teleport when they've caught the scent of their prey."

Pop! One of the bloodreaver cages filled with smoke as its occupant vanished. A second cloud appeared on the floor near the mages and the bloodreaver stepped out, fangs bared. Seven more *pops* echoed throughout the menagerie as more bloodreavers freed themselves from their cages and reappeared on the floor.

"They smell something," the mage with the book said. The pair scanned the room until they spotted me half in shadow near the door.

"Don't look at me," I said, doing my best to look offended. "I took a bath today. Okay, maybe it was a couple days ago."

As one, the bloodreavers gave a united howl and ran toward me.

26

Unexpected Rescue

"Providing another's alibi kindles a fire that burns
for life."

—Ancient par-Goblin proverb

I lifted my arm in the air and slammed a handful of smoke
pellets onto the stone floor. *Flash!* A thick white mist surrounded me.

I dove for the door, leaving the confused mages and
bloodreavers inside. In the dark corridor, the moaning alarm
ricocheted off the mordenstone walls so strongly that I could
feel it through my boots.

I held my hands over my ears and ran toward the warn
charm. I fought off the growing terror inside that urged me

to turn back. Aside from the fear, the noise upset my sense of balance, as it was designed to do. But I had to put as much space between the bloodreavers and me as possible, so I staggered on. Bounding into an intersection, I nearly ran into Maloch and Callie.

"I'm guessing you succeeded. They're playing the Grimjinx anthem!" I had to shout to be heard over the deafening alarm.

But Callie, face flushed, was in no mood to joke. "I thought I'd disarmed all the traps. I must have missed one."

"Two Sentinels appeared as soon as the alarm sounded," Maloch said, beaming. "And Callie set them on fire."

"I did not!" she said. "I was trying to do this spell that Talian taught me. It would have encased them in ice. But that's the problem with speaking magic. I said *cerata* instead of *ceraka* and, well—"

"Oh, relax," Maloch said. "They put themselves out. Eventually."

"Is that it?" I asked, pointing to Maloch.

His hands gripped a box about the size of a vessapede egg. The frame of the box was made of shining gold strips with raised magical sigils all along the edges. The walls of the box were thick, multifaceted crystal. Inside was the Sourcefire. At its core, a ball of dark blue flame churned and burned, surrounded by what looked like wisps of glowing green steam. Orbiting all of this were several tiny dots of red light that spun around the fire, leaving a comet-like trail.

"A mite smaller than I imagined," I said. "Let's go."

Maloch and I turned to run, but Callie stood her ground.

"Callie, you're an accomplice," I said. "You have to come too."

She shook her head. "I told you. If you don't stop Kolo, I can't let the people here die. Sundown is in one hour. You've got half an hour to stop him. If you don't show up at the palace gates to tell me you've succeeded, I'm going to warn the Palatinate and evacuate."

There was no arguing, and I couldn't blame her. She understood the risk of evacuating, but it was better than sitting around, waiting to get blown up.

"Let's move, Jaxter," Maloch said, charging down the hall. Callie threw an arm around my neck in a quick hug, and then I took off after Maloch.

"Do you know where we're going?" I asked.

Maloch nodded. "Callie and I passed the laundry room

on the way here. It's not far."

He led us down several long halls, through a spoke, and finally back to the corridor where we'd first entered.

"Down here!" he called.

But just as we were nearly back to the laundry room, the floor lurched. The stones ahead parted, as if shoved aside by invisible hands. From the crevasse sprang a new wall made of glowing red bricks that went all the way to the ceiling.

"I think," I said slowly, "they're onto us."

"Quick!" Maloch tugged at my arm, and we darted down another hall. It turned right. Then left. Then left again. Then right. It didn't make sense. When we'd first arrived, all the passageways in this area were straight and long. There hadn't been this many turns.

I thought of the wall that had just sprung up out of nowhere, blocking our access to the exit hole. They were altering the corridors. Guiding us to exactly where they wanted us to go . . .

"Maloch—," I said, trying to warn him. He took a sharp right, and I followed. The howling alarm stopped. A wall of red glowing bricks sprang up behind us, blocking the way back.

The room we were in looked like a garden. Topiaries and flower beds covered the grassy floors, all lit by a thaw-globe above. Festerelm trees, with their gnarled trunks that oozed sap, wove a latticework of twisting branches overhead. The scene looked so idyllic I expected to hear birds chirping. Instead, we heard a chorus of unearthly screeches from above.

Looking up, we spotted bloodreavers—eight of them—swinging by their arms between the festerelm branches, preparing to attack.

"Oh, yeah," I said. "Forgot to mention. I ran into some old friends."

Maloch's hand went for his ankle, where he kept his dagger. Then he remembered that Kolo had taken our weapons. Together, we dove under a topiary shaped like a mang, Maloch clutching the Sourcefire tightly to his chest.

The bloodreavers charged. The largest, who I took to be the leader, moved to the head of the pack and advanced on us. The arms that came up over his shoulders thrashed wildly at the air.

"Do something!" Maloch said, ripping apart my apprentice robes and exposing my pouches.

"Oh, yeah," I said. But I was doubtful I could concoct anything that might help us fast enough.

Shkk! Shkk! Shkk!

It was so soft I barely heard it. But the three rapid-fire shots hit their mark. The lead bloodreaver stopped advancing. Its massive pupils suddenly shrank to near nothing, just before its eyes rolled back in its head and it hit the ground, unconscious.

The other bloodreavers looked to one another, barking in some unknown tongue.

"Yeah!" I said, suddenly feeling quite brave. "Back off or there's more where that came from."

Maloch poked me. "What are you—?"

"Work with me, Maloch," I said.

I didn't know if the bloodreavers understood me. If they did, they weren't buying my bluff. The rest came at us, arms raised, fangs bared.

Shkk! Shkk! Shkk! Shkk! Shkk! Shkk!

The air came alive with the sound, and one by one the bloodreavers fell until just two remained standing. They looked around at their fallen brethren, faces contorted into what I could only guess were perplexed looks.

Just past the bloodreavers, I spotted a flower bed where Reena, on one knee, was hurriedly jamming more darts into her blowgun. Standing on a rock nearby, Holm lifted his chin and planted his fists on his hips.

"Do not fear and do not cuss. You'd be dead if not for us!"

The two bloodreavers howled and ran at their new quarry. In a flash, the Sarosans lifted their blowguns to their mouths and fired off enough darts to stop the creatures in their tracks.

Maloch and I crawled out from under the topiary.

"Are you all right?" Reena asked, running to us.

"Did Kolo send you to spy on us?" Maloch said with a sneer.

Reena's eyes flared for a moment, and then she looked genuinely hurt. "We came to help you. We overheard everything Kolo told you and . . . He doesn't speak for all the Sarosans. If our people were still around, there's no way they'd condone murder. Our parents personally would have stopped him."

Maloch rubbed the back of his neck. "Erm . . . sorry. It's . . . appreciated. Thank you for . . . you know, the poison darts. How did you find us?"

Reena shook her head. "We didn't. We were roaming the halls looking for you when we ran into the bloodreavers. They picked up our scent and chased us in here. It's just lucky you came in when you did. Gave us a chance to load our blowguns."

I agreed. "Yeah, thanks, guys. But we can't sit here. I'm pretty sure they can track the Sourcefire. I say we forget trying to find the laundry room and just get out any way we can. Any window, any door . . ."

Holm pointed frantically to the far side of the garden. Reena nodded. "When we were looking for you, we found the main gates. There's a gallery just through that door. The gates are beyond that."

We ran across the garden and into the next room. The hall was egg-shaped, long and round. Dark indigo fire from chandeliers high above offered barely enough light to show us the way. The purple glow gave the room the feel of a creepy museum. Paintings hung from the smooth marble walls, and a seemingly endless collection of glass statues on golden plinths stood between us and the far side of the room.

"If this art is valuable," I said, looking around, "there

could be traps in the floor to prevent theft. Move quickly—but carefully."

We tiptoed among the field of statues, the glass infused with the purple fire's glow. When we reached the midpoint of the room without triggering any traps, I guessed we were clear and urged everyone to move faster.

"Here's what we do when we get out," I said. "Reena, you and Holm go to Kolo and tell him that Maloch and I have the Sourcefire but won't bring it to him until he agrees to negotiate."

"Jaxter . . . ," Maloch said.

"Where will you be?" Reena asked.

"I dunno. In the woods somewhere. We can find a clearing and—"

"Jaxter!"

The anger that normally coated every word Maloch said had drained completely away. He sounded scared.

I turned back to see that we'd left him several paces behind, near the center of the room. He was gaping up, barely holding on to the Sourcefire.

Reena and I went back to him. I took the box, handed it to Reena, and snapped my fingers in front of his eyes. "Hey!

Angry mages! Stolen Sourcefire! Trying to escape! Any of this ringing a bell?"

Maloch remained quiet and slack-jawed. I followed his gaze up to a statue. It looked like a tall, balding man with huge muttonchops down his cheeks. He wore a cape that billowed and fine boots that went up over his knees. Unlike most statues, which normally looked pleasant or stoic, the face on this man looked clenched as if in pain. His arm was outstretched, his fingers curled inward to a claw. I squinted in the darkness and could just make out that his fingers were wrapped around a shiny tingroat.

Maloch breathed heavily. "It's my da."

27

The Labyrinth of Glass

"Forging a signature is smart. Forging a life is
brilliant."

—*Allia Grimjinx, master forger of Korrin Province*

Mr. Oxter wasn't alone. A semicircle of ten more statues, each gripping a tingroat, surrounded Maloch's
da. The Shadowhands. The only one missing was Dylis, who
remained trapped in the Covenant chamber of the Dagger.

"Why is he here?" Maloch said through clenched teeth.
"If Kolo hired the Shadowhands, why are they all *here*?"

"Maloch," I said softly, putting a hand on his shoulder, "we
can't help him. Not right now. We have to get out of here."

"I can't leave him!" His voice shook, and for just a second, he reminded me of when we were younger and friends.

It was Reena who finally got through. "We'll come back for him. Right now, we have to stop Kolo. If he blows up the palace, the Shadowhands go too."

Tears streamed down Maloch's flushed cheeks. He looked up at his father's frozen face and gave a single nod. Then he snatched the Sourcefire back from Reena, tucked it under his arm, and said, "Move."

We started back through the forest of statues, heading for the exit, when the sound of footfalls from the rear made us stop.

"Surrender!" a woman's voice rang out. "You can't escape."

I looked over my shoulder. Several mages, their spellspheres burning hot in their hands like miniature suns, filed into the room. They lined up against the wall, waiting for instructions. A woman in long flowing robes with an elaborate headdress stood in the center of the doorway, her spellsphere casting dark blue-gray shadows up into her stern face. Her right eye held a gold-rimmed monocle. I immediately recognized her. Her name was Nalia. I'd seen her after that business with the tapestry in Vengekeep. She was a member of the Lordcourt, the Palatinate's ruling council.

We could have slipped into the shadows to hide if Maloch hadn't been carrying a crystal box filled with magical fire that shot rays of multicolored light in every direction. Bit of a giveaway. As the mages fanned out, we ducked behind the plinths and waited.

"You'll never leave this room alive," Nalia said, an edge to her voice suggesting she very much meant that. "Surrender now. I won't ask a third time."

We looked to one another and cast furtive glimpses at the escape door. It was so close. Could we make it before the mages reached us? I nodded to Maloch, who nodded to Reena, who took hold of her brother's hand.

"Go!" I whispered. And as one, we ran for the exit.

The room exploded like fireworks on Grundilus Day. The mages lifted their spellspheres high in the air, and bolts of energy rained down, detonating all around. The first hit the floor in front of us, sending mordenstone shrapnel into the air. We scattered, diving for cover. I hid behind a statue of an Aviard, nobly holding a war hammer over its head. Fiery torrents of magic zeroed in on me, and I was thrown back as the statue and its plinth were reduced to dust.

Holm cried out as debris caught him in the forehead.

Hands over our heads, we zigzagged amid the statues and sculptures, trying to make it to the exit. I found myself with a straight path to the door, tucked my chin, and ran for all I was worth. I heard the sound of stone grinding on stone and looked up to find a statue and its plinth sliding across the floor to block my path. I took a hard left to go around, just as another statue moved to block me.

All the statues were sliding now, moving like game pieces on a board. Just as they had manipulated the palace halls earlier, the mages were creating a labyrinth, redirecting us back to the other side of the room where they all waited. I could see Nalia, whispering to her spellsphere. I tried to throw her off, faking one direction, then jumping in the other and sneaking around a statue already in motion. But it was like she knew exactly what I was going to do and blocked me before I could change directions. A new volley of magical lightning tore up the floor around me. I took a large stone to the forehead and stumbled down behind an empty plinth, its statue recently destroyed.

Breathing hard, I scanned the dimly lit room. The statues had stopped moving. I couldn't see Maloch or Reena, but Holm was crouched on all fours nearby. The room grew quiet as the assault stopped. I coughed on the smoke and dust that filled the air. Peering around my plinth, I could still see the silhouettes of the mages holding their spellspheres. But what were they waiting for?

Suddenly, beneath my fingertips, I could feel my plinth vibrate. It shook and shook until it finally shot straight up into the air, stopping just before it hit the ceiling. It hung there as if suspended by an invisible string. I jumped and joined Holm in his hiding spot.

The air filled with the sound of statues whooshing straight up as, one by one, the labyrinth of art was lifted to safety high above. Pretty soon, there'd be nothing to hide behind. I tapped Holm's shoulder and pointed in the direction of the exit.

He held up a fist in agreement. We watched as the statues continued to fly up off the ground. Finally, a group of three flew away and we could see the outline of the exit door. We could make it. Easily.

I took his hand and we sprinted toward the door. By now, the room was nearly bare, and as their shields flew away, Maloch and Reena joined us. I reached out to shove the door open. But then I blinked and in that instant, Nalia stood in front of us, staring through her monocle, arm and spellsphere outstretched.

She hissed a word, and four rings of blue light shot out of the spellsphere. The rings flew over our heads and down around our shoulders, pulling our arms tight to our sides. Slowly, all four of us began to rise, our feet kicking out to touch the floor that was now far below us. A wicked smile on her lips, Nalia stepped forward, and the magic rings that bound our arms pulled us backward toward the center of the room.

The other mages in the room formed a circle around us. We clumped together, our backs to one another. Nalia called out, *"Iossa!"* The room went pitch-black for a moment. Then the torches in the room burst to life with brilliant green-blue flames that banished the darkness.

I tried to reach my pouches, hoping to grab something— anything—to divert them. But the blue ring held me so tightly that my hands had begun to lose feeling. The ruby-eyed mage, still sweaty from his work at the forge, stepped forward with his spellsphere and barked a magical command. I winced, but nothing happened. He spoke again and still nothing.

"Cyric!" Nalia said. The forge master cowered under

her withering glare. "You can't use magic to summon the Sourcefire."

"Yeah, Cyric," I chided, having no idea why you couldn't use magic on the Sourcefire, "don't you know anything?" Ugh. Something in the Grimjinx blood made us flippant when faced with danger. It was going to get me killed someday.

Cyric walked over and snatched the box from Maloch's hands.

"What have you done to my father?" Maloch asked, glancing up at where his father now floated near the ceiling.

"Your father's a Shadowhand?" Nalia said, purring as she tilted her head. "He learned what happens to anyone who crosses the Palatinate. Just as you're about to learn. At least as a statue, he can be resurrected. I'm afraid that option won't be available to you."

I swallowed. "Uh, begging your pardon, Your Masterful Powerness, but—and I'm no law-advocate—I'm pretty sure that death is reserved only for treason and users of fateskein." I decided not to mention that technically—*technically*—I was one of the latter. *Technically.*

Nalia turned, her eyes burning into me. A thoughtful look

crossed her face. I guessed she recognized me but couldn't remember from where. "Yes, that is the High Laird's Law. But within these walls, the Palatinate owns a special brand of justice. Here, we can do as we please. . . ."

Nalia stared into her spellsphere, which burned so brightly I couldn't look directly at it. As she began speaking an incantation, I could feel heat rising from the sphere. I squeezed my eyes shut, bracing for the end.

"Stop!"

I didn't recognize the firm, commanding voice that filled the gallery. I dared to peek out with one eye, looking past Nalia to the exit door. Through the smoke, I saw armored men, bearing the standards of the Provincial Guard. They filed into the room carrying spears, swords, and crossbows leveled at the circle of mages. As they entered, the soldiers moved to flank a tall, lean figure in a very official-looking, fitted suit. The smoke cleared, revealing the Dowager.

The mages looked to one another and to Nalia, as if trying to decide whether they should fight. Finally, Nalia whispered a single word and the light in her spellsphere vanished, leaving it just a gray iron marble.

The Dowager strode regally across the room. I'd never

seen her in her full official state wear before. Around Redvalor, she only wore clothing appropriate to our experiments. In her formal garb, this occasionally absentminded, lighthearted woman looked downright formidable.

"Good evening, Nalia," the Dowager said, staring straight at the mage. She waited, lips closed tightly. After a moment of indecision, Nalia put one foot behind the other and bent at the knees in a curtsy. The Dowager continued, "By decree of the High Laird, these four children are under my protection. Release them to my custody at once."

Nalia's back was to me, so I could only guess at the look of shock on her face. I bet it was a good one. "The High Laird's Law allows the Palatinate complete sovereignty within the walls of this palace," Nalia said. "These four stole the Sourcefire. They are to be put to death."

The Dowager was not impressed. "That sovereignty, as you so rightly note, is granted by the High Laird. And it can be revoked by the High Laird. As it is, in this instance. There will be an inquiry, of course, into what has occurred here today. But I assure you that when you understand the scope of the situation, they will be exonerated due to . . .

extenuating circumstances." The Dowager shot me the briefest of looks.

Nalia stood her ground for two or three eternities, and the tension in the room mounted. For a moment, I actually thought she was going to order the mages to attack. But when she finally uttered a short, magical command, the blue rings binding the four of us disappeared and we fell to the floor.

The Dowager swept past Nalia and helped me up. "It's over," she whispered. "Kolo is in custody. Your parents are safe." Then she said a bit louder, "You four, through that door. The Grimjinxes are waiting for you." She turned and laid a cool smile on Nalia. "Nalia, I would speak with you. Now."

Reena and Holm hugged. Maloch stood still, staring up at the statue of his father above. I whispered in his ear, "We'll get this fixed. Okay? Let's go."

Maloch nodded. The circle of mages parted as the four of us, supporting one another, walked from the room.

28

Another Tribunal

"The High Laird's coffers are locked one key turn
at a time, same as everyone else's."

—*The Lymmaris Creed*

When the Dowager told Nalia that there would be an inquiry, I pictured something small and intimate, like what happened in Vengekeep after the whole mess with the tapestry.

Royal inquisitions, it turns out, are not small and intimate.

After the Dowager rescued us, I was whisked away—along with my parents, Maloch, Reena, and Holm—to Vesta, the seaside capital city of the Five Provinces. The next day, we were seated behind a long table in a cavernous room within the High Laird's palace.

Horns rang out. We all stood as a man in black robes—the Inquisitor General—entered, followed closely by the Dowager. They moved next to two fancy-looking chairs on a raised platform in front of us. Another fanfare sounded. We all bowed as the High Laird entered and sat on a throne between the Dowager and the Inquisitor General.

In all the time I'd lived with the Dowager, I'd never met the High Laird. Seeing him for the first time, I never would have guessed he was the Dowager's *younger* brother. His red-rimmed eyes watered constantly. His hair had gone white far too early. When he moved, he did so with great effort.

We were joined at our table by a pair of law-advocates who were defending us. Another pair of law-advocates, ones who wanted to see us imprisoned, stood near the platform. When the Inquisitor General banged two copper orbs together, we all sat and the inquiry started.

Our law-advocates were fierce, I'll give them that. They proved they could shout just as loud as those other law-advocates. I didn't understand much of what they were saying. There were long, long speeches with words so big they used entire alphabets. It was all very impressive. It was also more potent than any sleeping draught I could manufacture from my pouches.

I looked around. In a small gallery off to the left sat five chairs, where the High Laird's Chancellor and four of his closest advisers observed the proceedings. On the opposite wall sat the five members of the Palatinate Lordcourt. As if she sensed I was looking at her, Nalia snapped her head around and our eyes met. I flashed back to the first time we'd met in Vengekeep. Back then her gaze was cold. Today, it burned right through me.

The first few hours of law-advocates yelling at one another were all about our attempts to steal the Sourcefire. Each member of the Palatinate Lordcourt testified that we'd been caught trying to flee the palace with the magical fire. Of course, that was never really in question.

Our defense began with the Dowager explaining the rescue mission she'd mounted at my request and the threat Kolo and his plan had posed. She described how the Provincial Guard under her command had sneaked into the camp and quickly subdued the Sarosans before they knew what happened. Kolo, knowing he couldn't make it to the tinderjack in time, had surrendered.

Next, when called to testify, Ma and Da gave their . . . unique version of events. Da stood on his chair, arms thrust out, fingers curled as if strangling the air. He told the story of what had happened since they left Vengekeep in a litany of anguished shouts, each punctuated with slashing gestures like a madman conducting an orchestra. All the while, Ma wailed and gnashed her teeth. The performance rose to fever pitch and concluded with Ma falling to the floor in a well-rehearsed swoon.

I don't know if it helped our case, but it was very entertaining.

In the end, it was a signed confession from Kolo, who took all the blame for the plot, that convinced the Inquisitor General we'd acted under coercion. The Inquisitor General held up his copper orbs and banged them together twice, indicating that the charges regarding the attempted theft of the Sourcefire were dropped.

One charge down. Far too many to go.

We sat through several more hours of accusations, conspiracy theories, and questioning. Really, it was all quite plausible. Most days, my family was capable of just about everything we were being accused of. Not just capable but incredibly, unquestionably guilty. But for once, we had the truth on our side. We sat and listened as the Inquisitor General dismissed charge after charge. With each dismissal, Nalia's face grew darker and darker.

My stomach started to tingle, and I felt light-headed. "Ma," I whispered, "I feel . . . strange. What is this?"

She gave my shoulder a reassuring pat. "Don't worry, Son. It's just the feeling of innocence. It'll pass."

When I saw the court reporter, who had gone hoarse from reading out the very complex charges throughout the day, roll up the parchment he'd been reading from, I thought it was all over.

"What about my da?"

Maloch had been quiet from the moment the proceedings started. He'd sat perfectly still, his eyes never once leaving the five chairs where the Palatinate Lordcourt sat. Now, as we awaited the final dismissal from the Inquisitor General's copper orbs, he was suddenly on his feet and unleashing his anger on the room at large.

The Inquisitor General looked down his nose at Maloch. "You are in the presence of the High Laird, boy. You will speak only when granted permission."

Maloch pointed at Nalia and her brood. "They turned my da into glass. They've got him and all the Shadowhands in their palace."

Part of me expected the Lordcourt to emphatically deny the charge. But instead, Nalia rose with a smile that made me feel instantly sick.

"With your permission, I believe I can explain, Your Highness," she said, with a slight bow to the High Laird. He nodded, and Nalia continued. "After the break-in at the royal vaults, the Palatinate, seeking only to assist in the apprehension of the culprits, took it upon ourselves to launch an independent investigation into the matter."

The Dowager sat up straight in her chair. "Without informing anyone? Why is that?"

"We knew that the Provincial Guard had been charged with the task of tracking down those responsible," Nalia said sweetly. "We were afraid that if we made our investigation known, it would look as though we didn't have faith in the Guard's abilities. We acted in secret to save them from any embarrassment."

The Inquisitor General cast a look at the High Laird,

who nodded in approval. The Inquisitor General nodded as well.

Nalia moved to the center of the room. "As we reviewed everything we knew about the crime, we came to the conclusion that the thieves could only be those notorious renegades known as the Shadowhands. They were the only ones in the Five Provinces with the cunning and tenacity to even attempt such a heist."

I rolled my eyes. Exactly how much investigating did it take to come up with that gem? I knew newborn babies in Vengekeep who could have pieced that much together.

"Once we were able to determine their identities," Nalia said, "we laid a trap for each Shadowhand in the form of a shimmerhex, which we then used to apprehend them. It was only recently that this operation was completed, and I'm pleased to announce that it was a success!" She clapped her hands twice. A door at the back of the room opened, and four mages entered in single file. Each of them carried a red silk pillow, and upon each pillow sat one of the stolen relics: the gauntlets, the scepter, the coronet, and the orb.

The mages lined up along the High Laird's platform and held their arms out to present the relics. "As you can see,"

Nalia continued, "we have successfully recovered four of the five stolen relics."

The Dowager bowed her head only a fraction. I could tell she wasn't happy with this development. She didn't like having to give Nalia credit. "You've done an excellent job, Nalia. And the fifth relic?"

Nalia didn't bat an eye. "We hope to have it in our possession . . . very soon."

I leaned in to Maloch as he slowly sat down. "How? The Shadowhands never knew about the Vanguard."

Maloch didn't reply.

"Guards!" The High Laird, speaking for the first time, gave a wave. "Take the relics into protective custody until they can be returned to the vaults."

Before the guards could move, Nalia raised a hand. "Your Highness, it's an unimaginable tragedy that these items were stolen in the first place. The Lordcourt has studied them and they possess extremely powerful magic that, in the hands of the wrong person, could prove catastrophic. As your own vaults were compromised, might I suggest that you allow the Palatinate to take custody of these relics?" She shot a quick look at us. "I think we've proven quite capable of assuring that nothing gets out of our palace. And you would do us great honor by allowing us to watch over them for you."

The High Laird, looking tired, considered Nalia's proposal. "The relics were stored in the royal vaults for a reason. I will review the records left by my ancestors to learn why. Until then, they will be returned to the vaults." He nodded to his guards, who took the relics away.

Nalia nodded reverently to her liege and returned to her seat among the Lordcourt. It was the briefest of flashes, but something in her face said she was unhappy with the High Laird's decision. In that moment, I knew: she'd never wanted to recover the relics for the High Laird. She'd wanted them *for herself.*

Maloch slammed his hand down on the table. "All right, you've got your relics back. Now what about my da?"

The Inquisitor General glared at Maloch, a warning that further outbursts wouldn't be tolerated. Then he leaned in to the High Laird and spoke quietly. The monarch flicked his hand, and the Inquisitor General sat up tall in his chair.

"It is determined that there is sufficient evidence to suggest that the Shadowhands were responsible for the thefts from the royal vaults. This act alone is punishable by twenty years in Umbramore Tower. Given that the offense is made worse by the theft of *magical* items, it is the determination of the court that the sentence currently imposed by the Palatinate—in the form of the shimmerhex—will continue for the next twenty years."

The heads of the Lordcourt bobbed in approval.

"Furthermore," the Inquisitor General said, "in light of his father's incarceration, it is ordered that Maloch Oxter be sent to the Larkfire Orphanage until he turns eighteen."

Maloch looked ready to shout again, but Ma stood up brightly and said, "Begging your pardon, most excellent and wonderful of Inquisitors, but that won't be necessary." She produced a piece of parchment. "I have here a very legal document signed by Yab Oxter, which says that should anything happen to him, he grants custody of his son, Maloch, to Ona and Allia Grimjinx. That would be us."

Da waved to the Inquisitor General.

Maloch's head snapped around as he studied the document. "That . . . that's my da's handwriting."

"Why, yes it is!" Ma said. Then, softer, "Or a remarkable forgery."

She handed the parchment to our law-advocate, who in

turn gave it over to the Inquisitor General. He grunted in approval. "Very well, Ona and Allia Grimjinx will serve as young Mr. Oxter's guardians."

Stunned, Maloch took his seat, a storm brewing in his eyes. Ma leaned over and whispered in his ear. Whatever she said did the trick. Instead of another outburst, Maloch settled for a malicious scowl.

What else?

The Inquisitor General picked up his copper orbs. "If these matters have been put to rest—"

"They have *not* been put to rest!"

This time, it was Reena who leaped to her feet and caused gasps among the court with her protest. "If the Shadowhands stole the relics, then the Sarosans are innocent and should be freed."

Nalia cleared her throat. "There is no evidence that the Sarosans didn't assist the Shadowhands in some way. They may have provided shelter or food or—"

"That's a lie!" Holm now stood by his sister. He looked like he was wishing he had his blowgun right about now.

Nalia ignored the interruption. "And there is the question of their role in the attempted assassination of the Palatinate."

"Kolo confessed that he alone was behind that," Reena said. "The Sarosans are peaceful. You've locked our people up for no reason."

Nalia continued to ignore Reena. "Perhaps, Your Majesty, as this inquiry was called to deal with the matter of the Sourcefire and the Shadowhands, we could convene another session—a private session—to discuss the Sarosans."

The Inquisitor General consulted with the High Laird in a flurry of whispers, then announced, "These matters are now closed. The issue of the Sarosans will be addressed by the Inner Council in fifteen minutes." He slammed the copper orbs together and it was done.

As people began to file out of the room, I turned to Reena and Holm, who looked stunned. "They *have* to let your parents go. I'm sure you'll be with them in no time." But they seemed skeptical. I couldn't blame them.

While everyone else stood, Maloch slouched in his chair. I put my hand on his shoulder. "You okay?"

He looked down at the table. "Da always said the risk of gaol is the price of admission for the life of a Shadowhand. He was guilty. But I can't believe they won't release him from the shimmerhex. I can't even visit him. . . ."

As the High Laird's advisers gathered on the dais, the Dowager stepped down and joined us at the table. We all bowed respectfully.

"Thank you, Your Majesty," Da said.

"Annestra," the Dowager reminded him.

Ma smiled and took the Dowager by the hands. "Annestra, we appreciate all you've done. Rescuing us, saving Jaxter. Above and beyond the call of royal duty."

The Dowager blushed. She opened her mouth to speak when Nalia glided across the room and joined the semicircle of advisers who stood around the High Laird. The Dowager's eyes narrowed at the mage. "I don't like how Nalia has my brother's ear. The Palatinate's job is to govern the use of magic. In recent months, they've had too much say in matters of state. They've become more than counsel. The only reason the royal vaults were compromised in the first place is because of their intervention."

I froze in place. "What?"

"They're the ones who insinuated Vengekeep was under a curse," she explained. "They implied that every effort had to be made to keep the curse from spreading to the rest of the Provinces. It was Nalia's idea to send nearly all the Provincial

Guard to quarantine Vengekeep. If they'd stayed at their stations, the vaults would never have been compromised."

I'd been stupid. Completely and totally and remarkably stupid. But suddenly, I understood what was really going on.

The High Laird stood, and his advisers parted. The Dowager smiled at us. "If you'll excuse me. It looks like the Sarosan discussion is about to move to another room"—she turned and winked at Reena and Holm—"and I have more than a few things to say on the matter."

A member of the Provincial Guard approached me and bowed. "Jaxter Grimjinx?" she asked. When I nodded, she said, "The High Laird has granted the prisoner Kolohendriseenax a final request before sentencing."

My jaw dropped. "*Final* request?"

The Dowager placed her hand on my arm. "He's not being put to death. They're imprisoning him in a shimmer-hex like the Shadowhands."

The guard continued. "The prisoner has requested a meeting with you. I'm to take you to his cell."

Across the room, I watched Nalia bow respectfully to the High Laird. He smiled gently, hanging on her every word.

"Good," I said. "I need to see him too."

29

A Last Request

"If you quit while you're ahead, the mediocre thief
wins."

—*Gnillian Grimjinx, coauthor of the Grimjinx/Aviard Peace Accords*

I guess I'd imagined that the prisons at the High Laird's castle would be a step above some of the filthy places my family and I had been. But as we descended to the dungeon, the familiar scent of mold and dirt assaulted my nose. The air was moist, the lighting scant. There must have been some royal law I didn't know about, declaring that no gaol cell could be even remotely livable.

The guard took me to an iron door, opened it, and allowed me through. I found myself in a small room that smelled, if possible, a bit worse than the rest of the dungeon. Just across the way, a wall of bars separated me from Kolo.

The old man took great effort to rise. He winced, holding his lesion-covered arms. He drew a deep breath and leaned against the bars. "Thank you for coming, Jaxter."

I walked right up to him. "You could end all this. Just tell the truth."

"Jaxter, I—"

"The Palatinate hired the Shadowhands. Not you."

I wasn't holding anything back. Kolo said nothing. "Or rather," I continued, "the Palatinate hired you, *thinking* you were a Shadowhand, and you in turn hired Dylis and the others. It was the one thing I couldn't figure out. How did the Shadowhands know *exactly* when the vault security would be weak? How did they get accurate blueprints of the vaults? How did they know the ways to turn off the magical defenses? They could only have gotten that information from someone close to the High Laird."

Kolo remained stoic for a moment, then sighed wistfully. "When those terrible prophecies besieged Vengekeep, the Palatinate saw an opportunity to seize the relics. They advised the High Laird to send all his soldiers to quarantine the town-state. That left the vaults vulnerable."

"But they couldn't steal the relics themselves, in case something went wrong and they were caught. So they went looking for the Shadowhands . . . and found you."

Kolo shrugged. "It was all an accident, you know. Pure luck. I was sitting in a tavern in Smolderwick when I overheard some bumbling oaf making very awkward inquiries about hiring the Shadowhands. The gold rings on his fingers told me he was a mage. I guessed he was rogue, and I thought, *What does a rogue mage need with the Shadowhands?* So, on a whim, I asked him. Imagine my surprise when he spoke about five relics he needed stolen from the royal vaults. I knew only a member of the Lordcourt could provide so much detail about the magical defenses of the vaults. I thought they were stealing the relics to embarrass the High Laird."

I folded my arms. "Nalia says the four relics are full of powerful magic."

He shook his head. "I didn't know that then. I believed that stealing those four relics was a diversion, meant to hide their true objective: the Vanguard. I couldn't let them do that. And now they have relics that probably contain unimaginable power. . . ."

"But they don't have the Vanguard."

Kolo chuckled softly. "Like I said, I was very lucky. The Palatinate hired me to steal five relics. I, in turn, hired the Shadowhands to steal *four* while I went after the Vanguard. When the Lordcourt dug up the chest and found only four of the relics, they assumed they'd been double-crossed by the Shadowhands. Then I sent an anonymous tip to the Palatinate, revealing the Shadowhands' true identities."

Very clever. Kolo had gotten his two worst enemies— the Shadowhands and the Palatinate—to turn on each other while he got away. Except he didn't.

"And once they quietly got rid of the Shadowhands," I said, "the Palatinate told the High Laird they believed the Sarosans were behind the thefts."

Kolo nodded. "Because we represented the next biggest threat to them. People who hated magic and preached against it. People who knew how to fight magic *without* magic."

His thin fingers wrapped around the cell bars. "This has been happening a long time, Jaxter. Think of the spiderbats. Anything that can resist magic has been disappearing. This is no accident."

Kolo's words hit me hard. He was right. Silencing the

Sarosans was just the latest example. Even magic-resistant plants were dying out. That's why the Dowager was working to preserve them in her greenhouse.

"Why? Why are they doing this? And what is the Vanguard? A weapon? Where is it?"

Beyond the iron door, we could hear the jangling of keys and a muffled conversation.

"We don't have much time, Jaxter," Kolo said.

"I can get you an audience with the High Laird," I said, one eye on the iron door. "He needs to know what's going on. You need to tell him the truth."

"Jaxter, I can't—"

"Then I'll tell him," I said firmly.

Kolo could barely manage a rueful smile. "Jaxter, think of the lengths the Palatinate has gone to hide its involvement. They'll kill anyone they believe knows about what they've done. Even you. You can't tell anyone. Not yet. They must believe they got away with it. At least until you learn their true motives."

My chest tightened. Me? What did he think *I* could do? "What do you mean, 'true motives'?"

He moved to the cot where he'd been resting. He picked

up Tree Bag and held it out to me through the bars. "As part of my last request, they're allowing me to pass on the work for my next book. I'd like you to have it, Jaxter. You'll find notes on how to continue what I started."

I grabbed the shoulder strap. "They let you keep this in your cell?" Anytime my family or I had gone to gaol, we'd been stripped of all personal belongings.

"Oh, it's fine," he said, a hint of sarcasm in his voice. "The Palatinate used magic to search for anything harmful, and they *didn't find a thing.*" Kolo winked at me.

The door opened. I quickly slid Tree Bag over my shoulder as Nalia entered, eyes ablaze with malicious glee. A copper tingroat floated over her right shoulder, following wherever she moved.

Nalia ignored me and walked right up to the cell. With a flick of her finger, the cursed coin moved through the air between the bars and stopped close to Kolo's face.

"I'm here to impose the High Laird's sentence," she said coyly. "However, if you tell me where I can find the Vanguard, I might be able to intervene on your behalf. You could spend the rest of your life in Umbramore Tower. It doesn't have to end like this."

"What do you mean?" I asked. "'End like this'?"

Kolo's eyes never left the tingroat. "I'm old, Jaxter. Very old. When the Shadowhands are released from their shimmerhex prisons, they'll go on with their lives. If I'm ever freed, it's doubtful I'll survive the resurrection."

I wouldn't have been able to live with myself if Kolo had succeeded in blowing up the Palatinate. But that didn't mean I could watch him die either. "Tell her where it is, Kolo."

Kolo looked right at me and smiled. He must have known that if he didn't say something right there and then, I would blab everything I knew. He did the only thing he could to stop me. He muttered, *"Volo ser voli,"* and his hand shot up to grip the tingroat. A sound like ice cracking filled the room. A transparent shimmer turned his hand to glass, then raced up his arm and across his body. A moment later, it was all done.

Nalia spun around, as though noticing me for the first time. The smile disappeared from her face as once again our eyes locked. "It was wise of you to ask him to reveal the Vanguard's location. It would also be wise of you to tell me where it is . . . if you know."

The Palatinate had secretly acted to weaken the security

of the royal vaults, hire someone to steal magical relics, eliminate the thieves responsible, and incarcerate the Sarosans
who spoke out against them. I had no idea what that all
meant, but even if I'd known where the Vanguard was, there
was no way I was going to tell her.

"Sorry," I said. "He didn't tell me."

She wasn't convinced. "Then why did he ask to see you as
his last request? What were you discussing?"

I thought of Kolo's last words: *Volo ser voli*. A par-Goblin
proverb I'd never really understood. It meant "Yesterday is
today." Back when I first met him, Kolo asked me what I
knew about the Great Uprisings. He seemed to think it was
important I learn more about that hidden period of history. I
had a feeling the answers to my questions would be clear if I
did as Kolo suggested. True, information about the Uprisings
was forbidden knowledge. But I was a Grimjinx. Forbidden?
No such thing. I had some work to do.

"History," I told her. And I walked out of the cell.

30

Exile

"Exile is but the next great adventure."

—*Parika Grimjinx, first explorer-thief*

"**W**e should get back to the castle."

I sat on a bench near the docks, staring out over the vast Kroallis Ocean. The ports of Vesta bustled with activity: ships unloading imports from faraway lands, other ships taking on cargo for a long voyage ahead. A light breeze dotted my glasses with bits of sea mist that froze in the winter air.

Maloch stood with his hands in his pockets, pacing back and forth. "Just a minute. They're here somewhere."

He looked up and down the pier, where a long row of mang-drawn wagons had lined up. Each wagon was packed with Sarosans, newly freed from Umbramore Tower. The High Laird and his council had decided that while the evidence suggested the Sarosans had had no hand in the actual thefts from the royal vaults, they were still guilty of resisting arrest and the High Laird's will. It didn't seem to matter that the arrests were unwarranted.

The Dowager had argued ferociously for the Sarosans. In the end, the High Laird had decreed that the Sarosans were banished from the Five Provinces. As the wagons arrived, the Sarosans were escorted onto a waiting ship that would take them all across the ocean.

"We've been looking for them for an hour," I said gently. "I wanted to say good-bye to Reena and Holm too. But they could have found their parents. They might be on the ship already and—"

"There they are!" Maloch said, charging into the crowd. I jumped up and followed him. We wove between the masses until we caught up with Reena and Holm. They were looking around frantically. When they spotted us, they stopped.

"We can't find them," Reena said nervously.

"Wagons are still arriving," I said. "They'll be here."

Maloch, who'd been so eager to track the siblings down, suddenly found himself speechless. "I think . . . I think it's stupid that you're being banished. You didn't do anything. It's not fair."

Reena put her hand on his arm. "This isn't the first time we've been turned away. It's why we've always wandered the Five Provinces. No one wants to hear what we have to say. Even when we're proven right. It's part of being a Sarosan. No one understands us."

Maloch swallowed nervously. "I like to think . . . *I* understand you."

Holm and I shared a look and rolled our eyes.

Maloch's hand dove into his pocket. "Before you go, I want you to have something." He pulled out a silver triangle pendant.

"Hey," I said, "you stole that from the Dowager."

In his other hand, he held the red gem that went with the pendant.

"Hey," I said, "you stole that from me."

Maloch held out the pendant. "You don't really know

where you're going. It could be dangerous. And even though you're getting your family back, you might . . . I dunno. Get lonely. I thought this way we could, maybe, talk. Keep in touch. If you need someone to talk to."

Reena eyed the pendant queasily. "Thank you, Maloch, but . . . it's magic. It goes against everything the Sarosans believe. If I got caught with that . . ."

Maloch looked at his feet. "What if *I* need someone to talk to?"

His hard face softened, and Reena couldn't take it anymore. She looked around to make sure no one was watching, then slipped the pendant into a pouch at her waist.

Maloch turned to Holm and smiled. Lashing out, he threw a hard punch directly at the boy's head. But Holm deftly sidestepped the incoming blow, grabbed Maloch's arm, and flipped the bigger boy onto his back. Then he crashed onto Maloch's chest with his knee, sending the air shooting from Maloch's lungs.

"Not bad," Maloch said as Holm helped him up. "I expect you to be teaching me moves the next time we see each other."

All four of us fell quiet. We were all thinking the same thing. *If* we see each other again.

"You're moving in with Jaxter's family?" Reena asked Maloch.

He nodded. "Mr. and Mrs. Grimjinx are going to continue my training as a thief. When my father gets released from the shimmerhex, I want him to be proud."

Reena leaned forward and kissed him on the cheek. "He will be."

We all hugged. Then, from across the dock, we heard, "Reena! Holm!"

The siblings turned to find a man and woman, both tall and dark-skinned, waving frantically from the back of a wagon. Without another word, Reena and Holm ran to their parents. I leaned on Maloch's shoulder.

"You didn't tell her about what Ma did."

When Ma proposed that Maloch live at our house, she had more than kindness on her mind. During the fray when the Provincial Guard had stormed Kolo's camp and rescued my parents, Ma had used the confusion to slip the Shadowhand Covenant into her blouse. She showed it to us only last night, saying that even though she wasn't technically a Shadowhand anymore, she was the only one left to revive the organization.

"It's going to take a while to get things up and running again," she'd said to Maloch. "You're a mite young. Not sure the other Shadowhands would approve, but then they're not exactly in a position to protest, right? I could use some help recruiting and need someone besides myself who can enter the Dagger without setting off the defenses. You up to it?"

Maloch hadn't hesitated. He'd taken the quill Ma offered him, signed the Covenant, and joined the ranks of the Shadowhands like his da. Like he'd always wanted.

So it was decided that Da would return to his job as Protectorate and Maloch would continue to be Aronas's apprentice, and they would both use their positions in the Vengekeep government to divert suspicion away from Ma as she went about re-forming the Shadowhands.

Maloch rubbed the red pendant gem between his fingers. "Yeah, well, I figure that since the Shadowhands got her people banished, Reena probably wouldn't want to know I just joined. I'll tell her once there's an ocean between us."

We waved to Reena and her family as they walked up

the plank to board the ship. Then Maloch and I turned and
started the trek back to the royal palace.

★

In the promenade outside the palace, two mang-drawn
carriages were preparing for the long trip home. One would
take Ma, Da, and Maloch back to Vengekeep. The other
would bring the Dowager and me back to Redvalor Castle.
Footmen scurried about, loading up supplies for the journey.
I hugged Ma and Da.

"You doing all right?" Ma asked, brushing my cheek
with her hand.

"You mean because the man I idolized turned out to be
crazier than a sanguibeast during solstice?" I asked. "I'm fine.
His research will go on. The Dowager and I will see to that."

I had no guarantees that returning to Redvalor Castle
meant the Dowager and I would argue any less. We might
disagree, but the Dowager and I saw eye to eye more than
Kolo and I ever did.

"Do us proud, son!" Da said as he helped Ma into the
carriage.

Maloch shuffled up to the carriage door. "Thanks. For loaning me your room."

I frowned. "Don't touch my stuff."

"I don't want your ratty old stuff."

I held out my hand. "Good luck, Maloch."

He hesitated, then gave my hand a firm shake. "You're a lousy thief, Jaxter. But the rest of you's not too bad."

He climbed aboard the carriage, the driver cracked his whip, and they pulled away, Vengekeep bound.

The palace gates swung open, and the Dowager emerged. She was back in the blouse and slacks she wore when we worked in the laboratory. She rubbed her neck. "I think that will be enough official functions for a while. Can't stand to wear those formal uniforms. I think they squeeze my neck. Can you tell? Is my neck smaller? I think my neck is smaller."

"Don't worry," I said, "a couple of days sleeping in the back of the carriage will take care of that."

The Dowager giggled, then looked at me sadly. "The Sarosan camp was thoroughly searched. No sign of the Vanguard, I'm afraid."

Of course, we didn't know what it looked like, so who

really knew if it had been found? I suspected it was well hidden. And with Kolo gone, we might never know what it looked like. Or what it did.

The Dowager added, "My brother has given the Palatinate free rein to take whatever measures are necessary to recover it."

Whatever measures are necessary. I'd never cared much about the Palatinate before, one way or the other. Given everything I'd learned in the past few weeks, the idea of them being given that much power by the High Laird worried me.

I took her hand and helped her into the carriage. As we got under way, I pulled Tree Bag from under my seat. The Dowager's eyes lit up. I divided the papers between us and we started going through them, making notes and sharing ideas for how we'd continue the work.

"I don't condone what Kolo tried to do," the Dowager said sadly, "but I will say that he was brilliant." Then she turned and glanced out the window of the carriage. "You were thinking about it. Weren't you?"

"I'm sorry?"

"Quitting as my apprentice to study with Kolo." Although

she watched the passing landscape, I could see her studying me out of the corner of her eye. Somehow, she knew. One of these days I'd learn that she was always one step ahead of me.

I fumbled, trying to find just the right lie that wouldn't hurt her feelings. But the Dowager didn't deserve lies, not after everything she'd done for me. Instead, I just hung my head.

"I saw the way you paged through the notes for Kolo's new book," she said, smiling slyly. "You looked so happy and excited. Like when we first started working together. I don't blame you. The chance to work with a botanist as amazing as Kolo would be too good to pass up."

"I guess," I said slowly, "the apprenticeship wasn't *exactly* what I thought it would be."

"No one said being an apprentice was easy. In fact, I recall telling you it would be hard work. You can't give up the first time things get difficult. And I think you'll agree that while other opportunities may appear inviting on the surface, it's not so simple to see what lies beneath."

I nodded. The par-Goblins had a similar expression: *Aeris vul heshla noressa laneer.* It meant "Scratch the gold to find the tarnish." And *that* meant you had to dig deep to find true worth. From the first day of my apprenticeship, the Dowager had always been honest with me. And even though studying with Kolo may have seemed like a better situation, I knew now that I couldn't trust him. I hate that it took almost giving up a good thing with the Dowager to realize that.

The Dowager folded her hands in her lap and spoke softly. "I'll make you a deal. In a few months, you'll have been my apprentice for a year. If, after a full year, you don't want to continue, I'll do my best to help you choose another vocation and find a new mentor. But I hope we continue working together. I think we still have a lot to teach each other."

I raised an eyebrow. "Me? Teach you?"

"All teachers learn from their pupils," she said. "Sometimes, in ways that aren't so obvious. But they do."

I'm not sure I quite understood what she meant. But there was only one way to find out. I had a feeling our time together would go well beyond the first year.

"Are you still up for learning ancient par-Goblin?" I asked.

The Dowager's head tilted back and forth with childlike

excitement. "The minute we return to Redvalor."

She continued to peruse Kolo's papers. I skipped to the end to review his work on using blackdrupe pits to ease the symptoms of whiteflu. There, at the bottom of the page, was a hastily scribbled note that hadn't been there the last time I'd read these papers. I guessed Kolo had written it while in the High Laird's dungeon.

Jaxter—

Volo ser voli.

Yesterday is today.

Then, below that, in much darker ink and underlined many times, it said:

It's happening again.

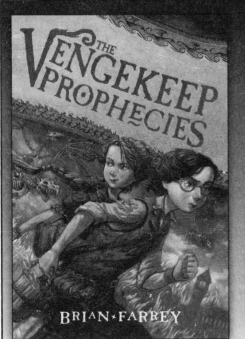